THE RED DEATH

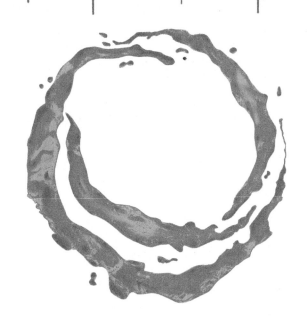

BIRGITTE MÄRGEN

THE RED DEATH Copyright © 2018 by Birgitte Märgen.
ISBN: 9781729311196 (paperback)

For Stephen and Morgana

"And now was acknowledged the presence of the Red Death. He had come like a thief in the night. And one by one dropped the revelers in the blood-bedewed halls of their revel, and died each in the despairing posture of his fall. And the life of the ebony clock went out with that of the last of the gay. And the flames of the tripods expired. And Darkness and Decay and the Red Death held illimitable dominion over all."

—Edgar Allan Poe

Prologue

New York City is one of the most densely populated cities in the United States, encompassing a land area of approximately 302.6 square miles, and inhabited with over 8.5 million people. The city sits on one of the largest harbors in the world, and with over 800 languages spoken, carries the highest number of foreign-born immigrants in the world.

Since the late 1800's when Ellis Island became the gateway to the new world, immigrants have continued to flock to the 151 ft. tall Statue of Liberty who promises to take the tired and the poor. With calloused hands and a suitcase of dreams, they envision the Big Apple as a new place to call home. A place where hard work earns you good wages and opportunity always knocks.

NEW YORK CITY.
AUGUST 18.

Rats. He could hear the sound of them squirming inside the bags of garbage. In the dark alley, trash bins were lined up against the cinder block walls. A few torn bags and their contents lay strewn across the ground. Juan Martinez stepped over a waded up T-shirt covered in oil, his foot nearly landing in a soiled baby diaper. He grimaced and moved to the other side of the alley. His eyes watching his shadow as it spread out in front of him. The shadow made him much taller than he really was. He was short and stocky, much like his father and his grandfather before him. A trait that ran in the Martinez family.

Juan looked up at the night sky. There was a partial moon peeking out from the dark clouds, but the stars were invisible because of the big city lights. He liked living in New York, it was an immense place compared to the poor farming town of Santa Ana Coatepec in Southern Mexico that he was from. Even his tiny one-room apartment was grand compared to the house he was raised in; a small two-room house made of adobe brick. The house had a latrine and no running water, meals were cooked in an outdoor smoke kitchen.

The living quarters were crowded, he was the oldest of six children and they all shared the one bedroom with their parents. Everyone in the family worked on their farm, a small patch of land where they grew avocados. Each weekend his father would drive around, selling the weeks crops.

Since he was the oldest, his father insisted that he get a better education than he had. Neither his father nor his mother could read. There were not any schools around the rural area Juan lived and every week he would take a bus to primary school. The school had shared housing where he would stay and return home each weekend to work on the farm. After graduating from preparatoria, high school, he moved to Mexico City and attended college at Universidad Nacional Autonoma De Mexico.

His dream was to be a doctor, and he had nearly finished his studies in the Facultad de Medicina de la UNAM when his father fell ill. His father had been working hard to put him through school, but with five other children and a drought that hit the family farm, Juan had no choice but to drop out of the university.

Many towns had been hit hard, and work was almost nonexistent where they lived. Determined to help his family, Martinez moved to the United States on a work Visa. After years of paperwork, he managed to become a citizen through the naturalization process and passing the citizenship test. He had never studied so hard in his life, but he learned enough English to be able to pass the test.

He was only a certified nurse assistant at Regency Hospital, but in Mexico, he was almost a doctor. Here in America, his partial degree was worth little, and he had to start all over with his schooling and even squeeze in language courses along with his studies. Although they had textbooks in Spanish, he had to know the English language if he was going to become a nurse. Even though he knew all the basics of medicine, he also knew that he had little chance of becoming a doctor in the United States.

He could always move back to Mexico and finish his degree, but right now his priority was to earn money to send back home to his family. Even the small wages he made in a day as a nurse assistant was more than he could make in a week in Mexico. Each week he wire transferred most of his check to his family. Although his father's health had been improving, he was still too weak to work.

Juan froze when he heard a scuttling sound, he looked behind him as two young men turned down the street at the end of the alley. He had to be cautious at this time of night, it was 4 AM, and robberies were rampant in his neighborhood. The sound of sirens was as natural here as the chattering of birds in the trees.

When he turned back around he noticed a gleam of silver lying next to one of the trash bins. He walked over to the bin and picked it up. Juan stared down at the profile of the man on the coin, the first president George Washington, he remembered from his citizenship test. In the small village he is from, there was a superstition that if you find money, you must pick it up, or you will anger the gods and all of your fortune will be taken.

There was more clamoring inside the bin next to him, and he jumped back as one of the garbage bags tipped over, leaking its contents onto the ground. All of a sudden a large black rat, the size of a chihuahua thrust its head out of the bag, a piece of tattered meat hanging from its mouth. It startled him, and he fell backward, landing on his back.

"*Chupacabra*," Juan said as he crossed himself. He watched as the rat disappeared back inside the bag. He quickly stood up and wiped his hands on his turquoise scrubs as he stepped away from the bin.

He continued walking, picking up his pace. One of the street lights above him buzzed softly and blinked on and off as he made his way toward his apartment. Juan rubbed his index finger across the smooth coin as he hummed a tune his mother sang to him as a child.

REGENCY HOSPITAL.
NEW YORK CITY.
AUGUST 21.

The emergency room doors of Regency Hospital slid open as a gurney shot through the opening flanked by three paramedics. One of the paramedics was holding a clear bag of liquid in the air attached to the man on the gurney. The other two paramedics took turns squeezing a bag valve mask while the other paramedic pressed down rhythmically on the chest of the man.

As they flew through the doors a nurse in scrubs hit her palm against a square button, and the next set of doors swung outward. After entering the ER room, Matthew Yates, the doctor on duty, held up a small light to the man's eyes as they rolled around. He grimaced when he saw that the pupils were unequal.

"Possible brain hemorrhaging," Yates said as he glanced up.

The nurses worked around him, one of them attaching electrodes while the other put an oxygen mask over the patient's mouth. The heart rhythm was irregular. He bent down watching the man's chest rise and fall as he gasped for breath. Yates removed the oxygen mask and opened the man's mouth, placing a tongue depressor against his tongue. He waved his flashlight around, checking for anything that may be obstructing the man's airway. *It was clear.*

"Vitals," Yates said as he glanced over at one of the nurses, who began calling out numbers. The blood pressure was low and falling, and the temperature was high. Yates' eyes shot back down as the man began going into convulsions, his corded neck twisting grotesquely. He restrained the man's arm, while the other nurses held the other arm down. The convulsions suddenly stopped. The doctor nodded to the nurse, watching as she injected the IV with dopamine.

"I need a CT scan of the brain," he said. He needed to check for swelling. He began examining the man's head, inspecting it for signs of injury. There didn't seem to be any cuts or abrasions.

Yates glanced up at the heart monitor as a loud beeping noise filled the room. The lines were showing erratic electrical activity with no distinct rhythm. Ventricular fibrillation, Yates thought. The man's eyes grew so wide that they looked like they were going to bulge out of his head. Then, the man grabbed Yates' arm. He shuddered at the look of terror in the man's eyes as he stared at him.

"¡Ayúdeme!" the man called out in a deep raspy voice.

Then Yates recognized the young man's face—he worked at the hospital. The man let out another guttural yell and his head fell to the side, his eyes staring vacantly outward. The grip on Yates' arm loosened, and he gazed back up as another noise filled the room—the flat line warning on the heart monitor machine.

"Code Blue," Yates yelled and the words echoed overhead. The nurse put an oxygen mask over the patients face as Yates pumped his hands against the man's chest. "Defibrillator," he called out.

The nurse handed him the defibrillator, placing the electrodes on the man's chest. The man's body bounded upward with the shock. He studied the heart monitor. No response.

"Norepinephrine," he hollered out to the Charge Nurse as she came running into the room. "Increase defibrillator to 360." He nodded to the nurse as the man's body jumped again.

Yates could feel sweat building on his brow as he stared up at the heart monitor still reading a flat line. He gazed down at the young man as he laid there unresponsive and shook his head. The rest of the team backed away. The look of defeat that he could see in everyone's eyes was something he always had a hard time swallowing.

Working in the ER, he had lost many patients before, but it was never easy. He was also bothered that he couldn't place the man's name when his face was so familiar. As the nurse removed the oxygen mask, he watched as a trickle of blood ran down the side of the man's mouth. Maybe he was wrong about the brain hemorrhaging, it looked like it was a problem in the lungs. The difficulty breathing . . . the convulsions could have been from lack of air. He ran through his head where he could have made a mistake. There was just no time, Yates thought. *No time.*

He looked over at the tray with the man's wallet, and picked it up, reading the name on his Regency Hospital Employee Card. "Martinez. Juan Martinez," he whispered. He remembered seeing the name before. We lost one of our own, he thought as he read the words NURSE ASSISTANT.

Yates didn't notice the silver coin that fell out of the wallet, rolled across the floor, and exited the ER room.

Samuel Greene whistled as he pushed the mop back and forth along the Regency Hospital corridor floor. It was almost midnight, and he had four more hours before his shift ended. He liked the quiet of the hospital at night, although there was always some discomfort some-where between the walls. His thoughts sailed to his new granddaughter Keisha who was born only a few days ago. He was now a grandpa. It had seemed just like yesterday that his daughter was small, and now she had a daughter of her own. He stopped moving his mop for a moment when he heard the sound of moaning coming from one of the rooms. He glanced up as the light next to room 318 flicked on.

He turned toward the nurse station, watching a red-haired nurse with a tattoo of a rose on her wrist texting on her cell phone, ignoring the blinking light. It wasn't his job to interfere with the way the hospital was run. Way he saw it, folks didn't take care of each other like they used to. Everyone was just out for themselves. There used to be a time that helping hands were given quickly and freely. Not anymore, Greene thought as he shook his head. No siree. Now there was a time when he would have had the right mind to pull that damn thing out of that woman's hand and point her in the right direction, but not anymore. He'd do better to just mind his own.

Samuel pushed the mop around the nurse's station and kept walking. As he rounded the next corner, he stopped and leaned his mop against the wall while he caught his breath. He heard the sound of numerous footsteps pounding against the linoleum floors. The hospital never sleeps, he thought. Sometimes on nights like tonight when a full moon was out, the hospital tended to get a whole lot busier. He wasn't superstitious, but there was something mysterious going on when that moon brimmed full.

It was hard to listen to all the suffering that went on between these walls. Folks dying, people injured. Sometimes the pain jabbed at his heart. It could wear on you if you thought too much about it. But he also knew that the walls held the secret of life, and new babies were born in the space between. Precious lives, like his new grandbaby, and that made everything all right. Life had a way of balancing itself out.

He began walking again, his mop shifting side to side in front of him. He liked to see the floor shine. Those bright hospital lights set like stars against his clean floors. Every so often he'd plunge the mop back into the bucket of gray water on wheels he pulled behind him. Then, he'd grab the handle and squeeze more grime and ugliness into the swirling mixture, erasing the pain that spilled between these walls.

Samuel stopped when he came to a door and rifled in his pocket for the custodial keys. He held the mop against his shoulder as he held out the ring of twenty keys in front of him. He thumbed through the keys until he found the right circular shape attached to the jagged rectangular blade. He stared down at his hand as it held out the key, it was knobby at the joints, and suddenly looked like a stranger's hand. Hands he didn't recognize. Arthritis, Greene thought as he opened his palm and closed it around the key. He gripped the key between his indistinguishable thumb and index finger and slid it into the door. When the door clicked, he pushed it open and switched on the light. He peered down at the floor next to the gallons of green and pink disinfectant liquid and pulled out a bright yellow caution sign. He locked the door and placed the sign in the center of the corridor, studying the image of a black silhouetted figure falling.

The sound of footsteps beating against the floor and the sound of doctors yelling drifted to his ears as he continued pushing the mop down the hall. He peeked inside one of the ER rooms as he strolled past. The sound of the voices became louder as metal trays clanked, and the screams of a man in pain echoed down the hallway. He paused for a few minutes, noticing it had suddenly grown very quiet. He shook his head. Then, he saw a silver coin rolling toward him from the ER room. His eyes followed it as it landed next to his feet. Samuel reached down and picked the coin up. 1974, he thought. A good year.

As he made his rounds back by the nurse's station, he noticed the red-haired nurse still hadn't answered the blinking light. Good Lord woman, Greene thought. He glanced at the counter where the nurse sat, there was a jar with the words RED CROSS on it. He held out the quarter in his hand and kissed it as he said a small prayer in his head for the man in the ER who dropped it. He grasped the quarter in those unrecognizable knobby fingers that he called his own and listened as it clinked in the jar against the other coins.

Samuel began whistling as he continued pushing the mop in front of him, turned down the corridor, and past the moans still radiating from room 318.

CHAPTER 1

OFFICE OF CHIEF MEDICAL EXAMINER.
NEW YORK CITY.
AUGUST 23.

Artsy framed posters of crime scene tape and gleaming stainless steel operating tables adorned the walls. Maggie De Luca glanced around the office, it was very sleek and modern—much different than the other coroner's offices she had been to in Atlanta. There were black shelves lining the walls and shiny black file cabinets. Even the secretary's desk was oversized with a large leather bound black chair.

She had recently transferred to New York and was still getting her bearings when she was called in to investigate the death of a man named Juan Martinez. The only information she was given was that Martinez was carrying a possible new strain of bacteria.

A heavy set lady with rosy cheeks gazed up from her computer.

"Hello, can I help you?" the lady asked as she sat a paper to the side.

"Yes, I'm—"Maggie said.

The phone rang and the woman held up her index finger.

"One moment. Yes, Detective Holloway I have the report ready to go . . . let me check, hold please." She got up from her desk, walked over to one of the file cabinets, and began searching through the files.

Maggie turned and watched as some people came in the front door and walked into another room. She looked up at a sign above the doorway that said THE BONE YARD. She noticed the lady was still busy on the phone, and walked through the entrance. In the center of the room were clothing racks with black T-shirts and jackets that had the word CORONER in yellow letters embroidered across the back.

She walked up to the shelves that had plastic skulls and arm bones. Another shelf had crime scene kits and signs that had NY CORONER emblazoned on it in bright yellow print. Maggie shook her head as she looked over at a cooking apron that had the words CRIME SCENE silk-screened across the front. These people are sick, Maggie thought. She had visited coroner offices many times in her line of work and had never seen anything like this. It felt wrong to make money off of the tragedy of others. She saw the couple that had walked in purchasing one of the Post-Its shaped like a body outlined at a crime scene.

She heard the lady calling for her and walked back up to the desk.

"Apologies for the interruption," the woman said. "How can I help you?

"I'm here to speak with the medical examiner about a recent inquiry made by the CDC regarding a man named Juan Martinez," Maggie said, watching as the lady typed something into the computer.

"Let me see, I remember seeing an inquest order just over an hour ago."

"Thank you," Maggie said as she looked over at a half-eaten double cheeseburger sitting on the desk.

"Okay, I see it here. And what is your name?"

"I'm sorry," Maggie said. "My name is Maggie De Luca, I'm an epidemiologist in charge of investigations." She pulled out her badge and held it up.

The woman leaned forward, studying the badge, and then began typing again.

"Thank you," she said as she stood up. "Right this way."

Maggie followed the lady as she led her through a long corridor. There was chipped paint on the walls, and the tiled floor was cracked. She glanced up at one of the long lights above that was flickering and burnt out on one side. It was obvious that the New York City OCME

2

put all their money into their front area and store—a facade they showed the public. The hidden back area behind the closed doors was antiquated, with a strong stench permeating the air of formaldehyde. But the dead don't speak, Maggie thought. Or do they? She glanced up as they stopped outside one of the doors at the end of the hallway.

The secretary opened the door and led her into an antechamber next to the autopsy area.

"Everything you need can be found on the shelves. I assume you've had Hazmat training—since you work for the CDC? Anytime we get a call from the CDC we take the utmost precautions."

Maggie nodded her head.

"Yes, of course." She looked over at two doors leading out of the antechamber. "Excuse me, which door do I use when I'm dressed?"

"The autopsy suite is the door on the right," the lady said, smiling. "I'm afraid the other one is just for storage."

"Thank you," Maggie said as she grabbed one of the surgical scrub suits and an impervious gown from the shelf. Impervious gowns were used quite frequently in her line of work, they have a barrier protection from fluids and microorganisms. After she tucked her head in the surgical cap, she put on the shoe covers, goggles, and double surgical gloves. When she was finished dressing she grabbed one of the N-95 respirators hanging on the wall, which was required to protect from airborne pathogens.

Maggie could feel her heart racing as she opened the door to the autopsy suite. No matter how many times she had viewed a dead body, it always hit her as hard as if it were the first time. She knew the person's soul had already moved on—there was an absence of presence and a vacant feeling—but it was the emptiness that scared her the most. She wasn't a religious person, but she knew something or someone had a hand in the world we viewed today. Sometimes she said a small prayer to the invisible force, and sometimes if things were going terribly wrong she cussed at it just the same.

The medical examiner was standing over a body on the autopsy table. She noticed he was wearing the same wardrobe she had on, along with a black rubber apron.

"I'd shake your hand, but I'm a bit tied up here," the man said as he pulled on the forceps, making a cracking sound as they forced the rib cage apart. "We're not very formal around here, my name's Jerry."

"Maggie," she said, averting her eyes away as he pulled the ribs the rest of the way apart. She knew someone had to do the job, but she couldn't stomach working in a place like this. As an epidemiologist, her job was dangerous at times, and she had been put in more than a few dangerous situations, but she still preferred to deal with the prevention of the spread of disease—not the after effects.

"I'm almost finished up here, but I wanted to open this area up a bit more to show you something," Jerry said as he pointed at red rings on the lungs. "These lungs look as damaged as a long-term smoker." He poked an area around one of the rings and a greenish colored pus came out. "And as you can see these red-ringed nodules are indicative of infection. This person didn't have a fighting chance of surviving the disease."

If her stomach was turning before, it had now decided to crank up the speed. She turned her attention to the medical examiner, before she lost her lunch in the snazzy N-95 respirator. The look must have registered in her eyes, and Jerry slid the clip down on the forceps, closing the ribs.

"I also believe this person had been infected for a short period of time, maybe less than a week," he said as he turned toward her. "This bacterial seeding of the lungs is usually caused by the inhalation of airborne bacteria which can produce inter-alveolar edema accompanied by abundant bacteria and acute inflammatory infiltrate."

"So you're saying this bacteria is airborne?" Maggie said. If this bacteria was airborne, that would make it a lot more contagious, she thought, running over the properties of bacteria in her head. *Bacteria are passed from host to host, similar to viruses, but very few bacteria are pathogenic. They live all around us in the water, soil, plants, animals, and even in our intestines and on our skin—but sometimes the bacteria can become deadly.*

"That's what I believe, yes, but I'll have my full report and tissue samples of the lung, lymph nodes, liver, spleen, and bone marrow sent to the CDC by this afternoon," Jerry said as he shook his head. "I must say—this disease is presenting itself much differently than any bacteria I have seen, but I will recommend a comparison is done of the blood and tissue samples to the pneumonic form of *Yersinia pestis.*"

"*Yersinia pestis*, you think this could be the plague?" She had heard of a small number of plague related deaths in the United States, but almost all of them were found in the Southwestern region and totaled less than 20 a year. Now, most cases of plague were in the sub-Saharan areas of Africa.

"Possibly, I've been fooled more than a few times," he said, shaking his head. "What I can tell you is that this man died from asphyxiation caused by blood hemorrhaging in the lungs."

CHAPTER 2

THE RED CROSS.
NEW YORK CITY.
AUGUST 23.

Amina Alaoui sat behind her desk in a small cubicle with five-foot walls isolating her from her surroundings. Even though she had her own space to work and think, she missed the outdoor air after being trapped inside an office all day.

As a child in Morocco, she used to sit under a lemon tree for hours at a time, listening to the slow trickle of the fountain in their Andalusian-style courtyard. The *riad* they lived in, or Moroccan traditional house, was private with walls made of mud brick that faced the open atrium. She remembered running her fingers over the zellige tiles on the walls bearing quotes in Arabic from the Quran.

But that was many years ago, and New York was now her home. Sometimes she enjoyed walking alone in Central Park, just to feel the openness of the city. Amina loved the open air, and when she closed her eyes she could almost smell the scent of the ocean buried underneath the smell of fumes from the cars.

She had made plenty of friends here, and although she missed many things about Morocco, she couldn't imagine ever moving back. New York was alive with an energy she couldn't explain. Besides, most of her family had moved to New York as well, including her parents.

Her brother Ahmed married and opened a business in Brooklyn and her sister Salma was attending college at NYU.

Amina's mother always asked her when she was getting married, but she hadn't found the right person yet. She knew she would have to marry someone Muslim in order for them to be accepted by her family, but she still had time. Her mother worried that she had bought into the western idea of being in love. In many ways her mother was right, she couldn't imagine spending her life with someone who she couldn't live without. There were a few men she had met over the years that she had feelings for, but things didn't seem to work out. Some of the men didn't want her to work, and she didn't want to quit her job at the Red Cross. She liked the independent feeling of making her own money—another western ideal. Amina glanced up as one of the other Red Cross workers named Greg Cooper sat a box on her desk.

"Here's another one for you," Greg said, the corners of his mouth curved upward in a smile.

"Thank you," Amina said, quickly averting her eyes away. She turned and watched as he walked back to his cubicle. She felt guilty for the light-headed feeling that Greg made her feel. She tried to transfer her thoughts to the work in front of her, but it was hard when the smell of his cologne filled her cubicle as if he was still there. He was a very handsome guy, and she found herself drawn to his light hair and eyes, but her family would never allow her to marry someone who was not Islamic. That was where they drew the line.

She glanced down at the metal box he had sat on her desk. She was in charge of cataloging local contributions and setting up banking deposits. Since the Red Cross is not funded by the government, many of the donations arrived as checks and money orders, but because of the many Red Cross donation stands, they also received a lot of loose change and bills.

She opened the container and began adding the coins to the counting machine. She watched for a few moments as the coins dropped down and disappeared. There had been so many wars over money, yet she knew money could also save lives just as well as take them. She stared at the cross symbol on her wall. The cross did not have any religious meaning to her the way it did to Christians and other religions, but she knew the Red Cross helped people and that made her feel good about her job.

Amina yawned as she separated the bills with images of American presidents and laid them on the table. Another thing she missed from Morocco was the coffee, the dark blend laden with warm spices. Even as a child, she used to relish taking sips of the fragrant drink. She took a couple of one dollar bills out of her purse and added one of them to the pile on the table. She reached into the metal box and pulled out four quarters in exchange. For now, American coffee would have to do, Amina thought as she pushed herself away from her desk and walked down the hall.

She didn't care for the employee room coffee, it always had a stale taste. The coffee vending machine, however, had flavored coffee which was much closer to the taste she was accustomed to. She stopped in the hallway in front of the coffee vending machine, studying the different flavors as she squeezed the coins in her hand. She liked the taste of the french vanilla coffee or the hazelnut. Today, she would have the hazelnut.

She turned, watching the yellow cabs and people as they walked by on the streets outside. She heard the sound of the coffee pouring, trickling out like the fountain in Morocco so many years ago. When the flow of coffee stopped, she slid the plastic door to the side, holding the warm cup against her palms. She relished in the fragrant aroma, took a sip, and walked back to her cubicle.

CHAPTER 3

THE CDC.
ATLANTA, GEORGIA.
AUGUST 23.

Microbiologist Michael Harbinger took off his shirt and jeans and folded them neatly; then, laid them in his locker along with his wedding ring, keys, wallet, and cellphone. Everything had to be stored away to enter the BSL-4 lab except eye-glasses—which was a good thing because he was blind without them.

Harbinger put on the green scrubs and white socks, and then reached for the yellow tape. He leaned down, pulled his socks over his pant leg, and taped the top of the socks. Then, he slid his hands into the gloves and ran tape around his wrists. He closed the locker, walked through the shower, and into the next chamber.

The walls in the chamber were lined with light blue Chemturion suits on long hooks. Harbinger lifted one of the suits carefully off the hook and laid it flat on the metal table behind him. He ran his hands down the positive pressure suit, examining it from head to toe. Satisfied there weren't any tears, he flipped the suit over and checked the back. It was important to visually inspect the suit each time beforehand, since they were only blown up once a week with air and tested for leaks.

Harbinger slid his foot carefully into the leg of the suit, followed by his left arm. He wiggled his fingers around in the attached glove until they were in place. Then, he began working his other leg into the suit and pulled the suit up over his other arm. After his fingers found their place inside the glove, he placed the helmet over his head. The suit weighed around 10 pounds and added a good 6 inches to your height. He always felt like an astronaut ready to attack alien invaders in the Chemturion suit—only these invaders were not from another planet.

It was very hot inside the suit, and his breath was already fogging up the face shield. Harbinger looked up at the red coiled oxygen hoses that were hanging from the ceiling and grasped ahold of the closest one. He pulled back on the collar on the hose and attached it to the front of his suit. The loud hissing sound of the air blocked out all the other noise around him. The suit immediately felt cooler, and the fogged up visor cleared.

He was used to the solitary confinement of working in the lab, but some people couldn't take it. Between the long hours without any communication and the inability to eat, drink, or use a restroom—many people found the job grueling. Add in the claustrophobia and the fact you're putting your life at risk dealing with the deadliest diseases, and they bolted for the door crying for reassignment.

He didn't know if it was the adrenaline rush, or just a suicidal tendency on his part, but he loved his job. He loved working in this self-contained box within a box. He had always been fascinated by the invisible creatures around us. Even when he was a boy, all he wanted was a microscope. He kept stealing his father's magnifier—anything to get a closer look at what lurks beneath, on top of, or all over the world around us. His parents finally broke down and bought him a microscope, and he began examining everything he could fit under the tiny lens.

Harbinger zipped the front of the suit and reached down, grabbing a pair of the green HAZMAT boots. He braced himself against the wall as he bent forward and carefully slid each foot into one of the boots. His thoughts went back to his first job as a microbiologist with the CDC, working with microbes on BSL-2. Those were the ones that caused mild diseases—annoying but curable bacteria that caused diarrhea, or a virus like you'd see with the common cold. Then, after a few years, he began working on BSL-3 with more serious diseases, all of them with a readily made vaccine or medicine available. He remembered getting vaccinated for every contagious disease they had: yellow fever, botulism, Rift Valley fever, and many others he hadn't heard of until he began working with them.

Back then, there was a sense of safety dealing with diseases that have a cure, but soon he was moved to BSL-4—the keeper of all the bad things you've ever dreamed of. It was the Hot Zone, also known as the life-threatening, no vaccine, and no cure zone. Housed in the confines of an isolated area in the CDC building, these were the dangerous and exotic microbes that were at high risk of causing aerosol transmitted infections. The safety net was pulled out from under his feet—one wrong move, and it could be his last. Now, all that stood between him and a deadly disease was a space suit.

Harbinger looked over at the plastic bin with pre-labeled tubes, reagents, and other equipment. His thoughts drifted to the new bacteria that had been sent in from the Bacterial Diseases Branch of the CDC. He always got his hopes up when he heard those words, it was a dream of his to make a new discovery, but most of the diseases that were brought in fell into a well-defined label. This particular bacteria he would be working with today fell under the Special Study *Yersinia pestis* Code CDC-10530. Unfortunately, it was probably not new at all—but a mutation.

There are 11 species of yersiniae, but only three of them garner the crown of being pathogenic to humans: *Yersinia enterocolitica, Yersinia pseudotuberculosis,* and *Yersinia pestis.* The later, *Yersinia pestis,* being the most well known, and the cause of Bubonic plague or the romanticized term the "Black Death." The name "Black Death," referred to the purple and black skin color of the victim which marked the person for death.

He turned and watched as Carl Whitman, another microbiologist, stepped into the chamber and began suiting up. He was usually teamed up with a lab "buddy" even though it was impossible to have any sort of communication with the noisy airflow in the helmet. After Whitman was set in his gear, they both began to inspect each other, like some form of primitive apes. Harbinger ran his gloved hand across the back of Whitman's helmet, and stood still as he returned the favor.

Carl Whitman was a young guy, still in his twenties, and probably raised with a silver spoon in his mouth, Harbinger figured, but the kid was a genius. Whitman made everything look easy and never seemed to look like he was working very hard. Whereas Harbinger took years to get to BSL-4, Whitman was moved quickly to the top in under two years. A true Harvard boy, with the badges to prove it, graduating *Summa cum laude* for Biological Sciences. Harbinger's USC degree didn't hold a candle next to his cool as ice co-worker, but he did have a fine eye for the smallest microscopic details often overlooked by others.

Whitman held up a gloved hand, giving a thumbs up. Harbinger returned the sign and pushed the button to enter the lab. Both men unhooked the red coiled hose attached to their suits. A metal submarine-style door with a biohazard symbol slid open, and they both stepped inside, each carrying a bin with supplies. The air pressure resistant door closed, sealing shut, and a green light lit up.

The air-tight BSL-4 lab has 10-inch double reinforced walls with a special epoxy coating on outside. The low-pressure air in the lab only runs in one direction and is pulled through HEPA filters that rid the air of any pathogens. Inside the lab are various workstations, most of them behind negative pressure work hoods or in a glovebox. A center area had computers and microscopic equipment. Green lights lit up two of the stations, and they both moved toward them. Harbinger grabbed the red coiled hose above him and attached it to the front of his suit. Hooking up to the air supply hoses and unhooking was required each time a person moved around the lab.

Harbinger turned toward the biosafety cabinet next to him. All microbes were passed through an autoclave and barcoded for security reasons. Every pathogen that was in use was placed in a log, and after working with a pathogen it had to be destroyed. A round container was inside the cabinet with his name on the label next to the code CDC-10530. He pulled out the plastic container and turned back toward the glovebox.

He sat down slowly, making sure the chair did not roll out from under him. He pressed on his stomach to expel the extra air, and then lifted the top of the cabinet, placing the container inside. He slid his hands into the long, heavy duty black rubber gloves that ran through ports into the container. Then, he carefully, opened the lid and lifted the tube out containing the blood contaminated with the bacteria. With a long plastic syringe, he placed droplets of blood and colored the smears on the slide with stain. He needed to check for the presence of bi-polar staining Gram-negative bacilli in the microscope.

Harbinger looked up at the gram stain on the microscopic screen as a number of long rod-shaped bacterium organisms appeared in front of him. At first glance with an almost safety pin shape, Harbinger also thought it was the Bubonic plague and could see why it came in under the guise of *Yersinia pestis*, but something was different. The individual features of the bacteria were more archaic and seemed to bulge out in sections. The appearance of the colony was also aligned differently. These details were small and easy to miss, but very clear from his perspective.

Harbinger pulled his hands out of the gloves in the port and turned toward the computer next to him. His eyes scanned down the coroner report:

No epidermal discoloration or buboes. Hemorrhaging in the lungs. Marked congestion of the lungs. Red ringed pulmonary nodules. Pulmonary edema. Excessive bleeding from body orifices. Recommend ruling out pneumonic plague caused by *Yersinia pestis*.

He typed in his report to the control room that was monitoring them from a different area:

Gram-negative, bacilliform bacterium. Starting comparison with
***Yersinia pestis* with culture media. Visual inspection of bacteria**
yields negative results.

Harbinger turned back to the microscope as he increased the magnification. Testing the bacteria for different byproducts was a common way to rule out the relationship of a bacteria. This can be done by inhibiting or encouraging the growth in the bacteria and comparing the two. He slid his hands back into the glovebox, carefully removing the vial of *Yersinia pestis* and placing it in the culture media. He had to isolate the bacilli in the tissue samples sent in from the coroner. He would then also check for diagnostic change in antibody titers in paired serum samples.

Since bacteria are microbes which are single-celled, they do not have a nucleus or membrane-bound organelles, all of their genetic information is in a single loop of DNA—unless they have a plasmid. A plasmid is an extra circle of genetic material which replicates individually and may make the bacterium resistant to some forms of antibiotics. *Yersinia pestis* has three different types of plasmids. From his visual inspection he counted four plasmids on the new bacteria.

He studied the acute-phase serum for the presence of antibodies against the specific *Y. pestis* F1-capsular antigen. While he waited, he watched the bacteria he had placed under a microscope. Two of them had already started dividing, which is when they release chemical poisons that kill human cells. Usually, it will also cause the symptoms the host will experience. *Yersinia pestis* carries a total of six toxins, called Yops, which are *Yersinia* outer membrane proteins. It injects these toxins across cell membranes by using a Type III injection apparatus. The new bacteria was also using a Type III injection apparatus, but the toxins were behaving differently. It's not using Yop toxins, Harbinger thought as he watched it invade a normal cell. His heart was beginning to race. If his observations were correct, this was not a mutant bacteria—this was a completely different bacteria.

He watched patiently as the new bacteria continued dividing. Bacteria reproduce by a process called binary fission. When this occurs, the bacterium divides into two daughter cells, each with DNA identical to the parent cell. He had seen bacteria divide rapidly, but this bacteria was dividing in half that time—faster than the *Yersinia pestis* bacteria. There was also something familiar about the characteristics of the bacteria, maybe it was the shape, but he couldn't place his finger on it.

Harbinger could feel his hands shaking as he started a new media with the two bacteria. He had to rule out the possibility that the media was causing the difference between the two. Each test he ran yielded the same results. He stared at the screen. It's not a match, Harbinger thought. It's a new strain. He turned and began typing:

Yersinia pestis -Yop toxins NEGATIVE. Recommend DNA sequencing.

Since the genome of *Yersinia pestis* had already been sequenced, it was the best way to completely rule out the bacteria as being a mutant form of yersiniae. The CDC was not quick to categorize new bacteria and it would need further testing. But he knew he was right, he could feel it in his gut. Then, he remembered where he had heard about similar behavior in a bacteria before.

Harbinger unhooked his hose and noticed that Whitman had already left the lab. He didn't realize so much time had passed. He had been working for eight hours straight. The thought made his throat dry up, he hadn't had a drink of water, food, or relieved himself in eight hours. This was a common occurrence since the only way to use the facilities was to completely un-suit and re-suit which was time consuming and discouraged.

Right now, all of his thoughts were on the new bacteria. He had to find out if his inclinations were true. Was it possible that James was right? That would mean this bacteria was not new at all, but an ancient one. He pushed a button that opened the sealed door, carrying his bin with him. He watched through the small window of the air pressure resistant door as it sealed shut, and a fog of formaldehyde vapor filled the air. He stepped into the shower, deep in thought as the mist from the chemical disinfectant rose up around him, once again clouding his vision.

CHAPTER 4

REGENCY HOSPITAL.
NEW YORK CITY.
AUGUST 24.

"He moves in darkness as it seems to me,
Not of woods only and the shade of trees."
—Robert Frost, North of Boston

I t was almost five o'clock in the morning. To most people, it was early, but to Samuel Greene it was late—the final end of a long night shift at Regency Hospital. He took off his name tag and dropped it in the center council of his Honda Civic where it found its place among a few paperclips, an old photo from his days in the marine corps, and a pack of spearmint gum.

It had been a difficult evening, and every push and pull of the mop required extra effort. Samuel knew he was sick, he had been feeling punky for days, and his muscles ached down to the bone like he had been beaten silly. But to him, taking time off of work was out of the question—he hadn't missed a day of work in 20 years. He planned to hunker down in the trenches and hold his ground, just like he was taught in his days as a soldier. He wasn't about to fall into the trap that some old folks fell into when they retired. Most of them wound up dead months later. If he didn't have a purpose, then he knew his soul would move on to the next world. And he wasn't ready to check his hat at the door just yet.

He turned on the ignition, stepped on the gas, and began heading toward the exit of the hospital parking garage. His foot slid over to the brake, stopping the car as a wave of nausea came over him. His eyes searched the interior of the car for a bag . . . anything. He opened the glove box and after seeing nothing but papers, he opened the car door. He had barely gotten the door open before the contents of his stomach came up. Greene sat there with his head hunched over and began dry heaving. The taste of stomach acid washed over his tongue and burned his throat.

He sat back up, resting the back of his head against the seat as he stared up at the interior light of the car. Vomiting made his throat smart worse, and his head was throbbing meanly at his temples. Something unsettled his tummy. Maybe it was the olive loaf, Samuel thought. He should have known it was too far past the expiration date. Three weeks might have been too long. He didn't like to waste food and never quite bought into those dates they stamped on the packages. Sell by dates . . . expiration dates, Greene thought. My Lord, if humans came with those stamps—my own expiration date probably passed long ago. He shook his head and wiped his mouth on the end of his sleeve.

He glanced down at the remains of Wonder Bread and packaged deli meat interspersed with a reddish colored liquid. At first, he thought it was blood, then he remembered the pimento in the olive loaf. He felt an urge to mop the mess up. He didn't like folks having to clean up after him, it was what he did. Others got queasy by human waste, but he had been cleaning up after people for so long it didn't bother him. The issue was that he had nothing to clean up the mess with, and all of his cleaning supplies were a long, long ways away.

Samuel glanced around at the parked cars around him, wondering how the situation could be remedied. He watched as a car whipped into a parking spot, taking up more than its fair share of space. The woman had a white coat slung over her arm. A doctor, he figured. The backlights of her car beeped and flashed as she rushed inside, not even

17

turning his way. After a few moments, he felt the sickness return, and his hand hit the hazard lights by accident. He saw red flashing on his panel and reached up and turned them off as he bent over. This time as he dry heaved only yellow bile came out. He leaned back in his seat and shut the car door. He was sweating profusely and clutched his stomach as pain twisted his innards.

One thing for certain—there was no way he could drive in this condition—he could barely straighten up enough to grab the wheel. He glanced around and saw an empty parking space out of the way in the corner. He backed the car up, cringing at the puddle of vomit he left behind as he pulled into the corner slot. He turned off the car and closed his eyes. It looked like he would have to sit here, at least until the sick feeling passed.

He didn't want to bother his daughter, she had her hands full with a newborn baby. Besides, she was the one who needed his help, and he tried to help her out whenever he could, even contemplating taking on a second job. Now that the baby was born, she would have to juggle her college courses along with raising a baby on her own. One thing that he did know—he didn't want her dropping out. He'd work five jobs if he had to. He had finally gotten her to agree to enroll in some night classes at the community college—he didn't want his daughter to end up like him. She was smarter than he was, she just got involved with the wrong folks.

As happy as he was to be a grandpa, the news wasn't good when he found out she was pregnant. He didn't particularly care for the young man she was with at the time—he wore his pants too low and seemed overly polite in person. The act didn't fool him, no siree. He could see that the young man would rather lie through his teeth than tell the truth.

One time he stopped by his daughter's apartment complex to drop off some of her mail and saw the boy hanging out on the side of the building. He saw some sort of exchange happen between him and two other boys. And he knew boys that age only exchange one thing—drugs. He blamed his daughter's behavior on his ex-wife. She had a free spirit, too. One day her spirit was so free that she packed up her things and left them both, never to be heard from again.

Samuel closed his eyes. He could feel pain building in his stomach again. He tried to stretch his legs out—they were cramped in the same position under the steering wheel. He rolled down his window for some fresh air. Then, he felt around for the lever on the side of the seat to lower it, but his knobby fingers weren't working well. He lurched forward as he began coughing. The cough was so deep, it felt like his innards were coming out. A tightness clenched his chest. If Samuel didn't know better, he would have thought he was having a heart attack. Whatever was happening to him, it wasn't good. He brought his hand up to cover his mouth as he continued to cough. He could feel something wet on his hand. When he moved his hand up to eye level, a wave of fear went through him. His hand was covered in blood.

A series of uncontrollable coughs rang out in succession, and it was hard for him to catch his breath in between. He felt himself going in and out of consciousness as the tightness in his chest increased. He saw dark shadows approaching in his peripheral vision—it was the walls closing in around him. He knew they were coming to claim him. His head landed on the steering wheel, and he stared out as the inky blackness engulfed him.

CHAPTER 5

NEW YORK CITY.
AUGUST 24.

*"I looked, and there before me was a pale horse!
Its rider was named Death, and Hades was following
close behind him. They were given power over a fourth
of the earth to kill by sword, famine and plague, and by
the wild beasts of the earth."*

—Revelation 6:8

Maggie De Luca read the email again from the CDC. She had read it numerous times, but she still couldn't believe the words she was seeing: UNKNOWN BACTERIA, PLAGUE PRECAUTIONS. The medical examiner was right, it seemed the CDC didn't even know exactly what they were dealing with. If this was a new strain of a plague-like bacteria, then the death toll could be much higher if it wasn't contained.

The mortality rate of the pneumonic plague is 100 percent if antibiotics are not given within the first 24 hours. An even larger problem is that antibiotics are not as effective against pneumonic plague and could be completely ineffective in the new bacteria. Since this unknown bacteria was airborne, it added a whole new level of problems, especially in a city the size of New York.

Maggie's head was spinning as she tried to remember everything she could about the plague. She remembered hearing a lecture in college about the plague and how it began. The history was sketchy at best, but some scholars argued it began when the Mongols catapulted corpses over the walls of the city of Kaffa. But it would be years later that the plague became known as the "Black Death," when trade routes were established between Europe and Asia, therein killing over one-third of Europe's population at the time. Famine and poor living conditions had already wreaked havoc across these countries, and the disease was able to spread and kill quickly.

The culprit was a deadly bacteria called *Yersinia pestis*, a bacteria that is present in some low types of rodents. The bacteria were then transferred to humans by fleas, which had feasted on the blood of the infected rats. The rats soon died and the fleas then began feasting on humans.

She felt overwhelmed, it was as if the entire world rested on her shoulders. She had to keep reminding herself that this was not the plague—only plague precautions. The words kept running through her head like a broken record: BACTERIA UNKNOWN. She couldn't get the image of the decimated lungs of Juan Martinez out of her mind. What the hell were they dealing with? Her psychologist always reminded her that she was not the savior of the world, but she couldn't help but feel responsible when things went wrong.

She had seen plenty of red alerts over the years, but none of them were related to the plague. The worst case she had seen was the Ebola epidemic that killed a little over 15,000 people between 2014 and 2016. Most of the deaths occurred in West Africa, but it did mark the first time the Ebola virus gained entry into a capital city. This was also the first time Ebola spread to a new country on the tail of an asymptomatic air passenger.

Ebola caused quite a panic, but never caught a grip on the U.S., with only one death in the states. But since the disease caused bleeding from all of the body orifices, including the eyes, it made for ungodly media sensation.

She had lost a few colleagues who worked as health care workers at some of the outbreak sites in Africa. A little over 150 workers had died. She was almost assigned to go to Africa with a team of scientists, but a case of yellow fever here in the states, just may have saved her life. Odd to think of it that way, she thought. *A disease that saved a life.*

She made a mental note to call Michael later. Dr. Michael Harbinger was a microbiologist she had worked with at the CDC before she was transferred. As an epidemiologist, she was considered a "detective" at the CDC and needed to have knowledge of many areas of research, including tracking down the cause of a disease by collecting samples and analyzing data. Michael taught new workers about laboratory procedures, handling dangerous microbes, and how to suit up in protective suits when she was first starting out.

She had always found him comforting to be around, and he had helped her more than a few times with cases she was working on over the years. Her eyes scanned down to the bottom of the email and saw his name as one of the workers on the case. She figured he would be, since all new cases of unknown airborne pathogens are sent to the BSL-4 lab of the CDC where he worked. He could tell her more about what was going on and information on how the CDC planned to handle the disease, but right now, she had work to do.

She looked over her notes again. She had a sinking feeling that Juan Martinez was not the first case of this bacteria—and definitely not the last. Too many cases were misdiagnosed and subsequently overlooked by the CDC. She read another section at the bottom of the email and nodded her head. Because of the plague precautions, she figured the CDC would be looking at the possibility of this being a biological warfare weapon. It was no secret that The World Health Organization, or WHO, had already classified the plague as Category A, which meant the disease required constant monitoring and was an ongoing threat.

Using diseases in biological warfare was nothing new. There were legends of dropping fleas infected with the plague from planes onto enemy territories below, aerosolizing the plague and other deadly pathogens during the Cold War, and most recently worries about pathogens getting into the hands of extreme terrorist groups.

There were even rumors going around the CDC claiming that the CDC did, in fact, have a vaccine against the plague, but kept it behind closed doors in case the plague was needed by our own government for biological warfare. These were rumors of course, but she found the idea of purposely hiding a cure for something appalling. If it were true, she could be working for the people responsible for a new plague emerging. Possibly even the bacteria they were now encountering. The thought sent shivers down her spine, and she tried to put the thoughts out of her head. After all, the CDC were the good guys, right?

She wasn't alone, even with the Ebola virus running its course, the thought of a plague re-emerging was even more frightening to most people, and she was no exception. The plague cases she had heard about in the Southwestern portions of the United States had been contained quickly and the loss of lives remained low, but the idea of a new plague breaking out in the heart of New York City . . . that was terrifying.

Would she be able to gather the needed information before it was too late? She had to think. Maggie clicked the button on her secure server and forwarded the email to her team, she would need all the help she could get. She tried to formulate a game plan. The hospital administrator she had spoken to reassured her that there were not any similar cases in their files. She asked them to comb through their database again, checking for hemorrhaging or any kind of deaths from asphyxiation.

The fact that Martinez also worked at Regency Hospital made her think there had to be a connection to the hospital itself. Even if he hadn't caught it there, surely it would have spread rapidly among the workers or patients he was in contact with. If it was the only death like it at Regency, it wouldn't be for long. Since they were dealing with an airborne bacteria, anyone who came anywhere near Martinez could have contracted the disease. All an infected person had to do was cough, and the droplets with bacteria would travel through the air, ready for the next host to inhale them in. The doctor and nurses who worked in the emergency room the night Martinez died were already in quarantine. So far, they weren't showing any signs of the disease. She still didn't trust it.

She emailed a message to two of her team members to get a list of all the patients at the hospital over the last two weeks and a list of all the hospital staff. The only way to be sure was to check each person out individually. If it were up to her, she would quarantine the entire hospital and move the patients who were cleared to another hospital, but the CDC was slow to make any move that would alarm the public.

It would help if she knew exactly what she was dealing with. Over the years, she had butted heads with the CDC more than a few times, and just like any company—there were too many fingers in the pot. The way every decision had to be approved, from one level to the next—she was surprised that anything got done. It was frustrating. Everything was categorized as a level to them, the diseases, the people in charge— each person answering to the next higher level up. The highest level was where the money was—the pharmaceutical companies.

Maggie tried to clear her head as she ran over the information. She also had to remind herself that this wasn't considered an outbreak until there were more victims—one death didn't prove anything—except that a deadly disease was out there. It would take many more deaths for the CDC to activate the Emergency Operations Center. The where, who, and how it started were left for her and her team to discover.

Her thoughts went back to what they had on Martinez. After one of her team members talked with a colleague of Juan Martinez, she had learned that Martinez was a quiet man, who mostly kept to himself—partly because he was trying to learn English. Originally from Mexico, Martinez was working as a nurse assistant.

He lived alone in a tiny apartment in a rundown area commonly referred to as "gangland." Martinez didn't fit the profile of a gang member and must have chosen the apartment because of the low rent. New York rents were some of the most expensive in the world, and the wage of a nurse assistant wouldn't go far. His apartment was sparsely furnished, with only a mattress on the floor which was splattered with blood.

The landlord had called 911 after finding Martinez unconscious on the floor of his apartment. The landlord, an elderly man with a thick Italian accent, said that Martinez was always on time with his rent, and he had become worried when Juan was late paying. The landlord was also put into quarantine until he could be cleared.

Since Martinez was a nurse assistant and nearly a doctor in Mexico, from the information they were gathering, she was surprised he hadn't gotten medical attention sooner. Unless, the new strain of bacteria presents as mild symptoms and kills swiftly at the end. She wondered if the bacteria hid under the guise of a cold or flu like the Ebola virus? This could be likely since its mode of attack is the lungs. This would also give the disease more time to spread to a variety of hosts. Although, if Martinez had been infected for less than a week, then the bacteria had a short incubation period and killed quickly. The incubation period is the time interval between the exposure to the pathogenic organism and the first onset of symptoms. The incubation period for the pneumonic plague form of *Yersinia pestis* was one to three days.

Martinez hadn't left the country for over a year, but she still had concerns about the Mexico connection. Luckily, each link to Mexico turned out to be a dead end. Martinez wire transferred money to his family in Mexico and didn't have any friends from Mexico that lived in New York. It was clear that Martinez was a hard worker, he didn't drink or hang out in bars. His landlord said that he never saw Martinez bring anyone home. In his apartment, there were stacks of college textbooks in Spanish and catalogs for the local community college, which painted a picture of him as a hard working man, who was continuing his education here in the states for financial reasons.

She still had to be sure, the last thing they needed was for a strain of plague-like bacteria to start spreading out to other countries. Or had it already? There was also a possibility that the disease didn't start in New York, but so far there hadn't been any incidents reported—Martinez was their only connection.

There was difficulty communicating between countries about diseases, and the information came in slowly. Some of the developing countries lacked the medical knowledge, and the fact that famine was rampant there made it a perfect breeding ground for disease.

Regardless, she knew that the Global Disease Detection unit of the CDC, could send in further information about another country with links to the disease at any time. There was always the possibility the disease had started somewhere else.

Maggie tapped the tip of her pencil against the desk in thought. Since they were taking plague precautions, she typed in the word PLAGUE. She moved in closer to the screen, staring at a black and white sketch on the computer of four men on horses. The caption under the drawing said PLAGUE OR PESTILENCE, ONE OF THE FOUR HORSEMAN OF THE APOCALYPSE. One of the horseman was a skull-faced man on a pale horse, wielding a scythe. Great way to start the search, she thought.

They had to find out where Martinez contracted the illness. First, she'd look into Regency Hospital, since it was the most likely place. She would also put in a request to move patients out of the hospital. It may do little, but at least she tried. Her team would need time to go through all of the patients and workers. At least Martinez hadn't taken any classes for a couple of months, that would have added a whole new set of problems.

She clicked on a map of New York City and enlarged the area around Regency Hospital. Her eyes followed the street that led to Martinez's apartment on 4th Street. She ran her finger between the two locations. There were only a few routes he could take to work. If the bacteria didn't come from Regency, then he may have picked it up somewhere else on the way to work.

CHAPTER 6

THE RED CROSS.
NEW YORK CITY.
AUGUST 24.

"Good sense makes one slow to anger,
and it is his glory to overlook an offense."
—Proverbs 19:11

The Metropolitan Transportation Authority Bus Company is the 11th largest bus company in the United States. With over 1200 buses and routes spanning from Manhattan to the Bronx, Queens, or Brooklyn, the MTA buses carry over 121 million passengers a year.

Melinda Howard stepped off of MTA bus number 23 and stared up at the buildings around her. She looked down at one last piece of bear claw pastry in her hand and added it to her already full mouth. Then, she washed it down with the last bit of coffee in her cup. She could feel her purse strap falling off her shoulder and grasped the strap, giving it a tug upward as she tossed the empty cup in the trash can next to her.

Even though her tennis shoes were extra wide, the laces still felt too tight. Next time, Howard thought, I'll buy the ones with velcro straps. Shoes were always a problem for her. They were always too tight or too cramped in the toes and almost every time—there wasn't enough arch support. Although she couldn't see her feet when she glanced down, she was sure they had swollen up again. She could always tell when this happened because the front of her shins would ache.

She was a big lady and she knew it. Dr. Patan made sure to make her aware of her size every time she saw him: 265 pounds. Her weight didn't fluctuate much, give or take five pounds—it was almost always the same number. Someone knocked into her elbow, and she realized she was blocking the other passengers from boarding the bus. She hoisted her bag up higher on her shoulder and stepped out of the way.

Looking back, she didn't know how the weight snuck up on her like it did. When she was younger, back in Kansas, she could put away two plates of food and still remain as thin as a bean pole. Her mother used to sew and would have to adjust the waist on her clothes because she was too thin and nothing fit. Now, she was on the other side of the spectrum, and the only way to find clothes that fit was to visit one of the big lady department stores.

She did try to lose weight, but no matter what she did, the weight just wouldn't come off. She'd tried Jenny Craig, Weight Watchers, and had even considered gastric bypass surgery. Maybe it was a good thing she had to walk a bit, the exercise wouldn't hurt.

She looked up at the street sign: Lexington Avenue. This was the closest stop she could get by bus to 42nd Street, but something told her to make the trip anyway. She called it a higher calling, that inner tug she would feel to help others in need—those less fortunate than herself. To see all the people suffering from different diseases like cancer on the news made her heart ache. Babies, small children, and the elderly were some of the worst affected. The most innocent souls, she thought as she walked down the sidewalk. She tried to donate twice a year, a regimen she had practiced for years after a little girl at the school she worked for was stricken with leukemia.

As a bus driver herself, she had just finished her shift when she decided to make the journey to the city. There were other blood donation centers closer, but part of her ritual was to go directly to the main Red

Cross downtown. The crosswalk light changed, and she walked with the crowd across the street.

She noticed that people in the city tended to keep a bit to themselves. She watched as a group of businessmen hurriedly walked by—all of them talking on their cellphones. Nobody talked to anyone else anymore, she thought. Everyone was always on their cellphones. She saw entire families in the restaurants, none of them talking to each other, instead, they were all texting on their phones. Melinda had learned that in general, people only worried about what affected them: panic was saved for those events that struck closer to home.

After what felt like an hour on her tired feet, Howard finally spotted the Red Cross up ahead. It was a plain entryway located on the lower level of a tall skyscraper, except for the bright white sign with the Red Cross symbol above the entrance. She made her way up the steps, feeling the full weight of her body as she lifted each leg. When Jesus calls, you listen, Melinda thought as she reached the top of the steps. As the doors slid open, the cool air blew across her cheeks. It was a welcome relief from the stifling humidity outside.

A white sign with an arrow in the entryway pointed her to a table with a long line of people. Praise the Lord, others were also hearing the call for help, Melinda thought as she stepped in line behind a young man wearing ear pods. She noticed he had a wrist full of different-colored bracelets and a peace symbol on the back of his shirt. She could tell he was a millennial—the new up and coming generation. She was happy to see someone so young helping others. She was around children much younger in her line of work and tried to instill what she could by setting a good example. The idea of helping and connecting to the people around her warmed her heart. She watched as a few people walked by with red heart-shaped stickers on their shirts that said I GAVE BLOOD TODAY. Soon, she would have one, too.

Howard walked forward with the line of people as it moved, following her group to a room with metal chairs lined up against the wall. She grabbed one of the white forms laying on the table and a clipboard before sitting in one of the too small metal chairs. After she filled out the information form, a thin woman with gaunt cheeks walked by, pushing a cart in front of her. The woman looked down at Melinda with a look she'd seen before, but usually ignored. She was used to the snickers and looks of disapproval from strangers because of her large size. She knew that most people thought she was lazy and looked down on her for being overweight, but she tended to think it was more about a fear they had inside themselves and had little to do with her.

The woman grabbed the white form out of Melinda's hand, sliding it into the plastic holder on top the cart. Howard turned her head as the woman tightened the band around her arm and asked her to make a fist. She felt the rubber pinching at her skin and then something wet and cold. The scent of alcohol wafted to her nose as the woman rubbed a cotton swab over her arm.

"Just a small stick," the woman said as she slid the needle into her arm. "Okay, you can relax now."

Melinda loosened her fist as her eyes glanced around the room at the other donor's in metal chairs, a stream of red blood flowing out of their arms. She had only come close to passing out one time and found it better if she didn't think about it as she sat there, since pulling her up off the floor would be a lot of work for anyone. She turned back around as she felt the woman put a bandage on her arm.

"Thank you," Melinda said. She was pleased she only felt slightly lightheaded. The woman nodded her head and handed her a small dixie cup of orange juice and a heart-shaped sticker.

On the way out, she pressed the sticker on her shirt, finished the orange juice, and tossed the cup in the trash. She was still feeling a bit tired and noticed a coffee vending machine down the hallway. She waited while a lady, with one of those thingamajigs on her head, got her coffee. Then, she pulled out her wallet from her purse. Two dollars and twenty-five cents, Howard thought as she slid a few one dollar bills into the machine. She glanced down as the coffee cup landed, and the dark brown coffee streamed out. While she waited, she checked the coin dispenser and pulled out three quarters, adding them to her change purse. She opened the compartment and pulled out the full cup of coffee, dabbing her finger inside to test the temperature. The coffee was luke-warm, but that was probably better on such a blisteringly hot day.

She walked through the sliding doors. As she walked back down the steps, she glanced down at the heart-shaped sticker. She had done a good deed today. It was a blessed day.

CHAPTER 7

ATLANTA, GEORGIA.
AUGUST 24.

Michael Harbinger read an out of date article in the "The Journal of Evolutionary Science," by Dr. J.D. Stallings titled "The Ancient Plague of Man."

Harbinger scrolled down the article which talked about an earlier plague that existed during the Bronze Age, thousands of years before *Yersinia pestis* first made its appearance. There was a photo of Stallings holding up a human skull. Next to the photo was a picture of various rod-shaped bacteria.

He sat farther up in his seat, clicked a button on the computer, and zoomed in on the photo. His eyes followed the shape of the bacteria. It had the same shape of the new bacteria, bulging out in areas. He knew the bacteria looked familiar—he had come across the article when he heard about Stallings and his research years ago. The article was not widely accepted by most scientists who argued that microbes and other bacteria commonly colonize human bones after death. At the time, he had found the idea of an ancient plague ludicrous as well.

James Stallings was one of his former roommates at USC and they hadn't spoken for over 20 years. Although they were both in the science field, Stallings had majored in anthropological studies, while Harbinger majored in molecular microbiology. He had read that Stallings later went into paleoanthropology.

He studied the photo of Stallings, his mind drifting back in time. He could picture their dorm room and the long hours spent sitting at a desk or in the lab. It seemed like decades ago. The article itself was from 17 years ago. What if after all of these years James was right? he thought.

Harbinger opened a file on his desktop and clicked on a photo with today's date and the code CDC-10530. He tapped on a photo of the bacteria he had sent to his computer from the lab, aligning the two bacteria side by side. There was no mistaking, it was a match. He could feel his pulse racing. He was on to something here. He had to find out more information about Stallings' research.

He scanned farther down the computer screen. In the article, Stallings' theory suggests that an ancient plague wiped out some populations of man, which led to the rise of other groups. He called the theory, "The Displacement of Ancient Tribes."

Stallings further explained that the ancient genetic material found in human bones from the Bronze Age contained the ancient plague. "Furthermore," Stallings hypothesized, "the ancient plague solves the mystery of the downfall of the Egyptian Empire, the Hittites, and the Mycenaeans, who traded frequently with each other. The ancient plague was why these ancient civilizations from Egypt to Greece, city after city, were burned to the ground. This explains why trade suddenly disappeared, societies shrunk, and entire areas were abandoned. These civilizations were merely trying to rid themselves of an ancient plague."

"This microbial DNA," Stallings stated, "was not only found earlier in the Bronze Age, but was also found before and during the reign of the Black Death. Traces of this ancient plague were found in human bones in Italy dating back to 250 to 270 A.D., in the time of the Plague of Cyprian. In Greece around 430 B.C., matching to the timeline of the Plague of Athens. And in bones from Istanbul from 541 to 542 A.D., the same year as the Plague of Justinian. It was also found in Central Asia in 1338—which marks the first time that the Black Death appeared. This, without doubt, explains," Stallings concluded, "why the plague was so successful throughout history—there was more than one. This ancient plague not only caused the deaths of millions of people—it gave rise to the plague known as the Black Death."

Stallings added, "The DNA extracted from bones, which contain this ancient bacteria, are also missing a gene that would make it capable of surviving in fleas. Some scientists believe that this would hinder the ability of the ancient bacteria to spread as well as *Yersinia pestis*, but I disagree. An ancient bacteria which is airborne and capable of spreading directly from human to human, such as the pneumonic form of the Black Death, makes it much more lethal and deadly, even today."

Harbinger scrolled farther down, there was a photo of Stallings standing among a group of partially naked men with bowl haircuts. Below the photo were the words DR. J.D. STALLINGS AND THE MOTOMBU. The next paragraph had two graphs with timelines of the Bubonic plague and the ancient plague, both of the timelines showing the first introduction of the plague in Paraguay and Brazil in 1899. Stallings spoke of a tribe called the Motombu, who live in Brazil, that were unaffected by the arrival of the plague, even as it closed in around them. There were some maps and charts, as well as photos of bones. It appeared the ancient plague spread even farther into the Amazon than the Bubonic plague.

Stallings attributed this immunity to the Motombu diet. Specifically, a plant that only grows in a remote region of the Amazon named *lapethria*. Stallings went on to explain that the Motombu grind the plant into a thick paste and chew the leaves.

Harbinger typed in the name LAPETHRIA on the computer, but it yielded no results, except the mention in Stallings' article and a few scientists who criticized the idea of an ancient plague. Many of them argued that the Motombu were only unscathed by the plague because of their isolation from the rest of the world.

He sat back in his chair, stretched his arms above his head, and took off his eyeglasses. He squeezed his eyes shut, and then opened them again, feeling a sting in both eyes. Then he began cleaning his eyeglasses on the bottom of his shirt. He hadn't slept for almost 24 hours, his mind just wouldn't quit racing. He had a nagging feeling that James was on to something.

He thought about the fact that almost all medicines come from plants, followed by fungi, vertebrate species such as frogs and snakes, and even from bacteria itself. The theory was not that far-fetched. There was a possibility that he was not only right about the ancient bacteria, but also about a cure. If only he had the *lapethria* plant, he could test Stallings' theory and possibly even make a vaccine. But, there was only one way to get the plant. He sat up in his seat, realizing what he needed to do—contact James.

CHAPTER 8

LAS VEGAS, NEVADA.
AUGUST 25.

It was early morning, and the sun was just starting to penetrate through the blinds. Stallings glanced over at Jeanine. She was lying on her stomach with the sheet covering her up to the waist, her face partially blocked by blonde hair. She was a nice lady—maybe that was the problem—she was too nice. Whatever it was, he wished she wasn't in his bed right now—he hated it when she stayed over all night. He liked to wake up in the morning to quietness—not the sound of someone yapping.

He couldn't kid himself, Jeanine was just someone to fill the space. It was a space that many different shapes and sizes had tried on, but none of them quite fit. The most bothersome thing about Jeanine was how much she needed to talk. All day long she'd ramble on about her friends and their lives—people he'd never even met.

Stallings sat up in bed when the phone rang and glanced over at the clock: 6 AM. Who the hell would be calling this early? he thought. He reached over and grabbed his cell phone. It was someone calling from Atlanta.

"James?" a dry voice said on the other line.

No one ever called him James anymore. He glanced over at one of the books he wrote that was sitting on the dresser, *The Displacement of*

Ancient Tribes, by Dr. J.D. Stallings. Well, not since he was a boy anyway, and that only occurred when he was in trouble. "James Delroy!" His mother would call out in a huffy voice. He remembered how she would always snort heavily through her nostrils when she was angry. But that was a long time ago. Now, he was 48 years old, and his mother was long gone. Then, it hit him: the sound of the voice and annoying pause—it was another ghost from the past.

"Michael?" Stallings asked hesitantly. Mike Harbinger was an old college roommate from USC. They had lost touch over the years, but damn if he didn't always call him James. He, of course, returned the favor and Mike became Michael—funny enough, the guy preferred it that way.

"It's been a long time," Harbinger said.

"Sure has," Stallings responded, his mind drifting back to those long ago college dorm days. The late nights studying and all night parties. Harbinger was more of a lab rat back then, with his nose always stuck in a book, whereas he was more of a field mouse, eager to explore. "How did you find me?" He noticed Jeanine was beginning to stir in the bed. He walked into the other room—he didn't want to wake her—or her mouth.

"I contacted the University and pulled a few strings. I told them it was an emergency," Harbinger said with a sudden urgency in his voice. "There isn't much time, and I hate to ask after not talking to you for so long. Listen, that deal with Karen . . . "

"Eh, that's the past," Stallings said as he stared at a piece of torn wallpaper hanging on the living room wall. Harbinger was referring to an old girlfriend of his named Karen Hamilton, who had found her way into Harbinger's arms. The ultimate betrayal at the time and the downfall of their friendship. "What can I do for you?" He immediately began to question his choice of words—he was practically offering his head to the guy on a silver platter.

"Can we meet in person this week?"

Stallings eyed a stack of blank typing paper on the corner of his desk next to a Remington typewriter.

"Can't-do. I'm in—"

"Vegas," Harbinger said, beating him to the punch.

"I forgot. You tracked me down," Stallings said as his eyes darted back over to the roll-top desk. "It's just that I'm knee-deep in writing an article that's due for a science journal," he lied. He hadn't touched a typewriter in months, and there weren't any academic journals that he was writing for at the time. The fact was, he was in a writing rut. Call it writer's block or whatever you want. Then again, maybe he just wasn't in the mood to write. Lately, he had been feeling stir crazy just sitting around the house. He preferred field work to paperwork.

"Still the procrastinator, huh, James?" Harbinger said.

Stallings winced at the comment. Unfortunately, it was true. Even in college he had sat on papers that were due until the last minute.

"Before you answer," Harbinger said, pausing, "it's about the ancient bacteria you discovered."

"That's another thing in the past—I shelved that work long ago," Stallings said. "If you read about it, then you should also know that my theory wasn't widely accepted."

"What if I told you it wasn't in the past," Harbinger said, his voice growing serious.

"How so?"

"There's too much to explain, and I'm still gathering data. I'll tell you more when we meet in person."

He remembered hearing a few years ago about Harbinger working for the CDC. He wondered if that had something to do with it.

"Like I always said, you're the lab guy, and I'm just a paleoanthropologist. You try to keep people from dying, and I study them long after they're already dead." He strummed his fingers on the desk. "I'll meet with you, but I don't see what I can—"

"Do you have any samples of the *lapethria* plant you can send me?" Harbinger said, cutting him off again.

Stallings always thought Harbinger was a pushy guy. He'd grab on to an idea like a Rottweiler even back in college. They had many heated discussions back then, and no matter what Stallings said to prove a point, Harbinger wouldn't listen once his mind was made up. He glanced over at the small jar of *lapethria* sitting on the book shelf.

"Yeah, I think I have some lying around. Where do I send it?"

"Thanks, James. I need it as soon as possible if you can overnight it. I'll text you my address and tell you more—"

"I know, I know. You'll tell me more when we meet," Stallings said, finally beating him to the punch. He sat the cell phone down and glanced out the front window, grimacing as he watched the neighbor's dog shitting in the front yard. It wasn't even a yard, really. In Vegas, it was rocks—making it all that much worse.

He had transplanted to Vegas after tiring of the Los Angeles bull crap. It was too crowded, and it took two hours too long to get anywhere. Once in Vegas, he bought an old house, circa 1950's. It was perfect for him, since he liked everything old. No wife, no kids, no pets, and no problems that came with them. He didn't need more hassles, and he didn't need someone to give the place atmosphere.

Soon after moving though, he realized that Vegas wasn't Vegas anymore. Not the Vegas he remembered anyway. It used to have great shows, and it had class. People dressed up back in the day when they visited from out of town, it was something to see.

Now, the place was run over with yuppies and their spawn in T-shirts and baseball caps. It was all Cirque Du Soleil and one big carnival ride—a far cry from the once desolate desert that it was built on. There used to be a mystique and that old mafia sense of danger—now it was costumes of Mickey Mouse and superheroes. But as an anthropologist, the people watching was colorful, and if he wanted to dig up some bones, he didn't have to stray too far into the desert to find them.

Stallings walked into the kitchen, grabbed a coffee cup, and added a spoonful of instant coffee. He filled the cup with water and stuck it in the microwave. He generally skipped breakfast, but needed at least one cup of joe to start his engine. *Lapethria*, he thought as he took the coffee out of the microwave and stirred it. Now, what the hell would he want with that?

CHAPTER 9

NEW YORK CITY.
AUGUST 26.

A long drawn out alleyway with oil stains and pit holes stretched out in front of Maggie De Luca when she stepped out of the car. She glanced down—luckily she was wearing flats. She learned the hard way to avoid heels. When a lot of your job is door-to-door questioning, the last thing you want is aching feet.

Large trash bins were placed periodically along the alleyway. The trash had obviously not been picked up for a while and was spilling over onto the ground below. As she walked, a strong pungent odor hit her nose—it was the smell of death. She had a keen sense of smell that was trained to recognize anything that had died, and the smell was getting stronger the farther she walked along.

Her eyes moved up and down the old run down buildings, some of them with boards covering the windows. This is not Park Avenue, Maggie thought as she stepped over some empty cans of beer. Some of the buildings had bright red graffiti streaked across them. One of the artists must have thought he was Picasso and had spray painted a dark-skinned man on one of the buildings. The man had a joint hanging out of his mouth and the words BROWN PRIDE in red letters that were outlined in yellow. Maggie cocked her head to the side, studying the painted figure.

"Not bad really," she whispered under her breath.

Farther down the graffiti got sloppier: hastily done symbols and Roman numerals with paint dripping down the wall. It was in a code for gangs, and each gang had their own dialogue to mark their territory. At least Martinez didn't fit the profile of a gang member. And since he didn't have a record—it made her job a whole lot easier. She had to interview gang members and criminals before, and they weren't the most cooperative bunch. As soon as they saw a badge of any kind, they either ran or became confrontational.

She scanned the graffitied wall. It was hard to imagine how someone could feel good about tagging someone else's property, but she'd seen it all over the world. Architecture hundreds of years old, ruined by a can of spray paint. It was sad, really. But some people had no respect for property that wasn't theirs, and she had no respect for them. She'd seen some beautiful murals in her travels, but she was positive that these "artists" didn't ask permission or have any "pride" in their work. They did it to make a statement. Sometimes it was political, and sometimes it was just a way to show how macho they were.

Metal stairs zig-zagged up the sides of the buildings, and a few makeshift clothing lines hung from one building across to a building on the other side. Some men's underwear and a bra hung from one of the lines, flapping in the wind like surrendering flags.

Maggie wondered if this alleyway reminded Martinez of Mexico as she listened to the sound of mariachi music. The faint cries of a baby drifted down from above. She had a gut feeling this was the route he walked each day to work. She was close . . . she could feel it.

She pulled out her cellphone and clicked on the photo of Martinez on his work identification card. She stared at the face looking back at her. Juan's large brown eyes looked kind, but the feeling that came over her was haunting. There were secrets behind his eyes and a story to tell, if only she could tune in to hear it.

"Speak to me, Juan. Where did you go? What did you see?" Maggie whispered as she looked back out at the buildings.

A humming noise was permeating through the air, joining the sound of the mariachi music. Maggie glanced up and saw a small fan propped in one of the windows above. She wiped a few beads of sweat off her upper lip and pulled the front of her blouse in and out to cool herself. It was a very hot and humid August day. Perfect weather for the spread of a pneumonic plague-like bacteria, she thought as she glanced over at more overflowing trash bins.

Maggie jumped when she felt her phone vibrate in her hand. She let out a deep breath and held it out in front of her. There were two texts from the other members of her team, who were following the other two possible routes Martinez could have taken to work. Both of the messages were the same—neither team member had found any new leads yet. I've got my walking shoes on, Maggie thought as she sniffed the air again. The unmistakable smell of death was definitely coming from somewhere close by, and it was almost knocking her off her feet.

She walked over to one of the overfilled trash bins. Flies were buzzing all over the garbage—another sign something was dead. Maggie held her hand over her mouth and nose as she got closer. There was a box with the words LIVE ANIMAL on the side of it. She batted the flies away and carefully lifted one of the flaps on the box. She quickly retracted her hand when she saw a few white rats. At first, she thought they were alive, and then she realized the movement was from the maggots covering their dead bodies. She felt a prickle on the back of her neck and slowly turned around. Directly behind her, there was a sign above a door that said REPTILE AND SUPPLY COMPANY.

She walked up to the door and saw another sign: CLOSED.

CHAPTER 10

NEW YORK CITY.
AUGUST 26.

*"And worship your Lord until there
comes unto you the certainty (death)."*

—Al Hijr 15:99

Amina Alaoui sat across the table from her brother Ahmed and his wife Safaa. Her mother and father were perched separately at each end of the long table. Her mind felt numbingly vacant as she nodded at the conversation going on around her. She had had a sweltering headache for a couple of days now and could feel the heat rising and simmering her head under the hijab. She longed for dinner to be over so she could take the headscarf off and lay down. She glanced over at her mother who was watching her with a worried expression on her face.

"Amina, what matter?" her mother asked in broken English as she leaned over the table toward her.

Amina usually corrected her, but that would require too much energy, so she ignored the urge to repeat the phrase correctly. She kept insisting that her parents try to learn English after her mother got lost one day. New York was a big city to get around, and the cab driver dropped her off on the other side of town on the way back from the market. Her mother finally agreed to enroll in some English classes, but her father still refused.

"Yes, *mâmâ*. I'm just tired," Amina lied as she looked over at her father, who had a look of disapproval at the exchange of English. She didn't want to cause her mother to worry, she always seemed worried enough. She turned back to her mother, who still watched her with concern, and lowered her eyes as she took a bite of the tagine.

When she glanced up, her mother finally looked away, and she quietly spit the rest of the Berber Tagine into her napkin. If she ate anything more, it would make her feel sicker. She squeezed the napkin full of food in her lap and sipped a bit of mint tea. The warm tea was soothing, and she held the cup under her nose, breathing in deeply.

She listened quietly as her brother, Ahmed, heatedly discussed a business venture with their father, the conversation growing tenser as they spoke. Ahmed had always been the willful one in the family and liked to consider himself an entrepreneur. He was always full of ideas, many of them not turning out to be what he'd originally thought.

Ahmed kept repeating in Arabic that it was an opportunity, his voice full of frustration. Amina looked over at their father, whose face was growing redder. She jumped when her father slammed his hand down on the table, spilling some of the drinks.

"*Shu hayda!*" her father yelled across the table. That meant he couldn't even contemplate what her brother was talking about, and the discussion was over. "*Ya Allah!*" Everyone knew not to press further, especially when he called out to God for help as he raised his arms in the air. The room went silent.

Amina glanced over at Safaa, who sat quietly with her eyes diverted downward. She was very soft spoken, and her family were very strict Muslims, much stricter than Amina's family. They also didn't approve of Ahmed's business ventures and felt no need to invest in the American lifestyle.

Another wave of sickness rushed over Amina, and the room began spinning like light through a kaleidoscope. She was having difficulty breathing as the pressure in her chest increased. She breathed in less air each time she inhaled, as if the air was moving away from her and out of reach. She held her throat and stood up as she gasped for breath.

The voice of her mother calling out to her in Arabic reverberated through her head as she fell to the floor. She stared out as her eyes glazed over. Through the fog, she could see a bloody napkin flash in front of her face. She could feel her mother's warm hand against her cheek. She heard someone calling out her name, but she couldn't respond. She willed her lips to move, but no words escaped. She felt someone pulling her upward, but she had already drifted out of the pain and far away. Somewhere far from Morocco, New York, and the life she once knew. A new place full of light.

CHAPTER 11

NEW YORK CITY.
AUGUST 26.

About an hour into her shift, Melinda Howard could feel the dryness returning to her throat. She grabbed the door handle, lifted the metal lever with her thumb, and pulled the handle to the side. She watched as the long metal bar attached to the door moved outward and pushed the school bus doors open. After the doors opened, two kids wearing backpacks walked up the steps and made their way to a seat without even glancing her way.

She peeked in the mirror above her head, making sure everyone was seated. Howard was about to move her eyes back down when she saw a boy shove another kid in front of him. The boy who had done the shoving was a blond kid wearing a black T-shirt with a skull on the front. She started to say something to the boy, but then the kid who was shoved began giggling and gave him a high five.

There were times that she had to break up fights or separate kids on the bus, but so far, today wasn't one of those days. She was relieved in many ways, she'd been feeling extremely fatigued since she woke up. She also didn't want to deal with the parents if the kid thought she was being too hard on them—the parents were quick to blame *her* if she interfered. This was mostly because many of the parents weren't around the kids like she was and felt it was normal to play around with their friends or tease. But she knew that there were kids who took things too far.

Bullying had become commonplace in the schools, and she was very aware of the impact it had on some of the less fortunate kids. Sometimes, she was the only thing standing between a bully and a victim of their taunts until they were dropped off safely at home or school. She could see the look of relief on the faces of some of the bullied kids when she stepped in. And she knew that kids were still learning how to interact and could be cruel sometimes. This was her school bus, and she would not tolerate bullying against one of her passengers.

She was very happy to see the anti-bullying campaigns that the schools ran. It was about time, Melinda thought. The bullying had been going on too long. Now, kids could be expelled for such contemptuous behavior. She would think the parents would be happy that she stopped it before the school stepped in, but that usually wasn't the case. Most of them told her to mind her own business. The bus and what happened on it *was* her business. Not on my watch, she thought. I won't tolerate it.

Howard stopped at the next block and opened the doors, waiting for the kids to board the bus. She leaned in closer to the mirror above her head. She noticed her eyes were glassy, and her cheeks were flushed rosy red. She shivered as a cold chill swept through her body. Well, isn't that the oddest thing, she thought, it was such a warm day. She reached down by her leg and grabbed a bottle of water. When she took a sip it burned her throat, and she felt a cough coming on. She coughed and wrenched forward in pain. She coughed again and held her hand against the side of her throat. The pain was unbearable, it felt like she had swallowed broken glass.

Melinda heard the sound of restless bodies and talking behind her as she leaned back in the seat. She slowly reached out and pulled the lever, shutting the doors. Then, she wiped away a few tears as she gazed out at the road in front of her. She tried to keep from thinking about coughing as she pressed her foot down on the gas pedal. She had to finish the rest of her route. The children were waiting at their bus stops, and it was her duty to get all the kids to school on time.

She counted the miles in her head—only two more stops before she would be heading back to Thomas Jefferson Elementary School. She made a mental note to stop by The Golden Dragon Restaurant after her shift. She always got a large egg drop soup when she was feeling under the weather, it would be soothing on her sore throat. Soup and some rest, Melinda thought. That should do the trick.

Up ahead, she saw a group of kids standing on the curb as they waited for the bus. She pushed the button to extend the stop sign on the bus and pulled over. Only one more stop left, and she could head back to the school. She pulled the lever and waited for the kids to step inside, squeezing the handle tighter as another painful cough came on. I rebuke this sickness in the name of Jesus, Melinda thought as she closed the doors once more.

CHAPTER 12

NEW YORK CITY.
AUGUST 26.

Song Le grabbed one of the small hand towels out of the kitchen, ran it under water, and began wiping off the front counter. He used his thumbnail to loosen a few dried marks of food from the previous day. He ran a very clean restaurant and prided himself on the "A" rating on the store window. His customers seemed to appreciate the quick service, and he knew many of the customers by name. If he couldn't remember a name, he usually knew what they ordered. It was a personal touch that he'd found worked well with his clientele.

Things were not always so easy for Le, he traveled a hard road to get to where he was. Opening his own restaurant in New York City was a large step, and he took great pride in the responsibility. He had a staff of ten workers: two cooks, five waiters, two busboys, and one dishwasher. Song tried to treat them fair and with the respect he would want to be treated with himself.

Originally from a small village located in Southwest China's Yunnan Province named Duoyishu, he was part of a group of residents known as the *Hani*. As a *Hani*, he worked on the rice terraces and in the wheat fields since he was a small child. He remembered his father's calloused hands as he showed him how to use a dribble stick to make holes for planting crops. After the crops were ready to be harvested, Song would help his father gather the long stalks of grain as he cut them with a sickle. Then, they would take the grain to a threshing ground and toss baskets full of wheat in the breeze to separate the seeds from the husks.

Sometimes he missed watching the fog roll in over the terraces and the feeling of water seeping up his bare legs. He also missed the Chinese New Year celebrations with his family in China, but his father and mother died long ago. Now, he had his own family to take care of, and he made sure his daughters spoke their native language and celebrated all of the traditions that he had celebrated as a child.

Song also joined in on the New Year's Eve celebrations that took place in New York City. He enjoyed watching the ball drop at midnight in Times Square and the sound of people blowing their paper horns. New Year's Eve was also a very busy day for his restaurant, and he welcomed the celebrating tourists.

However, today was a slow day so far, much slower than usual. He didn't know what it was, but there was a strange feeling in the air, like the calmness before a storm. He glanced over at the ceramic Lucky Cat sitting next to the potted bamboo plant, its paw held up in the air. He noticed some soil on the counter around the plant and wiped it off with the towel.

The door chime rattled, and Song looked up as a large woman hobbled toward the counter. He recognized the woman as a regular, but for the life of him, he couldn't place her name. Then, he remembered the woman ordered two large beef lo-mein dishes before. Howard, Le thought. He believed the name was Howard on the order ticket—it had struck him at the time as an unusual American name for a woman.

He started to speak as he nodded his head and noticed the woman looked very sick. Besides the fact that she was a very large woman, her skin was almost gray in color. She began to cough as she hobbled closer. All that extra weight's not good, Le thought. It's not healthy to be that big. He'd noticed that many of his customers were overweight, but he knew it wasn't from *his* food. He blamed it on all the fast food places that lined the streets, many of them taking good business away from him.

"Hallo Howard," Song said as the woman walked up and leaned on the counter. "Two beef lo-mein today?"

"No, thank you. I'll have one large egg drop soup, please," Melinda said as she placed her wallet on the counter.

"Ah, yes," Song nodded. He remembered now that she sometimes ordered egg drop soup. "Five dollar ninety-five cent please." He wrote the order and handed the paper to the cook in the back. He watched as the woman unsnapped her wallet and handed him a ten dollar bill. "Thank you very much."

She then added four quarters into the tip jar on the counter. The bell rang, and Le placed the round container with a lid into a plastic bag. He added an extra fortune cookie and a spoon into the bag, then handed it to the lady. The woman coughed, managed a small smile, and slowly walked out the front door.

After she left, Song asked the cook to keep an eye on the front while he loaded the dishwasher. The young man he recently hired had called in sick. Le decided he would place another ad for a dishwasher in the newspaper in case this happened again. Some people don't like to work, he thought. He watched as the busboy cleared a table and walked into the back. One of his waitresses was busy taking an order, so he walked by a couple at one of the corner tables and removed their finished plates from the table.

He took the plates into the kitchen and sat them by the dishwasher area. As he scraped the plates into the trash, Song noticed that a few pieces of chewed chicken were left on the plate. He would have to talk to the cook to make sure the chicken wasn't overcooked.

Some of the recipes his restaurant served were his grandmother's that he'd brought over from China. He tried to personalize many of the dishes and worked tirelessly after store hours to perfect them. He liked to invent new ones as well, but those were generally made as a chef special only. In general, the patrons of The Golden Dragon liked the same familiar Chinese dishes they had grown accustomed to in America. From his experience, he'd found that if he made something too exotic, the customer's didn't order it.

Song slid the tray of dishes into the dishwasher and stepped through the back door leading to the alley. He pulled a cigarette out of the pack in his pocket, lit it, and inhaled deeply. He stood, staring out at the alley, deep in thought. He still had the strange sensation that something bad was going to happen, it felt like a dark cloud hovering over his thoughts. He watched as a tan cat with a large black rat in its mouth walked by. The cat turned, staring at him with its golden eyes, and then scampered away.

"Lucky cat," Song said as he waved his hand back and forth through the air. He took a few more puffs of the cigarette, tossed it in an empty coffee can, and walked back inside.

CHAPTER 13

NEW YORK CITY.
AUGUST 27.

M aggie made sure she was early this time, she had to catch the reptile store before it closed again. Some small stores that were privately owned, danced to their own beat—including the hours they kept. She eyed a small sign next to the back door: PLEASE KNOCK FOR DELIVERIES.

"Well, not exactly," Maggie said as she started to knock on the door. She jumped as a rail-thin, middle-aged man, wearing a white tank top suddenly stood in the doorway, interrupting her mid-knock. She slowly lowered her hand, noticing that the man had nystagmus, a condition that caused uncontrollable eye movement. She tried not to stare as his eyes jumped from side to side.

"Yeah? What do ya got?" the man asked. He looked surprised to see a woman standing at the back door and quickly ran a hand through the top of his greasy hair.

"Oh, excuse me, sir," she said and took a step backward. She could smell his rancid breath and didn't want to get too close in case he was sick.

"Well?" the man barked out angrily.

Then she realized he thought she was delivering something. She cleared her throat.

"I'm not making a delivery, sir. My name is Maggie De Luca, and

I work for the CDC. I'm looking for information about a man that I believe may have passed this way."

"The what?" the man said as he held up a handkerchief, blew his nose, and shoved it into his back pocket.

"The Centers for Disease Control and Prevention," Maggie said. She always forgot that most people didn't have a clue what CDC stood for. "It will only be a few minutes of your time. Are you the owner of the store, Mr.—"

"Kaplan." He ran his twitching eyes down her body slowly, then back up, and sniffed. "Yeah, I'm the owner."

Maggie stood there, waiting uncomfortably. He finally nodded his head and stepped aside, holding the door open. She hesitated and then walked inside. Damn it, she thought, inwardly scolding herself. Where are your precautions, Maggie? She knew it was risky to enter a place that could be contaminated. She also knew the man would never let her inside if she put a face mask on.

She glanced over at some crates and boxes that were stacked against the wall, partially blocking the back entrance. A couple of the empty boxes fell over as she brushed by, and she saw the words FRAGILE and LIVE ANIMAL imprinted on the sides. They looked like the box that was in the trash bin.

She held her hand up to her nose, the place reeked of animal feces. Don't act up on me now, she thought. Her stomach was doing back-flips, and she could only imagine what the restroom looked like in this place.

Kaplan closed the door behind them. She stepped aside as he squeezed past and then followed him into the store. Once inside, she walked past different-sized vivariums on the shelves, some of them with glowing orange heat lamps. In one of the smaller tanks, a large tan and brown snake with a red tail was doubled over itself, barely fitting in the enclosure. It reminded her of a rundown zoo with displays too small for its inhabitants.

A few of the other glass habitats had plastic green plants in them. At first, she thought they were empty, but then she noticed two lizard eyes staring back at her, both of them going in different directions. It reminded her of Kaplan's eyes, the way they wandered around aimlessly. She must have surprised the lizard as well because it turned from a dark brown to a light green, camouflaging itself to match the backdrop of plants.

"You say you're looking for someone?" Kaplan asked as he walked up behind her.

"His name is Juan Martinez," Maggie said as she turned around and held up her phone with Martinez's photo. "We have reason to believe he may have walked this way each day. He worked at Regency Hospital, a few blocks away, as a nurse assistant. I'm questioning anyone that he may have come into contact with over the last few weeks."

He leaned in as he studied the photo, his red-rimmed eyes twitching sporadically.

"Missing, you say?" He straightened back up, his mouth turned downward at the corners.

"No, I'm afraid he passed away two days ago," Maggie said, watching the man for any changes in his expression. Sometimes it was easy to read the shock on someone's face if they knew the person, but other times, people were good liars. In some situations, the person just didn't want to be involved in an investigation—especially if there were some shady dealings going on. She had gotten pretty good over the years at knowing if someone was hiding something. Whether it was the way their eyes drifted upward when they spoke, or the awkward pauses before answering a question—she could usually sniff out a liar from the pack.

"No, I haven't seen him. Name doesn't ring a bell either," Kaplan said. "But listen, I get a lot of customers in this place. Many of them looky-loos, as I like to call 'em." He pulled the dirty handkerchief out of his back pocket and blew his nose again loudly. "They think I'm running a zoo here. Come in just to look at the snakes and such."

She believed him, he wasn't lying.

"Are you feeling okay?" Maggie asked as she took a step back, trying to keep as far away from the man as possible. He kept standing too close and invading her personal space.

"Eh, just a little cold. Can't seem to kick it," he sniffed.

She nodded her head and walked farther into the store. She couldn't help but think of Martinez and wonder what his symptoms were. But at this point, there wasn't any proof that he'd been anywhere near this place. She still couldn't seem to shake the idea of the word PLAGUE. Since there were plague precautions and this was a plague-like bacteria, shouldn't there also be rats in the equation? After all, that was how the Bubonic plague spread. Well, there *were* the fleas . . .

She walked up and down the store aisles, the floor creaked loudly under her feet. There were more snakes and lizards, but not any rats like she'd seen in the trash bin.

"Do you sell rats too?" Maggie called out over the shelf. When she turned, her heart felt like it was going to leap out of her chest—Kaplan was suddenly standing right next to her.

He stared down at her blouse, his eyes lingering too long, and said, "In the back, I don't display feeders."

Maggie put her arm across her chest and took another step backward. She didn't know what was scaring her more—the fact the man was sick or his google-eyed stares. She walked over to one of the vivariums against the far wall, watching as a small green snake on a rock flicked out its tongue toward her.

"Feeders?"

"For the reptiles to eat," Kaplan snapped, as if it was a silly question to ask.

Bingo, Maggie thought, her pulse racing.

"Can I see them?" she asked as she cleared her throat, trying not to sound too excited.

He gave her a strange side glance.

"Yeah, all right. Nothing special to see, really. I usually keep the area off limits." He walked to the back of the store, tugged on a short black curtain, and pulled it aside. "Makes my sales go down when the customers realize the snakes gotta eat."

Maggie walked past the black curtain while Kaplan held it open. She noticed the back wall was lined with more glass enclosures. There was also a strong scent that smelled like urine. When she got closer, she saw some black rats curled up on some tan bedding. One of the rats yawned, showing its long yellow incisors.

"I also got mice and pinkies for the small snakes."

"Pinkies?" Maggie said as she walked over to one of the mice habitats. She stared at one of the mice, it was gray and one of its eyes was crusted over.

"Yeah. Newbies without fur, that's what we call 'em," Kaplan said as he grabbed the mouse by the tail that she was looking at. The mouse began squeaking as it wriggled in his hand. Then, Kaplan swiftly swung his hand down, knocking the mouse against the side of the metal shelving. The mouse went into spasms for a few seconds and then went limp.

Maggie quickly turned, covering her face. She could feel her stomach revving up, until it became a full-blown circus. She glanced over, peeking through her fingers as Kaplan walked back into the store with the mouse. She pulled the curtain aside, watching as he opened the lid of the vivarium housing the oversized snake and tossed the lifeless mouse inside. The snake flicked out its tongue, opened its mouth, and swallowed the mouse whole.

"A snack," Kaplan laughed, seemingly enjoying the horrified look on her face. "Got frozen ones, too. I keep em' 'round for the queasy folk, like yourself, that are too scared to do the knockin."

Maggie let go of the curtain and walked back over to the glass enclosure housing the rats. The black rat she had seen yawning earlier was awake now, its nose wiggling as she approached. It seemed just as interested in her. The way its black beady eyes stared at her, sent chills running up her spine. There was an intelligence behind the eyes.

"Do you mind if I buy one of these rats?" Maggie asked. She needed to cover all of the bases and send at least one of the rats in for testing, it was the only way to rule them out. The black rat she was watching walked closer to the glass and stood up on its hind legs. As creepy as she thought rats were, there was something cute about the way the rat was so curious about her. It reminded her of the way a puppy would look at you at a pet shop.

"As long as you're pay'n lady," Kaplan said, wiping his hands on his jeans. "I don't see what a rat has to do with that fella you're looking for though."

"I'd like one of the white ones," Maggie said, remembering the dead white rats in the trash bin. She felt her phone vibrate in her pocket. She held the phone up and looked at the text, it was one of her team members letting her know that there was another possible related death. That's not good, she thought. But deep down, she knew it wouldn't be long before another victim surfaced.

Kaplan looked at her sideways.

"What are you, one of those PETA people?" he chuckled. "Little buzzards grew on ya that quick, huh?"

Maggie smiled and shrugged her shoulders as she typed a text back to her teammate, letting them know she'd call them back shortly.

"Thought so," Kaplan said as he pulled the lid off one of the rat enclosures. "Just don't go thinkin' I mistreat the lil' critters. Snakes gotta eat, too." He reached his hand into the tank, grabbing one of the white rats. "White ones haven't been doing so good, gotta bad batch. Sure you want white?"

She looked at the white rat he was holding, its fur was discolored, and it had dark rings around its tail.

"Yes, one white rat and . . . that one," Maggie said as she pointed at the black rat that was still watching her.

CHAPTER 14

THE CDC.
ATLANTA, GEORGIA.
AUGUST 27.

From an outside perspective, it looked like Michael Harbinger was waiting patiently in the lobby—but inside his mind was going a million miles a minute. He kept going over everything in his head as his eyes wondered down, rechecking his notes.

"Dr. Harbinger?" the secretary called out.

He stood up, and then glanced down as one of his papers drifted to the floor.

"Yes," he said, reaching down uneasily. He picked up the paper and returned it to the top of the stack in his hand. He looked down at the page he dropped. Of all the papers to lose, he thought, it would be the one containing my formula. He could feel his eyeglasses slipping, he used his pinky finger to push them back onto the bridge of his nose.

"Do you need some help?" the secretary asked as she gazed at him awkwardly.

He walked forward, noticing the secretary had her nutmeg colored hair pulled back neatly at the nape of her neck and her make-up perfectly set. He figured that he must seem like a disheveled mess to the lady. He even had a stain on the front of his shirt from a coffee spill this morning. He watched as her eyes traveled down to the brown spot and met his eyes again.

"No, I'm fine," he said, pausing uncomfortably. "Thank you." He followed the secretary as she turned quickly on her heels and waited as she opened the door. He eyed a plaque on the wall next to the door:

Harold Bowman, M.D.
CDC Director

Harbinger had only met Bowman a few times, but he had a reputation as a ruler with an iron fist. He heard that Bowman worked his way to the top, and after a tenure in different departments, he became the director of the CDC. He replaced the last director, Jan Albright, who was caught trading stocks that were linked to a lobbyist for a tobacco company.

When he saw Harbinger enter through the door, Bowman quickly stood up and reached his hand across the desk. Harbinger shifted his papers in his arms and extended his hand out to meet Bowman's. It was a constricting handshake, but he tried not to show any signs of discomfort. He was relieved when he could finally pull his hand away.

"Dr. Harbinger," Bowman said, glimpsing at the schedule on his desk. "Please, have a seat."

Harbinger glanced down at a set of chairs in front of the desk. He started to sit in one chair, and then moved to the other one. He could feel his glasses beginning to slide off his nose again as he sat down. He used his thumb and forefinger to push them back into position.

"How can I help you?" Bowman said, his steel gray eyes narrowing.

Harbinger glanced over at the plaques and various framed degrees, then shifted his attention back to the director. He noticed that Bowman had very tan skin, and his dirty blond hair was bleached golden from the sun. He was wearing a dark blue suit with a yellow tie that reminded Harbinger of a hangman's noose. He could almost feel it slipping around his neck as he tried to gather his thoughts.

"Yes. I'm here . . . I'm here to speak with you about a vaccine," he said, peering down at his notes. For some reason his mind had gone blank for a second.

"Go on," Bowman said, his chin tilting upward.

"Well, Director, I believe . . . I mean, I can . . . make a vaccine for the new bacteria we've encountered," Harbinger said and cleared his throat.

"The Martinez bacteria?" Bowman said, glancing down again at his desk.

"Yes. You see, I had worked on a similar vaccine for *Yersinia pestis—*"

"We don't have a vaccine for the Bubonic plague."

"I understand, sir, but that was because it was incomplete and—"

"Then it wasn't a vaccine—it was research," Bowman said, crossing his arms over his chest. "In any case, as you know, vaccines aren't as commonly used for bacteria as antibiotics. And this new bacteria is far from being a plague—I've only seen one confirmed case. Unless, you've seen other cases I don't know about."

"No, that's correct, sir. But, I've discovered a vaccine—"

"Another research vaccine?"

Harbinger handed a paper to Bowman that outlined the vaccine. He watched as the director's eyes skimmed quickly down the page.

"The vaccine weakens the toxins and disables the bacteria from making more."

"I must admit this is an interesting idea, Dr. Harbinger, but what do you need from me? Right now, as it stands, it's just inkblots on paper."

"Well, sir, in order to make more of the vaccine . . . I'm missing a key component," Harbinger said as he shifted uncomfortably in his seat. "A chemical derived from a specific plant."

"And . . ."

"When I say missing . . . I mean it doesn't exist in the United States."

"And where is this mysterious plant?"

"South America, sir."

Bowman laid the paper on his desk and stood up.

"Dr. Harbinger, we've only seen one case of this bacteria, which may very well end up as nothing more than a dead end. Now, I can't possibly be expected to fund research into an area that doesn't call for it. Frankly, we can't afford to make a vaccine for every disease that blows through here. Put your mind to good use. If cases are caught early enough with this new bacteria, we can treat the patients with antibiotics like we do the Bubonic plague. If there are any more cases, that is."

"But this bacteria is a pneumonic form and fluoroquinolone and tetracycline are ineffective on—"

"That will be all. Thank you for coming by, and here's your research back," Bowman said, holding out the paper.

Harbinger grabbed the paper, stunned at being dismissed so quickly. He turned as he stood in the doorway.

"I think you're making a big mistake. This bacteria could cause widespread devastation in a city the size of New York."

"We'll see, Doctor. We'll see," Bowman said, his eyes staring at him coldly.

CHAPTER 15

NEW YORK CITY.
AUGUST 27.

Kaplan put the two small boxes with the rats inside a larger un-marked box, then punched two holes in the side with a box opener.

"Here you go," he said. "Sorry, I'm all out of pet carrier boxes."

Maggie handed him a twenty dollar bill and stared down at the box. She could hear the sound of nails scratching on the cardboard. The fact that people catch two-thirds of all diseases from animals, and the fact they were dealing with a plague-like bacteria, didn't make her feel any better about carrying the little vermin. She was still scolding herself for not wearing protection.

The problem was, if she pulled out a face mask and gloves, then the people froze up and started freaking out. After that, it was damn near impossible to get any information out of them. She was positive Kaplan wouldn't have sold her the rats, had he known what she wanted them for—he would have feared being shut down more than the disease.

Regardless, it still felt like a long shot that Martinez had come into contact with the reptile store or the rats. He didn't have any pets, and he wasn't poor enough to dig around in the garbage. She just didn't want to leave any stones unturned. She carefully picked the box up, holding it away from her. When she turned, Kaplan was holding the back door open.

Maggie handed her card to him.

"If you think of anything—"

"I'll let you know," Kaplan said as he slammed the door.

Nice guy, she thought. She glanced over at the trash bin. Well, if she really wanted to cover all of her bases . . .

Her phone began vibrating, interrupting the thought. She shifted the box to one arm, balancing it on her hip. She could hear the rodents slide from one side to the other. She righted the box and clicked the phone.

"Got anything yet?" a man's voice said on the other line. It was Jason Conner, one of her ground team members.

"How 'bout two rodent friends?" Maggie said as she peered down at the box, half-expecting one of the rats to have already chewed its way out the side. She didn't imagine the cardboard boxes would hold them for long.

"Seriously?"

"Dead," Maggie said as she walked over to the trash bin. "Hold on." She put the phone on speaker and slid it in her front pocket. She quickly turned around, making sure Kaplan wasn't watching. Then, she sat the box on the ground. She grabbed an evidence bag, plastic gloves, protective eyewear, and a face mask out of her purse. After checking behind her again, she quickly slid the face mask on, pulled the strings around her ears, and slipped on the goggles.

She carried safety equipment everywhere, especially since she didn't know where the next lead would take her. Over the course of her career, she'd been put into more than one precarious situation, and learned to never leave home without it.

She slipped on the gloves and slowly reached her hand toward the box in the trash bin. Just thinking about the maggot-infested rats made her skin crawl. She just had to get it over with as quickly as possible. She reached into the box and picked up one of the dead white rats by the tail. She turned away as she slid it into the plastic bag. She could hear Jason talking on the other line, the sound of his voice emitting from her pocket.

"You're really taking this whole plague thing serious, huh?" Jason said, laughing on the other line.

Maggie placed the bag containing the dead rodent inside the box and threw the gloves in the trash bin. Then, she pulled out fresh gloves and took the phone out of her pocket. She picked up the box with her other hand.

"You have no idea," she said, her voice sounding muffled through the face mask. "Problem is that the reptile store owner claims he's never seen Martinez before. But the fact he sells rats, and it's on the route Martinez could have taken . . . "

"I know, I get it. Well, kudos to you—I know how squeamish you get around those things. By the way, did I ever tell you how sexy your voice sounds when you're talking through a face mask?"

Maggie laughed.

"More than a few times."

"Did you get my message about another possible related death?"

"I just got it. Fill me in."

"Samuel Greene, African American, mid-sixties, and get this . . . he worked at Regency Hospital, like our friend Martinez. They found him still sitting in his car—in the employee parking garage, he'd been dead for two days."

Maggie let out a deep breath, fogging up her goggles and making it hard to see. She clenched her teeth together when she almost tripped over a garbage bag. She held the box lower so she could see—the last thing she wanted to do, was chase little vermin through the streets of New York City.

If both connections were at Regency Hospital, then maybe it had come from a patient, and not from somewhere on Juan's route to work. She just couldn't shake the nagging feeling in her gut about the rat connection, but maybe she was fishing too hard. She had to keep her mind open to other ways the disease could be transmitted. In reality, it could have been caught anywhere. At this point, it sounded like the hospital was the most likely place, since there wasn't any proof that Martinez had been anywhere near the reptile store—or the rodents.

She looked down at the box. She'd still send the rats to the NC, maybe they could at least rule out the connection and put her mind at ease. The NCEZID, or the National Center for Emerging and Zoonotic Infectious Diseases, was equipped with labs to test animals for disease. Everyone called them the "NC," since no one could remember all the goddamn acronyms at the CDC.

"All right, I'm heading back in," Maggie said as she came to the end of the alleyway. She sat the box on the ground next to the trunk of her car. "Let me know if they get a positive on Samuel . . ."

"Greene."

"By the way, what did Mr. Greene do at Regency?"

"He was a custodian."

"Uh-huh."

She placed the box in an airtight portable container in her trunk that she used when she was carrying contaminated items. She figured the rats had enough oxygen to make the journey to the NC. She used it to transport mice before during a Hantavirus investigation in North Carolina, and they survived a much longer trip.

Maggie looked down at her hands and slipped the gloves off carefully, pulling them inside out. Then, she tugged off the face mask. She always found it hard to breathe in those damn things. She took one last look at the alleyway as she took off the fogged up goggles. She could still hear the sound of mariachi music in the distance. She closed her eyes and massaged them with her fingers. When she opened them, there was a man with dark hair and green scrubs, walking down the alley. The man turned and waved at her, his brown eyes glistening. He danced a couple of steps before continuing to walk; then, disappeared behind one of the buildings.

"Juan," Maggie said.

CHAPTER 16

NEW YORK CITY.
AUGUST 29.

*"He who sacrifices his conscience to ambition
burns a picture to obtain the ashes."*
—Chinese Proverb

The New York City subway system is the largest system of its kind in the world, encompassing 472 train stations and 26 subway lines. The subway system is also one of the longest, covering over 850 miles of railway track. As one of the busiest subways, it carries nearly 2 billion passengers a year to their destinations.

Song Le swiped his Metro Card through the reader. He waited until the display said GO and put the card back in his wallet. He'd been feeling run down for a few days and could feel a tightness in his chest, making it harder to breathe. Now that he was 64 years old, his body just didn't bounce back like it used to. He'd been drinking ginseng tea all morning and taken the Chinese herbal remedies Zhong Gan Qing Pian and Yin Qiao Jie Du Pian, hoping the sickness would pass.

It was already mid-morning and he had to unlock the restaurant in an hour. Regardless of how he felt, his restaurant would need to be opened, people depended on him. His family, his customers, and his staff of workers. If he wasn't feeling better by tomorrow, he would go to an acupuncturist. He preferred to try natural Chinese methods before going to a doctor. He always thought some of the medicines and their side-effects did more harm than good.

He passed by a trash can and saw a homeless man sitting next to it, holding out his hand. The man had dirt under his nails and smelled foul. The stench alone made Song want to walk away, he was feeling nauseated already, but then he saw a head peeking out next to the man. It was a white, scraggly dog with one eye. The dog wagged its tail at Song and made a whimpering sound. He found it touching that the homeless man, who had so little, was taking care of the dog. He looked down at a lid full of water next to the man.

He had to throw out food daily at the restaurant, it always bothered him when there were so many people starving in the world. In China, some of the places around his village were ravaged by famine and disease. He would never forget the images of children with bloated bellies on their skeleton frames. Rice was a lifeline for many people where he was from, and his father used to help feed other families whenever he could. He remembered the people's joyful expression when he'd help his father carry bags of rice to their doors. His father was a kind and giving man. Le hoped he was remembered the same way by his own daughters.

Song pulled out some coins that he'd taken from the tip jar, handed them to the man, and patted the dog on the head. Then, he boarded the subway train. He held the metal bar in the center and glanced out the window, watching the man pet the dog.

Once the subway doors closed and the train began to move, he had difficulty standing and wished he had taken one of the seats. His eyes shifted over to an Asian woman wearing a face mask. Seeing the woman reminded him of his last trip to China after the SARS outbreak, he'd never seen so many face masks. What most Americans didn't know, was that the face masks were usually worn to keep the wearer from spreading an illness. It was a courtesy to other people around them. He should be wearing a face mask, too, he thought. How quickly customs die out when you're so far away from home. He knew that if he wore a face mask in the restaurant, his customers would never return. Americans didn't understand the Chinese ways.

A wave of fatigue washed over him, and it was only the beginning of his day. He cleared his throat, but he could still feel a tickle deep down. He tried to resist, but he couldn't keep the cough from escaping. It started as one cough, and then he found that he couldn't stop. People began to move away from him, staring at him as he continued to hack. Their faces distorted, becoming larger, as they watched him with accusing eyes. Karma, Song thought. Punishment for his own thoughts about the homeless man. Maybe he wasn't as good of a man as his father. His father never recoiled when he was in the presence of a sick or needy person. He grasped the bar in front of him, squeezing it tightly. The subway shook side to side as he continued to cough uncontrollably.

At the next stop some people exited, and he spotted an empty seat. He quickly sat down, trying to escape the prying eyes as he coughed. The woman on the seat next to him covered her face and stood up. He glanced over as she moved to the other side of the train. Through watery eyes, he looked out at all of the people staring at him. He'd never felt so ashamed. When he lowered his head, he saw blood all over his sleeve and the front of his shirt. Blood, Song thought. *Blood.* He held his hand over his nose and mouth. He noticed two feet standing in front of him, and when he gazed up, a young man was looking at him with concern.

"Are you okay, sir? Do you need help?" he asked.

Song, too scared to speak, shook his head and turned away.

He was relieved when the subway train came to a stop. He pushed his way through the crowd, exiting the train, just as another series of coughs came on. He grasped his throat and sat on a bench, hoping it would pass. He held his hands out in front of him, they were covered in blood. The restaurant, Le thought. He had to make it to the restaurant. He stood up on shaky legs, made his way up the steps, and onto the sidewalk.

As he stood on the sidewalk, he stared out at the restaurant with the red and gold dragon sign that he designed. Through his cloudy vision, it felt like a dream. He clutched his stomach as a series of sharp pains shot through it. He hunched over and stumbled across the street. When he reached the sidewalk, he fell to his knees and crawled toward the bright red door. He gasped for breath as he reached up and stuck the key in the door. He grabbed the doorknob with both hands and leaned against the door, it swung inward forcefully from his weight. When he landed on the floor, he heard the familiar door chime ring out. He was the first and the last person to enter The Golden Dragon.

CHAPTER 17

REGENCY HOSPITAL.
NEW YORK CITY.
AUGUST 29.

W hen the emergency room doors of Regency Hospital slid open, Maggie was surprised to see the number of people waiting inside. New York City hospitals were known to be busy, but this emergency room was literally overflowing with people. There was a long line of people continuing outside who were waiting to check in, some of them lying on the ground with blankets—most of them hacking and coughing. She turned as she walked toward the administration building, watching as more people lined up outside. Jesus, Maggie thought, has the epidemic already started?

If the new strain of bacteria did start here—things were going to get a hell of a lot worse—the place looked like a war zone. Maybe it was, she thought. Bacteria and viruses are our tiniest and deadliest enemy. The most successful germs kill only some of the hosts they infect. Otherwise, there wouldn't be a way to continue spreading. But what if the bacteria had an almost unlimited supply of hosts—billions of human beings? The death rate could be extremely high, and the disease would still successfully spread. The thought sent a cold chill up her spine.

She watched as two hospital workers helped an elderly woman into a wheelchair and began pushing her inside. If all of these people knew about the plague-like bacteria found in the two employees who worked here, they'd be running from the hospital, not flocking to it. One of the hardest parts of her job—was keeping her big mouth shut. She didn't want to see more deaths because of a bunch of bullshit red tape. She was on pins and needles, waiting for the CDC to give the green light to shut down Regency and move the patients to other hospitals. Now that they knew Greene was positive, it shouldn't be much longer.

Maggie scanned the area looking for Jason. Then, they both spotted each other at the same time. He was hard to miss, with his sandy blond hair, six-foot-three frame, and silly grin. He stood out like a sore thumb next to the line of sickly people. As she got closer, she saw Barney Benson standing next to him.

Barney was one of the best workers on her team. He was soft-spoken, always got the job done, and never complained. Her only grievance was that he always smelled like cigarettes—the guy was a walking chimney. It was especially hard to take when she had to work with him in a confined space over an extended period of time. God did she hate the smell of cigarettes.

"Sorry it took me so long," Maggie said as she walked up and got a good whiff of second-hand smoke. "Since the garage is under quarantine and the parking lot is full, I had to park two blocks away. Not hard to miss though, I think I illegally parked in front of the B of A." She handed Barney some papers. "I need you to send these over to the CDC. Can you tell them to move their asses down there, too? I need that order pronto. Did you see the goddamn emergency room lines?"

She noticed that not only his teeth were stained yellow from the nicotine, but also his fingertips as he took the papers. She supposed that everyone had their own vices and dealt with stress in different ways. An epidemiologist had to deal with death and disease on a daily basis, and it took its toll on everyone. Her psychologist gave her Alprazolam and an endless cycle of various tricyclic antidepressants to deal with the stress, but she hated taking them. She couldn't do her job if her thinking was fogged up with drugs. All of her senses needed to be on high alert—even if it was painful sometimes.

Barney nodded his head.

"I'll do my best. Do I need to sign anything?"

"No, it's already covered, they know it's on the way." She turned back to Jason, who was still wearing a silly smirk on his face. Well, not everyone needs drugs, she thought. He never took anything serious, not even a doomsday scenario. He was the polar opposite of her. She was an alarmist, and everything was a potential crisis; he was the joking, reassuring soother.

"Hello Darlin', I missed you," Jason said in his worst Conway Twitty voice.

"Would you stop," Maggie said, hitting him on the shoulder as they walked through the administration building. She looked over at him when they got on the elevator. "Well, where's the paperwork on Greene?"

"It's on the way, he's bringing it. Calm down."

"Calm down? I told you to have everything ready to go when I arrived. I don't think you understand how quickly we need to move on this. Do I need to spell out the words PLAGUE and PNEUMONIC to everyone?" She bit her lip, trying to hold back the anger, but she was furious. Everyone was dragging their ass. "I mean, hello people? Remember the Black Death?"

"I said he's bringing it. Don't you think you're overreacting a bit? Don't forget the Mason case where you—"

"I know, but this is different," Maggie said as she ran her hand through her hair and looked away. Jason always brought up her past obsession with a strain of flu that they had worked on together. At the time, she thought the new strain had the potential to wipe out thousands of lives. The first victim in the United States was a five-year-old boy named Billy Mason who brought it back to the states after a trip to Thailand. She was still haunted by the boy's face before he died and was determined not to let unnecessary deaths happen on her watch again.

The virus went on to claim the lives of the boy's parents and twenty other passengers on the plane. She begged the CDC to place travel restrictions, but they wouldn't listen. They said it would only delay the flu from spreading for a couple of weeks. Maggie remembered the feeling of panic she felt at the time. She thought the CDC wasn't taking the flu seriously and even put in calls to WHO, but all of her pleas fell on deaf ears.

After a few months, the death toll raised to a few hundred; then, for some unknown reason, the flu disappeared. She knew that viruses and bacteria can mutate rapidly and would still find herself combing through news articles, looking for cases that might be overlooked as the same flu strain. She admitted that sometimes she got too caught up in a case. Jason likened her to Chicken Little running around, screaming, "An epidemic is coming, an epidemic is coming."

She glanced up as the elevator opened. They walked down the hallway and were led to an office where the hospital administrator was waiting. He was a stuffy looking man in a drab brown suit, and the frown on his face was easy to read—he was less than happy to be dealing with the CDC.

The hospitals send any alarming information to their local public health organization, who in turn hand it off to the CDC. Direct communication between the CDC and the hospital signaled a high alert problem. And if there was a complication, they usually blamed it on the highest guy on the totem pole—the hospital administrator. Just like any big money business, a private hospital ran on money from companies, but they also relied on government funding, and they liked to keep their nose clean. The hospital administrator handed her a folder with papers.

"Here's a copy of the papers you requested."

Maggie looked down at the man's name tag.

"Thank you, Mr. Carter. I believe we met on the phone, Maggie De Luca," she said and held out her hand.

The man shook her hand firmly and tried to manage a half-smile.

"Yes, we did," Carter said. "I'm sorry, but I don't quite follow why you're here. I already sent the same paperwork over to the CDC hours ago, as well as our employment record for Mr. Greene." He straightened his shoulders. "I have a hospital to run, and as you can see, the blockage of our parking structure alone has caused undue stress on our emergency room. Now, I can send over anything else needed by the CDC, but—"

"If you'll please allow me to explain, Mr. Carter," Maggie said, her eyes stern and holding his. "I'm an epidemiologist, and I investigate the cause of the disease, so we can contain it and stop it from spreading any further."

"I understand that, but—"

She held up her hand.

"Just a few more questions, and we'll be out of your way." She scanned down one of the papers he gave her and flipped over to the next page. As she read the autopsy report, the words RED RING-SHAPED NODULES ON THE LUNGS immediately jumped out at her. She looked up at Mr. Carter, who had begun pacing the floor behind his desk like a caged animal. She felt like he was hiding something. Why didn't he just say what it was? He seemed to be in denial about what was happening. She pulled out another paper and studied the photo of Samuel Greene, who unlike Mr. Carter, had a warm and inviting smile. Greene was a handsome, older man with hard-earned streaks of gray in his hair. Under the photo were the words SAMUEL GREENE, CUSTODIAN, REGENCY HOSPITAL.

She stared down at the post-mortem photos of Samuel Greene. His face was bloodied and swollen. The warmness of his smile was gone, and his mouth was agape. The next group of photos showed the inside of his car—the windshield and dashboard were covered in blood. It looked like he'd been massacred by an ax murderer.

"Mr. Carter, did you already contact Mr. Greene's family?" Maggie said as she looked up from the photos, trying not to let her distrust show.

"Yes, we only have his daughter's phone number. He was divorced."

"I'll need to get her information. How well did you know Mr. Greene? It says that he was employed here for . . . over 20 years?"

"Not very well, I . . . um, handle paperwork and Mr. Greene generally worked the graveyard shift. But I hear he was a very good worker and never missed a day of work in all those years. That is until . . . "

She could see the way he purposely sidestepped the words.

"The new strain of bacteria killed him?"

"Well, uh, . . . yes. I suppose that's correct."

"Did Mr. Greene live alone, or did his daughter still live at home?"

"I believe, from what I remember, that he lived alone."

"I'll need to have that verified," she said to Jason, handing him one of the papers. "And have a search started on Greene's residence."

Jason nodded, stood up, and then walked out the door.

She looked back over at Carter.

"I'll need Greene's work schedule for the past month. As far as you know, did Mr. Greene come into contact with Mr. Martinez while working?"

"Well, who's to say?" Carter said as he loosened his tie. "I suppose they could have crossed paths. Mr. Greene cleaned all of the hospital floors, as well as the employee area."

"Mr. Carter, we'll need all of your employees to be tested for the bacteria—before they can be allowed back to work." If they weren't going to give the order, she was going to make it hard for him to stay open.

"That's impossible to do," Carter snapped. "I have a hospital to run, I can't shut down."

"You'll have to figure it out—unless you want to take a chance of another related death at Regency—possibly a patient this time."

Carter lowered his eyes and shook his head.

"Good. I'll also need a print out of admissions over the last few weeks. I believe one of my team members already contacted you requesting the information?" Maggie said, giving Carter a knowing look. His sidestepping game wasn't going to work with her.

"Yes," Carter said, his eyes shifting uneasily.

Maggie turned around as Jason came back into the room. He winked at her.

"Thank you for your cooperation, Mr. Carter. I'll be in touch if I need anything else. You can send all the requested documents to the same email I gave you."

Carter turned to leave.

She looked down at the paper Jason handed her. It was an order to evacuate the hospital. Yes, she thought.

"Oh, one more thing, Mr. Carter . . . we'll also need to quarantine the entire hospital," she said, handing him the paper. "Evacuation begins immediately."

From the look on Carter's face, you would've thought she told him to hang his balls over hot coals. He turned abruptly and left.

She stood up and glanced over at Jason, who was watching her and smiling.

"You're so hot when you're mad," he said as he handed her another paper.

"Well, that guy's an asshole. He's more worried about his job than saving lives. He should've gone into banking." She looked down at the paper Jason gave her. It was Samuel Greene's driver's license, but it said New Jersey. "New Jersey?" She curled the paper in her fist. "I knew that prick was hiding something. Why wouldn't he tell me that? Do I have to drag every bit of information out of him?"

"I think you scared him," Jason said, smirking.

"Yeah, all five foot-three of me." She shook her head. "Damn. New Jersey. That means only two people out and we're already in two states. Get some of the team members on it. We have to cover all of the bases before this gets out of hand." If it hasn't already, she thought. New Jersey. Why did he have to live in fucking New Jersey? Her mind drifted to Greene again, picturing his warm smile.

When she looked up, Jason was watching her. She hated it when he looked at her like that. They shared one kiss after a night of too much alcohol, and he seemed to think there was more than there was between them. She told him she was married to her job, but he was persistent. It struck her as odd, the way he could seem so emotionally removed from what was happening around them. Didn't he see the red flags at all of this situation?

"Would you knock that off and get to work," Maggie said as she hit him with the papers.

"Knock what off?"

"I know that look. Now stop it, it's distracting."

She flipped through the papers again. There was a connection right here at the hospital between these two men. She put the photo of Samuel Greene back on top of the papers, staring at the image. Talk to me Samuel, she thought. How well did you know Juan? Both of you worked menial jobs at the hospital, but what was the other connection? Why both of you and not others? The doctor and nurses who worked the emergency room were negative. She bit her lip. Maybe they worked the same hours . . .

"What are you thinking about Maggie Gene," Jason said, still grinning.

"Don't call me that—I hate that name. How'd you find that out anyway?"

"I have ways," Jason said, tapping his temple.

"Well, I wish you'd use those detective skills to help me out here."

"How 'bout we wrack our brains over dinner?" Jason said as he grabbed her by the shoulders. "Look, we can discuss the case and figure out a strategy together." His tone got serious all of a sudden. "I just want to be near you—even if you do think I'm annoying."

She looked into his crystal blue eyes, noticing they had tiny flecks of green. She was attracted to him, but she couldn't clear her head enough to allow anyone in. She thought of the last talk she had with her mother, who worried that Maggie would die alone. Her mother was scared that there wouldn't be anyone around after she passed away. Now, she knew where she got her obsessive worrying from.

"All right. But work only. Friday, my place at seven—and don't get any crazy ideas in your head," Maggie said sternly.

Jason pumped his fist in the air.

"Yes!" he said and looked over at her. "I know. Detective work. I'll even bring your favorite—Chinese."

She couldn't help but smile at the excited look on his face.

"Whoa, cowboy. I need you to find out what shifts and days Martinez and Greene worked. Let's see if they match up. Did we find out more about Greene's family?" As they walked out of the administration building, she noticed the lines of people were gone and ambulances and vans were lined up outside, loading patients.

"I tracked down Greene's daughter," Jason said, pausing. "She said that she had a baby recently, and the last time she saw her father was last week when he dropped off some of her mail. No symptoms, but we're having her tested anyway to clear her. I also spoke with the head of the custodial department, who spoke highly of Greene. Said he didn't speak much, but he was a hard worker."

"Another quiet one. What about his car? Any news about how they found him?"

"One of the doctors found him when they were walking to their car. Said they noticed the same car had been parked there for a couple of days. Then, they saw all the blood and called it in. Big mess from what I hear."

"Yeah, I have the pics. Pretty gory scene, it looked like he lost every ounce of blood in his body—just like Martinez." She felt her phone buzzing and held it up. "Shit," Maggie said as she read the message. She glanced over at Jason as his phone buzzed as well. "We got another one." She read the rest of the text. "Oh, this is bad."

Jason read the text on his phone.

"Melinda Howard, Caucasian female, 49 years old—"

"And—an elementary school bus driver."

"Aw, shit," Jason said as he shook his head. "This *is* bad."

"You know what I'm gonna say."

"I know, I'll get on it."

"Please, don't use those words when you're around me," Maggie said as she glanced around, suddenly realizing her car was gone. She looked up at the B of A. "Goddammit. They towed my car." She turned and saw Jason beaming.

"Need a lift?"

"Well, I'm not taking a bus." She felt her phone buzz again. She was almost scared to look. She was relieved to see it was a text from Michael. He said he needed to meet with her about something important.

CHAPTER 18

NEW YORK CITY.
AUGUST 29.

"There but for the grace of God go I."
—John Bradford

Tom Franklin squeezed the coins in his hand as he watched the Asian man walk away. He noticed the man had a limp as he boarded the train. After the train pulled away, he opened his hand, staring down at the four quarters. One buck, Tom thought as he picked up the empty plastic McDonald's cup and dropped the coins inside. It was a slow day, he'd only made a few one dollar bills, and what little there was in the cup.

He looked over at his dog, Biscuit. She was panting and had long strings of drool hanging out of her mouth. It was a very hot and humid August day, with temperatures reaching over 90 degrees. He pushed the lid of water he had filled at one of the fountains in front of her. The dog lapped up the water with her tongue and wagged her tail. He named her Biscuit because it was her favorite treat. He scratched the scruff under her neck as she nudged him. Then, he watched as she spun in a circle and laid down next to him.

Biscuit was one of the many surprises Franklin had found while rummaging through trash bins. He was hoping to find food at the time, but instead found one eye staring up at him. She was only a puppy when he found her, and she'd been beaten badly. One of her eyes was sealed shut and never reopened. He never tried to open the eyelid, but judging from the way the skin hung around it, the eye was missing. Her white fur was patchy with pink bald spots where the fur never grew back. He remembered her whimpering as he took her out of the bin and tucked her under his coat. And that was where she stayed for many months.

Now, Biscuit was full grown and way too big to fit under his coat. She was the only friend he had. His faithful companion that walked the streets with him day after day and never complained. At first, he wondered how the hell he would be able to take care of a pup, when he couldn't even take care of himself, but the dog didn't eat much and took a real liking to him.

There were benefits to having a dog around as well—she was very protective of him and kept people away who might try to steal. He also found he made more money since having her around. Many people thought of him as disposable but had a real concern for the welfare of an animal. He knew that having a pet dog made him human again in people's eyes. They could see that under all the dirt and grime, he actually had a heart.

Tom did have a heart, but it had been broken too many times and he finally gave up. There was a time when he thought he could conquer the world, but now he was content just to make enough money to fill his belly and a semi-private place to sleep. Sometimes, he thought about how things could have been different, but those thoughts usually disappeared after his first sip of whiskey.

Now, he liked to think of himself as a simple man, who dropped out of society. He was no longer a part of the corporate rat race. He was no longer tied to a cell phone, trying to uphold people's high standards. Even his family had disappeared from around him, the memories of them barely holed up in the recesses of his mind. Sure, his sister had tried to help him, but after a while without succeeding, she gave up, too. *A lost cause.* Tom knew she was right. He was a lost cause, and he damn well planned to stay that way.

He glanced up as another subway train pulled into the station, the loud sound of its brakes echoing off the walls. He looked over at Biscuit panting next to him and held out his hand as the people passed by. Everyone's always in a hurry, Tom thought. *Rush, rush, rush.* Some of the people went out of their way to avoid him, as if he had a catchy disease. Others looked at him with pity—that was the hardest to take.

He had to listen to the religious talk at the mission he stayed at sometimes, but the sisters were nice to him. Tom didn't mind them praying for him—he needed it. Hell, he even attended AA meetings at their urging. But it all came down to one thing, and that was willpower. Will and power. He didn't have the will, and he certainly didn't have any power. His mind drifted back to the present when some coins landed in the cup next to him. He glanced up and saw a man wearing a suit walk away. That could be me, Tom thought. That could've been me.

He picked up the cup of coins and shook them.

"Will you look at that Biscuit, we're rich."

Biscuit stood up on all fours, wagged her tail, and licked Tom on the lips. He patted the dog on the rump and reached in his front pocket, pulling out some crumbles of biscuit. The dog sniffed the morsels of bread and ate them out of his hand.

"There you go, girl," Tom said, watching as the subway train pulled away.

CHAPTER 19

LAS VEGAS, NEVADA.
AUGUST 30.

At 2 AM Stallings found himself sitting at a dark corner table. A busty blonde, who had gotten too much sun over her lifetime and was aged beyond her years, approached.

"J.D.?" the woman said as she sat a glass of his favorite scotch on the table. "You're in late. Couldn't sleep?"

He nodded and said, "You could say that. Late night call tonight, I'm waiting for an old . . . acquaintance." Stallings stopped himself— he wasn't sure if he would call Harbinger a friend. He looked down at the gold name tag on her cleavage-baring uniform: ALICE. Fitting, he thought, like the old TV show. Why couldn't he remember that name? He'd seen the lady almost every week for the last few years. Then again, he'd never been great with names. He wasn't a real people person, and he didn't care for small talk either. He glanced up, realizing she was still standing there.

"Thank you, Alice."

She seemed to take the hint and finally walked away. He stared out at the blinking machines lining the walls, their bleeping sounds filling the air. One-armed bandits, Stallings thought. That's what they called the slot machines. No one was going to make him pay them to take his money. He knew the sound of the clinging and beeping wasn't even real coins anymore. If you got lucky and won—they gave you a ticket. A measly ticket, that you handed to a person sitting in a batting cage. He was a blackjack or poker man. Better odds and he could hold his own. As if reading his thoughts, two men in tight, ill-fitting suits approached, both of them wearing their hair slicked back.

He glanced up as they walked up to the table, and then turned away, facing ahead.

"Where's our money, J.D.?" a man asked in a husky voice.

Stallings took a sip of scotch and kept staring ahead. The other guy reached forward to grab him.

"I wouldn't do that if I were you. That's too nice of a suit you're wearing," Stallings said as he took another sip. The man straightened the bottom of his suit jacket and looked over at the other guy. "Besides, I'll have it next week. I already told Vinnie," he lied. He had no intention of paying the bastards a dime. The Bertonelli brothers were a rough group of wanna-be mobsters, who swindled him out of ten thousand dollars during a poker game—a game he knew he won. They kept upping the ante, claiming he could pay them back later if he lost. A real racket.

"Until next week," the brother with the husky voice said. "Or you know what."

"Yeah, I know. You'll stick a horse head in my bed," Stallings said, watching out of the corner of his eye as the two men walked away. He wasn't worried. Most of those guys were all talk. He glanced up and saw an old lady sit at one of the bandit machines and shook his head. Robbing the old, he thought. He looked down at his watch. He'd been waiting for half an hour. Harbinger was taking a red-eye flight and meeting him here, at Binion's. It was one of the few places he could stand—he only frequented the place for a stiff drink and the nostalgia.

Binion's was one of the last holdouts against the encumbering Disney-esque takeover. A classy joint so many years ago—that is until Ted Binion got whacked by his stripper girlfriend and her boyfriend, who wanted to stake a claim on Ted's hidden silver. Back in those days, Binion's was called Binion's Horseshoe, but now it was known as Binion's Gambling Hall and Hotel. The place looked like a neon-lit dinosaur compared to the new hotels with roller coasters and fake Euro-style facades. But, he didn't mind, dinosaurs were just his style.

He glanced up as a man approached with a receding hairline and a briefcase in his hand. Stallings recognized the face and stood up as the man grew closer.

"James," Harbinger said as he sat his briefcase down and opened his arms out wide to the sides.

Stallings reached out his hand, and then felt his body stiffen as Harbinger wrapped his arms around him, embracing him in a bear hug. He wasn't the hugging type either.

"You look . . . wonderful," Harbinger said as he backed away, still holding onto his shoulders with a firm grip.

Stallings thought he should return the kind words, but in all honesty, he hardly recognized the pudgy, balding guy in front of him. No, the years had not been kind to Michael. He straightened his sport coat and managed a small smile as he waved his hand in the air to get the attention of the waitress.

"Alice," he called out as she passed by. What do you know, he remembered her name. She sauntered over as they sat down. He watched as Harbinger grabbed a cocktail napkin off the table and began blotting his upper lip. "Vegas heat," Stallings said as he looked up. "But it's a dry heat. Right, Alice?"

Alice stood with her weight on one hip, chewing a piece of gum and gave him a side smile.

"That's what they say. What can I get for you handsome?" she said and placed a few more cocktail napkins in front of Harbinger.

Handsome? Stallings thought. Well, what do you know? Someone actually finds the chump attractive.

"Just a glass of ice water, thank you," Harbinger said. "With a lemon if you don't mind." He sat his briefcase on the table and wiped his forehead.

"I don't mind at all, hun," she replied and walked away.

Stallings rolled his eyes.

"Still not a big drinker, eh?" he said, remembering Harbinger's inability to hold down his liquor. Then he noticed the strained expression on Harbinger's face. The guy always looked like he was ready to take a shit—not exactly someone he'd call handsome. He didn't get it. "Well, you're looking at me, and it's . . . 3 AM," he said as he glanced down at his watch. "Do you mind telling me what the hell's so urgent?"

"The ancient bacteria you discovered . . . "

Stallings could almost hear the drumbeat rolling.

"Yeah, ancient history, like I said. What about it?" He tipped his glass toward Harbinger and took a swig of scotch. The comforting burn settled on his tongue and warmed his throat as he swallowed. Even after all these years, something about the guy just irked him. Maybe it was because he was so fidgety, like he couldn't sit still in his seat, or his sweaty palms and upper lip. But more than likely, it was because he'd learned the hard way that the guy wasn't trustworthy. Two years in a relationship and a guy like this just comes along and takes it all away. Stallings had learned after that not to trust people. Give them enough rope, and they'll hang themselves, he thought as he tapped his finger on the glass.

Harbinger leaned across the table.

"It's back."

CHAPTER 20

LAS VEGAS, NEVADA.
AUGUST 30.

"**W**hat do you mean it's back?" Stallings said as he looked across the table. Harbinger opened his briefcase on the table and handed him a computer printout of a bacteria. He immediately recognized the shape of the bacteria. "Yeah, so that's the bacteria I discovered. Anyone could print a photo from the different articles. Harbinger handed him another paper.

"Correct. And this is a photo of the bacteria that was recently sent to the CDC."

He held up the two pictures side by side. Both of the bacteria were identical.

"All right, you've got my attention. Where did the bacteria come from?" Stallings asked as he continued staring at the two images.

"New York City."

"New York?" Stallings repeated as he glanced up. He would have expected Africa or somewhere in Asia, but New York? His head was reeling. When he discovered the bacteria it never occurred to him that it could come back—he was just trying to prove it existed. His mind drifted to what it did to past civilizations.

Harbinger straightened up in his seat, his eyes darting to the left.

"So far, there are only three known victims, but I think the bacteria is more widespread than they think," Harbinger said, his voice only slightly above a whisper, as if he were worried someone was listening. He reached into his briefcase and pulled out another paper and handed it to Stallings.

It was a line graph showing the increase in the number of deaths over the past 30 days. His eyes followed the line of the graph which ascended upward and ended at the 50,000 range. He glanced over the page and back up to Harbinger.

"But this could be an increase due to anything—the U.S. has high rates of heart disease, cancer, car accidents—"

"This is only New York City," Harbinger said as he pulled out another paper. "None of these are accident related or any of the others you mentioned. Most of them are classified under respiratory arrest and hypovolemic shock, also called hemorrhagic shock—the loss of more than 20 percent of your bodies blood or fluid supply—which can cause organ failure. James, everything you thought about the bacteria is true. It's pneumonic, lacks the gene to be carried by fleas, and it's highly deadly."

Stallings squeezed his chin, rubbing it with his thumb and index finger in thought.

"What about the antibiotics they give to people with the Bubonic plague? Have they ruled them out?"

Harbinger nodded his head.

"That's part of the problem with this new strain of bacteria—not only because it's pneumonic, but also because the antibiotics we have are ineffective. I believe that somewhere along the line, both strains of bacteria were being carried by a single host. Antibiotic drugs can be a powerful ally against bacteria, but because of the overuse of the antibiotics used to treat *Yersinia pestis*, we also ran the risk of encountering an antibiotic-resistant strain. Some countries, including our own, were careless with the antibiotics and didn't use them properly, which allowed the bacteria to build up resistance."

"So let me get this straight," Stallings said as he ran over all of the information in his head. "Something out there is carrying around both the Black Death bacteria and the ancient bacteria?" Just the thought of it set his hair on end. Harbinger was right, this could be very bad indeed. He'd come across both strains of bacteria during his research in Europe, Africa, Asia, and South America—it was undeniable how many lives were lost. He'd seen mass graves filled with thousands of human bones that were heaped on top of each other, many of the bodies burned.

"Yes."

"And these new cases are from the ancient bacteria, not the Black Death bacteria?"

Harbinger nodded his head again.

"Yes. *Your* bacteria—which is more deadly. The Black Death killed almost all of the hosts that were carrying the disease—the most successful germs kill only a few. That's why it was mostly the fleas that spread the Black Death, the original carrier . . . the rats—were all dead or dying."

"If this ancient bacteria doesn't kill the host, and we know it doesn't need fleas, how the hell do we know where it's coming from?" Stallings shifted his weight in the booth, the back of his neck felt hot.

"That's the problem. We don't know who or what the host is. It's not well understood how some diseases are spread. There are too many variables in the environments they're found in. This is also true with the Black Death—there are still disagreements about how it was spread. Some diseases can be carried around by the host undetected, yet still be just as lethal to anyone coming into contact with them." Harbinger pulled out a small vial and handed it to him.

Stallings held up the vial, it was full of a slightly yellow liquid.

"What's this?"

"Your *lapethria*."

"What did you do to it?" Stallings asked as he tilted the vial to the side.

"I made it into a vaccine. Not only were you right about the characteristics of the bacteria, James. You were also right about the chemical properties of the *lapethria* plant—it destroys the bacteria and keeps it from replicating."

He was in shock.

"You tested this?" Now he understood why Harbinger had him send the *lapethria* sample.

"Well, not on people. The CDC won't back my research, since there are only a few cases that tested positive. However, I can assure you it works. An inoculation will prevent it from not only spreading further, but the vaccine destroys the bacteria already present as well. All I need is more of the *lapethria* plant; then, I can prove to them that it works." Harbinger looked at him like he was waiting for an answer.

"I see where you're going. You want me to help you find more," Stallings said. His head was spinning. "And if you get more *lapethria* you can make more of this . . . this vaccine?" He held up the vial, staring at the cloudy liquid. He'd spent a great deal of time in South America doing research, but that was many years ago.

"Exactly. I need someone who is familiar with traveling to remote areas of the Amazon, and someone I can trust," Harbinger said, his eyes wide with anticipation.

The word "trust" hit him as a poor use of words considering Harbinger's track record, but he *was* the one who discovered the ancient bacteria and the plant the vaccine would be made from. There was also a big part of him itching to get back to working in the field. What better excuse than to prove his theory about the ancient bacteria was right?

"Some of my best years were spent trekking through the Amazon. I don't know if you know about my work with the Motombu—"

"Say no more," Harbinger said as he pulled out a back issue of a science journal titled *Science in Review*.

Stallings glanced down at the words DR. J.D. STALLINGS AND THE MOTOMBU PEOPLE. He grimaced at the photo on the cover of the journal. He had a full beard and was surrounded by the Motombu tribe. All of the tribe members had bowl haircuts and were wearing loin cloths barely covering their painted bodies. Some of the men held long spears in their hands.

"That's quite a briefcase you've got there."

"James, there's more than one reason why I came to you for help—you're the only one who can do the job, and this is just as much your discovery as mine."

CHAPTER 21

NEW YORK CITY.
AUGUST 31.

A crescent moon hung low in the dark purple sky. The night grew blacker as a large group of clouds drifted by, blocking out the small bit of light radiating from the moon. Most of the light was now stemming from the boxy outline of skyscrapers in the distance. From where Tom Franklin was sitting, shadows ran across the sidewalk as cars streamed by on the overpass above him. The sound of motors gunning and the smell of gasoline filled the air. He watched as pieces of trash were tossed down the road by the wind—used and no longer needed like him.

Tom pulled the blanket tighter around his head, bunching it up in his fist under his chin. Even though it was a warm summer night, he was shivering. He'd been coughing and wheezing for a few days now, and no end was in sight. His head throbbed, his throat ached, and the only thing that helped him with the pain was whiskey. He looked at the Bhatia Liquor Mart across the street as he drained the last swig of whiskey from the bottle. He always thought the store was perched on the corner like a small ship that had docked and got stranded on the stained sidewalk. But at least it came to town, he thought.

"Stay," Tom commanded as he stood up on shaky legs and dropped the blanket next to Biscuit. Biscuit barked twice in response, wagged her tail, and laid down.

Franklin felt unsteady on his feet and took two steps backward before moving forward. He stepped awkwardly off the sidewalk and stumbled into the street, not bothering to check for traffic. If they want to hit me, let 'em hit me, he thought. He caught his balance, stepped onto the sidewalk, and grabbed the door handle. The door swung open with too much force, nearly taking him with it when it opened.

He staggered forward to the counter, where an Indian man with a white turban and a long black beard was standing. Tom had been in the market many times before, and the owner never looked pleased to have his business. Sometimes, he could hear the sound of air freshener being sprayed as he left. It didn't bother him though, he was used to people not wanting him around.

"Can I help you?" the Indian man asked tersely in a British accent.

Tom felt chills rush over him, even though his body was drenched with sweat. He eyed the bottles of liquor lined up on the shelf, but everything looked blurry. He leaned against the counter for balance.

"One bottle of Old Crow," Tom said, slurring the words. His tongue felt thick and numb.

The Indian man frowned and pulled a bottle off the shelf. He sat it on the counter as he tapped the keys on the register.

"Twelve dollars and twenty-five cents."

Tom reached into his pocket and pulled out some waded up bills. He was too tired to count them and shoved the entire wad across the counter. The Indian man scowled and spoke in another language as he reached for the bills. Then, he began to unfold each dollar bill and line them up on the counter.

He wished the man would hurry up, the room felt like it was moving around him in waves, and he didn't know how much longer he could stand there. Suddenly, he started coughing and felt his knees buckle. He grabbed the counter to keep from falling as he continued to cough. Tom began to shiver as more chills ran up his back. When he glanced up, the

Indian man's dark eyes flashed at him angrily. He watched as the man unfolded the last one dollar bill and tapped the counter.

"This is one dollar and twenty-five cents short," the Indian man said as he pushed the money back across the counter and picked up the bottle to put it back.

Tom felt sweat stinging his eyes, and his hands began to shake. The Indian man put the Old Crow back on the shelf, and he started to panic—he *needed* the whiskey. Then, he remembered the coins from the subway station that he had put in his other pocket. He reached into his jeans and pulled out the coins, tossing them on the counter at the man. The Indian man looked at the six quarters and placed the bottle of whiskey back on the counter.

"Keep the change," Tom said as he grabbed the bottle. He twisted the bottle open before he even reached the door and chugged a large gulp. When he stepped off the curb, a horn blared loudly as a car swerved, almost hitting him. He froze and waited for another car to pass that was approaching. The car had dark tinted windows and was low to the ground. The sound of music thumping grew louder as the car slowly cruised by. The driver stuck their arm out the window, waving their middle finger through the air as they passed.

"Yeah, fuck you, too," Tom yelled as he crossed the street. "Fuck all of you."

He picked up the soiled blanket and wrapped it around his shoulders as he slid down the side of the mailbox. Biscuit wagged her tail and laid her chin on his lap. His eyelids felt heavy as he raised the bottle of whiskey to his lips. He needed to block everything out and sleep. He closed his eyes and immediately began to drift off.

His eyes jolted open at the sound of the glass bottle hitting the sidewalk. He turned his head to the side, watching helplessly as the brown liquid flowed over the curb and down the storm drain. He grabbed his throat as another series of coughs came on. His eyes shot downward— the blanket was covered in blood. Suddenly, his airway felt constricted, and he had to fight for each breath. He began to gasp like a fish out of water. A moment later, everything went black.

When he opened his eyes, he realized his cheek was smashed against the sidewalk. He saw Biscuit's large nose grow closer and sniff; then, she began to lick his cheek. His back arched upward and his body stiffened as he began to shake uncontrollably. The last thing he heard was the sound of Biscuit howling.

CHAPTER 22

NEW YORK CITY.
AUGUST 31.

Jaspreet Singh Bhatia watched the homeless man as he stumbled out the door. The man's body odor was very offensive, leaving a pungent smell permeating throughout the store. He grabbed the bottle of air freshener next to him and began spritzing the jasmine scented mist into the air. He needed to get rid of the odor before another customer came in.

After Bhatia was satisfied that the foul smell was gone, he glanced down at the money laying on the counter and noticed something red on the bills. He picked up one of the dollar bills and held it up to the light—it looked like blood. Jaspreet pulled a paper towel from the roll next to him and cleaned off the dollar bill, leaving a pink streak across the towel. He wadded up the paper towel, threw it in the trash, and added the coins and bills to the register. He didn't notice that the homeless man was bleeding and wondered if it was from a red marker. Then, he realized the man could have been digging through the garbage and gotten the money from anywhere.

He glanced up as one of the lights above him began to flicker. He sighed and walked into the storage room, grabbing the ladder. When he reached across the shelf to grab a lightbulb, he winced in pain. He looked at his hand, it had a small cut across two of his fingers. He stuck each of the fingers in his mouth, sucking on them until the bleeding stopped. Then, he reached in with his other hand and grabbed the pieces of the broken bulb, tossing them into the trash can behind him. He picked up another long fluorescent light bulb and examined it to make sure it wasn't cracked. Seeing that the lightbulb was fine, he picked up the ladder under his free arm and brought it into the store. He placed the ladder under the worn out light fixture and rested for a minute.

As Jaspreet climbed the ladder, he thought of the homeless man again. He wondered why, with all of the opportunities in America, that people would choose not to work. In India, he understood why—there were more people than jobs. But in America, he didn't understand. Why choose this life? He pulled off the rectangular covering over the light, removed the long burnt out bulb, and took a few steps back down the ladder. Besides serving God, Sikhs were taught to work hard and never beg. He laid the covering on the floor, climbed back up the ladder, and pushed the new light into place. Maybe it's the alcohol, Bhatia thought as he grabbed the covering and placed it back over the light.

The man wasn't the only homeless person that came into the store, but this man seemed different. He got the feeling that it was a choice, not something forced on the man. The man talked like he was educated—on those rare occasions he wasn't intoxicated. He also didn't seem to be mentally ill like some of the other homeless people who came into the store—many of them talked to people who weren't there and had a craziness in their eyes. But, he did notice the man seemed more inebriated than usual. He thought again of the blood on the money and shook his head.

As a Sikh, he wasn't allowed to drink alcohol or smoke. He was grateful that he never had—if this is what it can do to people. He picked up the ladder and sat it back in the storage room. He felt bad for selling things that could make people sick, but cigarettes and alcohol were what kept his store open. There were a few neighborhood kids that would come in and buy a candy bar or soda, but that made up a very small percentage of his business.

After he saved enough money, he would move back to Punjab and get married. He didn't want to raise a family so far away from India. When he walked back into the store, he saw a tall man standing at the counter. Jaspreet stepped behind the counter, noticing the man was very well dressed for this area. He was wearing a dark blue business suit and had a cellphone pressed to his ear. The man was very clean-cut, even his face had a shine to it—a stark contrast to the last customer.

The man turned away from the counter, pressing the cell phone closer to his mouth.

"Then get me the next flight," he said in a low, snappy voice.

The man had a scowl on his face as he slid his phone into his pocket, straightened his tie, and ran his hand through his hair. He looked through Jaspreet as if he wasn't there, staring at the shelf.

"How can I help you?" Jaspreet said.

"One pack of Marlboro Red," the man said as he sat his briefcase on the counter, opened the latches, and handed him a twenty-dollar bill.

Jaspreet put the pack of cigarettes on the counter and tapped the keys on the register. He grabbed a crisp five-dollar bill and a some ones, avoiding the stained dollar bills from the homeless man. The man watched him impatiently, making Bhatia nervous.

"Nine-dollars and fifty cents is your change," Jaspreet said as he took a couple of quarters out of the register and handed the money to the man.

"Thank you," the man said as he closed his briefcase, his cellphone ringing as he walked out the door.

Jaspreet watched as the man stood outside smoking a cigarette. Ten minutes later he saw the man getting into a taxi cab. After the cab pulled away, his eye caught some kids spraying paint on the front of the store window. He ran outside the store, waving his fist in the air. He watched as the three boys ran under the overpass. Then, he turned and saw the word TERRORIST in bright red paint. He shook his head angrily as he walked back inside.

"They damage my store and I'm a terrorist," Jaspreet said as he grabbed the paper towels and window cleaner.

CHAPTER 23

NEW YORK CITY.
AUGUST 31.

Ethan Goldberg slid a Zippo lighter out of his pocket as he stood outside of Bhatia Liquor Mart, ignoring the ringing sound of his cellphone. He lit the cigarette, inhaling deeply before blowing the smoke out. The smoke drifted in front of him, and then disappeared in the breeze. He stared out at the dark street, noticing a homeless man sitting on the other side. He was in a real shithole, thanks to the last cab driver. He took another puff of the cigarette and clicked the cellphone.

"Ethan? Are you there?" Bethany said on the other line.

Bethany was his secretary and his connection to the rest of the world.

"Go ahead," he said, exhaling the smoke.

"Next flight to London leaves in two hours. Can you make it?"

"I'm leaving now," Goldberg said as he flicked the cigarette on the ground and headed toward the street.

"Um, Ethan, there is one more thing. Emily called and asked if she could use your Platinum Visa. She said hers hit the limit."

He tilted his head to one side, then the other, listening to his neck crack. His daughter, Emily, was always blowing through money. A spoiled princess, whose best chance at making it through life was to latch on to some rich dumb ass, who could put up with all of her

demands. She'd never known what it was like to work for things; everything was always given to her. He supposed it was his fault for always
giving in. He sure wasn't raised that way. His father had money—a lot
of it—but it was never just handed to him. No, he had worked hard
to get where he was. His father did pay for him to attend the best ivy
league schools, but after graduating from Harvard with a degree in law,
it was his own idea to get into entertainment law. Now, he had already
surpassed what his father had made in his entire life—he didn't need
handouts from him or anyone else.

His clients paid big bucks, and it showed in his jet-set lifestyle.
Celebrities did need a lot of hand-holding, since they felt there was
always someone out to get their money or get them. Family and friends
come out of the woodwork when you're rich and famous, and many
of them didn't fit the persona the celebrities wanted. Goldberg had ar-
ranged many deals between relatives, most of them being paid to go
away. He was like a net, protecting his clients not only from unwanted
acquaintances, but also from bad business deals. None of his clients
signed a contract of any kind—unless it passed through his hands first.

Being artistic didn't mean celebrities knew how to handle a bank
account, let alone their army of staff that kept them going. It took a lot
of people to keep up the facade and none of the celebrities were what
they seemed. Smoke and mirrors, Goldberg thought. That's what they
called it. If it didn't fit the persona that made money, it was kept out
of the public eye. Whether they were homosexual, mentally ill, or on
drugs—none of it existed. The hard part was convincing the tabloids of
this, which rang more truth than lies.

One of his clients, Julie Moray, is an Oscar and three-time Golden
Globe winner. She's portrayed, by a well paid publicist, as a charity-
giving humanitarian with a big heart. Little does anyone know, she also
has a big drug habit. If he'd seen it once, he'd seen it a million times.
Some people just can't handle fame—it had a way of bringing out the
worst in people who were weak—or not quite there to begin with.

The celebrities were just like everyone else, only their insecurities
were hidden behind a wall of million dollar mansions, Bentley's, and a

lot of people who were paid to pretend to care. Just like him—he didn't give two shits about any of them as long as the checks kept rolling in. Besides, if it was easy for them, he wouldn't have a job to do.

If George Durham wanted to blow his wad on prostitutes, that was his prerogative. But when things went sour, that's where he stepped in. Deals were struck, money was paid, and mouths stayed shut. Anyone will stay quiet if you wave enough green in front of their face.

In a couple of hours, he had to fly to London to talk some sense into another client, Zoe Levine. Levine was a once bit part actress that hit it big on a television show. She had mistakingly hired the wrong business manager and just found out that she was damn near bankrupt. Of course, it had nothing to do with the fact that she had bought five houses around the world and spent twenty grand a month on clothes alone—at least that's what she claimed. The fight went public, with both sides calling each other the problem. Words were exchanged, lawsuits were filed, and now it was his turn to fix things.

"Just give her what she wants," Goldberg said as he waved his arm in the air to hail a taxi and hung up. He had no time right now to deal with one of Emily's tantrums. God knows he got enough of those in his line of work. He could only imagine the state that Levine was in. A yellow cab stopped, he opened the door, and sat in the back seat.

"Where to?" the cab driver said as he stared at him in the rearview mirror.

The driver had a very heavy accent. Probably Eastern European, Goldberg thought as he glanced over at the photo clipped to the dashboard. *Vladimir something.*

"JFK Airport. I have a flight to catch for London in less than two hours. Do you mind?" He held up the pack of cigarettes and shook them.

The driver eyed him in the mirror.

"Go 'head. Just crack the window."

Goldberg rolled down the window, staring out at the buildings as they whipped by. His mind began drifting off to the work ahead of him. He had to be tactful in how he approached Levine. He took a few more puffs of the cigarette and flicked it out the window as they rounded the off-ramp toward the airport.

He only smoked when he had to fly. Something about those damn winged birds scared the hell out of him. They say it's safer than driving, but it doesn't feel like it when you're on one. Maybe it was the lack of control he felt. It also didn't help the way the news droned on about how decrepit the old planes were, claiming some of them shouldn't even be flying. He just didn't have time to charter a private jet, this was an emergency. He shook his head. As much as he flew, it would seem like he would be used to it by now. Usually, he flew back and forth between L.A. and New York at least twice a month, but duty calls in London.

He forgot to tell Bethany to put in a call to his housekeeper, Rosarita, to make sure she checked on the dogs—and Emily. My little princess, Goldberg thought as he glanced over at the airport. He pulled out the bills he'd gotten back at the market, along with his last twenty. When the cab stopped, he looked at the meter. Shit, he thought, I'm out of cash. He grabbed the rest of the coins he was given and handed them to the driver. He'd have to hit an ATM when he got inside.

Goldberg put a stick of gum in his mouth, grabbed the door handle, and exited the car. As he made his way through the airport, he watched some of the other people with trailing luggage. He looked down at his briefcase, he completely forgot about packing a suitcase. He'd just gotten out of a meeting when all hell broke loose with Levine. He'd have to get a few toiletries when he arrived. Looks like he'd also have to buy another suit, since he'd be there for a few days. He rolled his head across his shoulders, cracking his neck again. He needed a new suit like a hole in the head.

CHAPTER 24

NEW YORK CITY.
AUGUST 31.

A large map of New York City and New Jersey was spread across Maggie's apartment wall. She eyed the map briefly, and then put the tape down as she unrolled a second map—a world map. She just hoped she didn't have to use it. She held the map flat against the wall and taped it next to the first map. Then, she pulled out the photographs she had blown-up of Juan Martinez and Samuel Greene and taped them on the wall.

Maggie picked up the blown-up photo of Melinda Howard and studied the picture. Howard had a round face and a paltry smile. She was still waiting for more information, but as of right now, it appeared Howard didn't do much—except drive the bus at Thomas Jefferson Elementary School. She wasn't married, and she didn't have any children.

Some of her team members were still tracing the school bus route and interviewing the parents of children who took the bus Howard drove. Anyone who had been near the bus or in class with the kids who took the bus, were already in quarantine. The school was shut down until all the students and their families were cleared. Unfortunately, two of the kids already came back positive. Why did she have to drive a bus full of kids? Maggie thought. And how the hell does this connect to Regency Hospital? She had found out that Martinez and Greene worked some of the same graveyard shifts at Regency, but a school bus driver was completely out of left field.

She taped Howard's photo on the wall next to Greene and Martinez. Then, she sent a message to Jason, asking him to find out if Howard had been hospitalized recently or if anyone she knew worked at Regency. Her name wasn't on the list Maggie received of recent patients, but it wouldn't hurt to double check.

She took a sip of Michelob Ultra and picked up the red marker, hitting it against the palm of her hand. She drew a large box around the three-mile area surrounding Thomas Jefferson Elementary School on the outskirts of the city. She stared at the photo of Martinez, his large brown eyes beaming back at her. Her eyes shifted back to the map of New York City and the area around Regency Hospital. She moved in closer, straining her eyes, but the print was too small. She walked over to the desk and pulled her reading glasses out of the drawer.

The glasses were only a 1.00 in strength, but made all the difference in the world. She noticed that she could read better under good light, but if it was even slightly dark, she was as blind as a bat. With her glasses on, she zeroed in on the block surrounding Regency Hospital and put a red box around the entire block. Then, she drew another red box around the area where Juan Martinez lived. She paused for a moment, moved her hand over to New Jersey, and then drew a red box around the area where Samuel Greene lived. She studied the four red boxes, and then shifted her attention to the photo of Greene. Talk to me Samuel, Maggie thought, staring at his kind eyes and warm smile. How do all of you connect?

She jumped when there was a knock on the door. Then, she let out a deep breath. Jason or Michael were probably early. She ran her hands through her hair and adjusted her shirt. She opened the door, expecting to see Jason's silly grin, but no one was there. She stepped into the hallway and looked in both directions, but it was deserted. She started to shut the door; then, she heard the sound of whistling. She stepped back out into the hallway, listening. She recognized the tune as "Dixie's Land."

"Hello?" Maggie called out as she walked toward the stairwell.

She leaned over the rail and realized the whistling was coming from a man walking down the steps. The man turned, smiled up at her, and tipped his Derby hat. She watched as he tossed a coin in the air before disappearing through a doorway below.

"Mr. Greene! Wait!" Maggie yelled down the stairwell, her own voice echoing back. She quickly turned to follow him and ran into Michael standing directly behind her.

"Are you okay?" Harbinger said. He had a worried look on his face.

"Michael," Maggie said as she turned, staring down the stairwell. The whistling had stopped. "Yeah, I'm fine. I just thought I saw someone I knew." She walked back to her apartment and opened the door, letting him inside. "Come on in. It's good to see you." She glanced down the empty hallway again, listening as she shut the door.

"The infection zone is growing," Harbinger said, studying the map on the wall.

"Unfortunately," Maggie said as she pointed at one of the red boxed in areas. "We just got two more confirmed cases here . . . at Thomas Jefferson Elementary School. We don't have enough confirmed cases yet, but I expect that number to start rising exponentially." She handed him a paper off her desk.

Harbinger glanced down at the graph.

"The start of a propagated curve."

"Exactly, although I was also plugging in cases that may not be related. These are all of the deaths that included hemorrhaging or respiratory failure at Regency Hospital over the last three weeks." She handed him another piece of paper. "And this is what happened to the curve when I plugged in the same symptoms for the entire city of New York."

Harbinger looked down, then his eyes jumped back up to meet hers.

"This matches my findings. It would put the death count to over fifty thousand already."

"That's what I'm worried about—all of the cases that are still hidden," Maggie said as she stared at the map on the wall. "Not only that, but most of these deaths are clustered within 50 miles of our confirmed cases. Checking out each of these deaths one by one will take time. The time it takes pouring over autopsy reports is one issue, but trying to get court orders to exhume bodies is another. Then, of course, there's the issue of cremation." She turned to face Harbinger. "So far, Martinez is still the first victim, but I'm following up on all of the leads. With Martinez and Greene both working at Regency, it's the start of a trail, but I still don't know how Howard, the bus driver, fits in."

"Sounds like you've got your hands full. Good work, Maggie. I won't take anymore of your time, but I wanted to come by to give you something before I leave," he said, his voice growing quieter as if someone was listening. "I needed someone I could trust."

"Where are you going?"

"Maggie," Harbinger said, pausing. "I have a vaccine."

"Michael, that's great! When will we have it available to the public?"

"Well, I need this to be kept between us for now," he said, then cleared his throat. "I've run into some—"

"Let me guess—red tape with the CDC. Those bastards."

"There's more. I have to acquire a special plant in order to make more of the vaccine and the only place it grows is . . . " He picked up the red marker and drew a small box around an area in Brazil.

"South America?" Maggie said as she leaned in closer to the map, eyeing the area. "Okay, so it's good you know where to find it, right?" She turned to face him. "And you're going yourself?"

"That's where the problem with the CDC comes in. They won't back an untested vaccine when there's only a handful of confirmed cases—regardless of what my results show."

"But the foundations—"

Harbinger shook his head.

"They won't back me either."

"That's all they're ever worried about is money. I knew it."

"Listen, there's more," he said, pausing dramatically. "An old colleague I know, discovered a bacteria plague that goes back much further than the Bubonic plague. He found traces of it in the bones of some ancient human teeth from the Bronze Age."

"Our bacteria?" Maggie said, shocked. "If they knew about the disease before, why hasn't it been talked about?"

"It has been . . . by my colleague, Dr. J.D. Stallings. When we were in college together we had similar interests," Harbinger said as he pushed his glasses back up on the bridge of his nose. "We were both interested in disease in humans, only James is a paleoanthropologist. After his discovery, he went on to publish his findings, and a theory about an earlier form of the plague, but it was dismissed and not widely accepted. Instead, the disease was considered an earlier, unsuccessful form of the Bubonic plague—even though he proved that the two plagues were not related at all."

"Are you saying the bacteria we're dealing with was the original plague?" Maggie said, astonished. Harbinger let out a deep breath. She couldn't believe what she was hearing. "What about the theory that rats and fleas were carriers?"

"Rats made a perfect carrier for Bubonic plague in Medieval times, but this bacteria is missing a gene that would make it capable of surviving in fleas."

"That's why it's pneumonic," she said under her breath. "Is there a possibility that the rats acted as a reservoir for the disease and may have contributed to it re-emerging?" She bit her lip, thinking of the rats she sent in for testing.

"It's possible," he said. "The natural reservoirs and vectors of a plague, however, are not usually known. This is mostly because we lack understanding of how the ecological conditions assist in the progress of transmission. There are widely held theories that rats and fleas helped spread the Bubonic plague. But with bacteria in this form, it could possibly survive in rats that were carriers—without them being affected by the disease." He removed his glasses, cleaned them on his shirt, and then put them back on. "It's also possible that the rats and fleas were a confounder. Especially with this particular bacteria, since they weren't necessary in order for the disease to travel from host to host, unlike the Bubonic plague."

Maggie was deep in thought. If the rats were a confounder, that meant they were just present at the time, but not the reason for the spread of the disease. She still couldn't help but think there was some connection to the rats she found. She wished she had the test results on the rats back from the NC while Michael was still here. Why was everyone dragging their ass? She didn't want to throw out information to him when there may not be any link at all.

Harbinger continued, "James also studied an isolated tribe in the Amazon basin known as the Motombu. Even after both plagues had ravaged the people of South America, the Motombu remained unscathed. He theorized that this immunity was because of the Motombu diet after he discovered a rare plant that they chewed in a paste. Once I linked the new bacteria to the same one that he'd found, I tested the plant from a sample he sent me. What I discovered was that it had remarkable characteristics—it destroyed the biochemical processes in the bacteria and kept it from feeding—and therefore replicating."

"All of this information and they still won't listen?"

"Not until it's tested and I can find enough of the plant to make more of the vaccine. I was unsuccessful at synthesizing the chemical make-up of the plant. So far, from what I've found, the chemicals have to be derived directly from the plant in order to work successfully," Harbinger said as he put a small box and some papers on her desk. "Keep this in the fridge. There's one kit in the box ready for use if you need it. It's some of the vaccine, enough for one dose. I'm also giving you the only copies of my research. As I mentioned, I needed someone I could trust. Someone who believes this bacteria is as much of a threat as I do. That's you, Maggie. I leave for South America in two days." He walked toward the door.

"Thank you, Michael. Not to worry, everything is safe with me."

When she opened the door, Jason was standing there, his hand in mid-air ready to knock. He had a bouquet of yellow flowers balanced in one arm and a white plastic bag in his other hand. He looked over at Harbinger, surprised.

"Jason. This is Dr. Harbinger, a microbiologist from the CDC." She turned back to Michael. "Jason is one of my team members."

"Nice to meet you Dr. Harbinger. I'm sorry both of my hands are full."

"That's all right, I was just leaving," Harbinger said as he eyed the flowers and started to walk away. "Maggie, please be careful out there, both of you."

"We will. Have a safe trip, Michael. See you when you get back." She watched as he disappeared around the corner, then turned to Jason. "You're taking this whole date night thing a bit far, don't ya think?" She shut the door behind them and grabbed the flowers out of his hand. They had a sweet floral smell. She hated to admit it, but the guy was getting to her.

"And," Jason said as he held up the plastic bag, "I come bearing Chinese." She narrowed her eyes at his use of words.

"Lucky for you—I was ready to shut the door."

"Nice glasses! They new?" Jason said as he moved in closer, messing with his hair as he looked at his reflection.

"Would you knock that off," she said as she grabbed the bag of food. "They're for reading."

"You look worried. I know that look."

"Just thinking about something Michael told me." She had to keep quiet about it for now, but her mind kept circling back to the ancient plague—which started with the bacteria they were dealing with. She looked in the bag. "Hey, where's the chopsticks?" Maggie said, changing the subject. Her heart jumped when she saw Jason walking toward her desk where the box containing the vaccine and papers was sitting. She dodged around him, quickly grabbing the box and papers off her desk. Then, she walked around the corner into the kitchen, opened the fridge, and placed the box on the lower shelf. She put the papers on top of the fridge and grabbed two Michelob Ultra out of the fridge.

Jason pulled the chopsticks out of his jacket and held them out.

"Got started without me, huh?" he said, motioning to the maps on the wall. "Why is part of Brazil boxed in? We don't have a case there do we?"

Maggie swallowed hard as she took the chopsticks and handed him a beer.

"No, nothing related, just some rudimentary markers," she said, almost biting her tongue. Jason gave her a strange side glance. "Did you find out any more information about Howard?" She turned away, avoiding his stares. Then, she pulled the chopsticks out of the wrapper and ate a bite of noodles.

Jason held up the bottle, toasted her in the air, and took a swig of beer.

"She was remarkably large—weighing almost 270 pounds. I talked to her doctor, said she was pretty healthy, except the weight she was carrying. His biggest concern was diabetes and heart disease, not something like this. Same manner of death as Martinez and Greene—heavy blood loss followed by asphyxiation. The ground teams are still searching her apartment. Last I heard, they were following some leads regarding her recent whereabouts. No word yet about any connection to the hospital though. We should be hearing more any minute now."

Maggie nodded her head and took another bite of noodles. The room grew very quiet. Her phone buzzed, breaking the silence.

"See, there it is," Jason said, grinning.

She grabbed her phone, reading the text out loud.

"Melinda Howard's death has been linked to another confirmed death. Song Le, owner of The Golden Dragon restaurant. More details to follow." She looked up at Jason and dropped the chopsticks. "Where did you say our Chinese food is from?"

CHAPTER 25

NEW YORK CITY.
AUGUST 31.

Vladimir Kuznetsov brought the cab to a halt and turned to the dark-haired man in the backseat. He guessed the man was a handsome man by American standards, but something about the guy rubbed him the wrong way. The man seemed nervous and clutched his briefcase like he was scared someone was going to snatch it away from him. Vladimir never trusted nervous people, it usually meant they were hiding something. It also hit him as strange that the man was flying internationally with only a briefcase.

After the fall of communism, Russia became a free-for-all and a dangerous place where people were easily erased. He was a drug runner for a Russian drug cartel, and he learned real quick who to trust and who not to trust. He had to—his life depended on it. One shaky man could kill a deal and him along with it.

He watched in the rearview mirror as the man riffled through his briefcase. New Yorkers were strange. He'd have a much harder time snooping out the crazies here than in Russia—there were too many of them. One time he picked up a lady, along with her two oversized pink poodles. The lady talked on and on about the dogs like they were her children. Saying how she didn't want them to tire out. Didn't dogs need exercise? He thought at the time, but he just listened while she droned on about how special the dogs were. The dogs even had on nail polish and smelled like perfume. Crazy, Vladimir thought. Just plain crazy.

Another time, he picked up two women, at least he thought they were women—until one of them flashed his cock at him in the rearview mirror. He'd never been so happy to get rid of two people. He was appalled when the one who flashed him handed his phone number to him. Not that there weren't some strange people in Russia, but New York allowed the behavior openly, and there wasn't a price to pay.

The man in the backseat handed him some bills. Vladimir looked over at the meter and counted them, it was the exact amount—twenty-nine bucks. He looked up as the man reached out his hand. Vladimir took the change and glanced down at his hand as the man got out of the car. Two quarters for a tip on a twenty-nine dollar fare. He threw the change in the seat next to him. Cheapskate asshole, Vladimir thought as he pulled away from the curb. I hope your plane crashes.

If he didn't like the guy at first, he didn't like him any better now for giving him a chump change tip. It was an insult the way he saw it. He knew the man had money, he could tell by the way the man dressed in his stuffy top designer suit and shiny shoes. The richest were usually the cheapest, probably how they got so rich, he thought as he circled around the airport and headed down the ramp toward downtown.

He didn't feel like getting into a thirty car line up of other cabs waiting to pick up passengers. One airport jerk was enough for the day. Then, he thought of Milana. Maybe he'd stop by the club to see her before it got too late. If he went by late in the evening, she was always with a customer in the back giving a dance.

He brought Milana over from Russia years back. She was a nice girl from a poor family who lived in Velsk, a small town in the Arkhangelsk region. It made him feel like he was doing a good deed by giving her a fresh start here, a real chance at a good life. Not long after they moved to New York, she got hired at a club on the East Side called Top Hat. It was a gentleman's club—at least that's what they called it—he thought it was a place for gawkers and losers who couldn't get a real girl, so they settled for paying to be near one.

He didn't like Milana earning more money than he did, but it helped take some of the stress off of him. He thought at times of asking her to marry him, maybe even starting a family, but something about her had changed since they came here. He couldn't quite place it, but she was different. He could see it in her eyes. There was a darkness there, like she hated him. He didn't know if it was because she held it against him that he didn't make more money, or if it was because she didn't need him anymore.

Vladimir made a U-turn and veered down a side street. He ignored a man trying to wave him down on the side of the street. He looked out his side mirror, watching the man's frustrated expression. He thumped his hand on the steering wheel a few times and chuckled. He liked to see how the people reacted when they realized the world didn't stop for them. When he pulled around the corner, he saw the flashing sign for Top Hat and searched for a spot to park.

He kept looking around, but all of the spaces were full. It looked like he'd have to walk a few blocks. He backed into an empty spot on the street and turned off the car. He eyed the two quarters laying on the seat next to him. Maybe it's time to pass on the good fortune, he thought as he scooped up the change on the seat.

He nodded at the security guard, who recognized him and stepped aside as he approached. When he stepped through the doors, he could hear the sound of loud thumping music. The place was so full of smoke and the lights were so low, he was surprised they could see anything. Milana told him the dark lights made the dancers look better. He guessed so, you could put a chimp on the stage and they'd probably hoot and howl.

He turned to the stage, watching as Milana sauntered slowly down the center. He gritted his teeth as she undid her top and gyrated her hips over a man sitting at the stage. The man reached up and tucked a bill into the side of her bikini bottom. Sometimes Vladimir could take it, but today wasn't the day. He stuck his hand in his pocket and hurled the coins across the stage. The customers sitting around the stage turned, staring at him as the coins clanged loudly. Milana glanced up and quickly grabbed her top, covering herself when she saw him.

"Filthy bitch," Vladimir hissed at Milana as one of the security guards grabbed his arm. He jerked his arm away. "I know the way out."

"Come back when you've calmed down, Vlad," the security guard said as he followed him out.

He stared back at Milana, who was still cowering on the stage. He told her the customers weren't allowed to touch her, and she promised him they never did. Lying bitch, Vlad thought as he stormed out the door.

CHAPTER 26

NEW YORK CITY.
AUGUST 31.

Milana Mikhail watched as Vladimir was escorted out. She knew he was overly jealous and had been dealing with his behavior for a long time. Sometimes he acted like her line of work turned him on, other times he acted like she was the biggest slut that walked the earth.

She didn't mind working at Top Hat. It wasn't the best club in town, but the bosses left her alone. She'd heard rumors that some of the other clubs expected you to sleep with the owners, managers, and even some of their bigger clients. Basically, anyone who wanted a piece. At this club, she came in and worked a shift like any other job—she clocked in, clocked out, and left the 8-inch heels behind.

To her, dancing was easy money. Sometimes it was hard on her emotionally, but during those tough times she'd have a couple shots of vodka, and the feelings would usually subside. Most of the girls she worked with either drank or were on drugs. There were also a few who she suspected dabbled in prostitution. Milana tried to stay away from the real bad apples, especially since there were always fears of a police raid—she didn't want to be caught with the wrong company if something went down. She also knew that if she was caught, she'd be shipped back to Russia. Her Visa had run out long ago, and she was now living here illegally. Vlad said he could fix it where they could stay here forever, but until he did, she had to walk on eggshells.

She had some regular customers, some of them just wanted someone to talk to. They liked to complain about their jobs or their wives. She didn't mind, but it made her feel like a shrink at times. Her English was pretty good, she had to learn quickly upon Vlad's insistence, but sometimes she had trouble following what people were talking about when they spoke too fast. She also had a few scares with stalkers. They would send her flowers, bring her gifts, or wait for her when the club closed. But overall the men behaved themselves. She laid down the rules before each lap dance, although not all of them listened.

Now, her main concern was dealing with Vlad when she got home. He had a bad temper, and it took him a long time to calm down. He could be cruel at times, making her feel even worse about herself and where she came from. He was always quick to remind her that she came from trash. He was right, her family in Russia were very poor, but she still missed them. It hurt her that he forbid her to have any communication with them. He told her that if he ever found out that she had contacted them, he would ship her back to Russia for good.

He wasn't always like this. When she first met him, she thought he was her knight in shining armor. She thought he was everything she could possibly want in a man. He was older, handsome, and promised to take care of her by giving her a better life in America. But soon after they arrived in New York, he wasn't able to get the jobs he thought he could and settled on driving a cab. They could barely afford a tiny apartment in a very dangerous area on his income. She'll never forget the sound of nightly gunfire. Then she saw an ad in the paper and offered to get a job at the club. Vlad pretended to be bothered about it, but she knew he was happy to have the extra income. They were able to afford a better place in a nicer part of town, and she could sleep better at night. But it came with a price—sometimes it wedged distrust between them.

Milana glanced up as one of the dancers named Candy approached. She was one of the nicest dancers at Big Hat. Most of the other dancers were very competitive and would shove you out of the way to get to a customer, but Candy usually had the men crawling to her. She looked like a stick-thin Barbie doll with breasts that were too large for her body. Her hair looked like straw, and her face was painted on—but the men loved her.

"That guy's such a jerk, Eva. I don't know how you put up with him," Candy said, calling Milana by her stage name as she helped her pick up the money on the stage. None of the dancers used their real names, it was the one part of them that remained private.

"Thank you, Candy," Milana said as she picked up some dollars by her feet.

"You know what I'd do with this . . . I'd shove them up old Vlad's hairy ass if I were you," Candy said as she handed her the coins he threw on the stage. "Of course, the slimy fucker would probably like that."

Milana laughed and pulled the rubber band off her ankle with rolled up dollar bills. Then, they walked down the steps and through the dressing room. One of the dancers had her feet up on the table and was smacking on a piece of gum. She stared at Milana and blew a large pink bubble as they passed. Candy reached over and popped it. Pink gum spread out all over the girl's face. The dancer jumped up, part of the gum hanging down her chin.

"Bitch! You could have gotten that in my fuckin' hair!"

Candy looked over at Milana and rolled her eyes as they walked into the locker room. Another dancer by the lockers was wiping her crotch vigorously with a baby wipe.

"Goddamn disgusting prick," she hissed as they passed.

Milana walked over to her locker. She still had her swimsuit top in her hand. She pulled off the bottoms and stepped out of the platform high heels. Her feet were killing her. She put the bikini and heels in a bag in her locker and grabbed her jeans, sweatshirt, and flip-flops. She looked up as the House Mom approached. She was in charge of keeping the girls in check in the locker area.

"Leaving already?"

"Sorry, Angie," Milana said as she handed her a stack of one dollar bills. "Can you give half of this to the bar for me? The rest is for you."

"All right," Angie huffed, "but the bosses aren't going to be happy about this. You can't keep leaving early."

"Club's dead anyway," Candy said as she winked at Milana. "I mean where the hell is everyone?"

Angie shook her head as she left.

"Thanks, Candy. See you later," Milana said as she finished getting dressed and walked out the door. Now, she had to go home and deal with the wrath of Vlad.

CHAPTER 27

McCARRAN INTERNATIONAL AIRPORT.
LAS VEGAS, NEVADA.
SEPTEMBER 2.

McCarran International Airport is one of the busiest airports in the world. Located five miles south of Downtown Las Vegas, it spans over 2,800 acres of land. After the airport was built in 1942 it underwent a series of expansions to accommodate the growing number of visitors tempted by Sin City.

In Stallings' mind, the airport was a jumbled mess. It wasn't always this confusing, he thought as he drove into the parking garage. Why couldn't they leave well enough alone? Now you needed a goddamn Sherpa to find your way around the thing. He grabbed his bag out of the trunk and headed out of the garage and over the ramp.

He remembered when flying used to be a comfortable way to travel, but after 9/11 the entire world had changed. The days of walking right on to a flight and relaxing in comfort were gone. Meals served on trays—long gone. Flight attendants in sexy little outfits—nope. Now, it was a strip search just to get on a plane and everyone studying you like you were the next terrorist. What they did give you was a high ticket price—just to be flown in a tin can box.

Not only had flying to another country changed—he'd also become a pin cushion over the last two days. He had to get yellow fever shots and an anti-malarial vaccination, since yellow fever and malaria were the largest threats in the Amazon. And he also took Harbinger's advice and got vaccinated against typhoid, rabies, and influenza. His ass and arms still hurt. Now, twenty years ago, you could pop a couple of malaria pills and be on your merry way, but times have changed. There were even checkpoints to make sure you were vaccinated against yellow fever.

Stallings begrudgingly took off his shoes, placing them in the gray plastic container and sat his bag in the next one. He never carried a large luggage, making sure to keep his bags below the required size for carry-ons. They could keep their peanuts as far as he was concerned, and he wasn't about to pay an extra seventy-five bucks for a checked bag either.

He glanced up at the metal contraption they made you walk through, watching as the heavyset lady in front of him beeped and was pulled aside. He shook his head as he looked over at the lady, her arms and legs spread wide apart while one of the security guards ran a detector over her. Where the hell did they think she was hiding the bomb— under her fat rolls? Stallings thought as he walked through the scanner without much ado and grabbed his shoes and bag off the conveyor belt.

He glanced down at his ticket, eyeing the number 30. Speaking of which, he hoped he wouldn't be seated between two fat slobs who needed to purchase extra seats for their oversized asses. This happened to him once before on a flight to L.A., and it was a plane ride from hell. Considering this was a 14-hour plane ride and not an hour long one, it would take hell to a whole new level. That's the other thing— Americans were getting bigger, and the seats were getting smaller. Hell, maybe airplanes should charge by the pound, he thought. Regardless, he wasn't buying into that technology crap and checking in early online—he'd take his chances.

Harbinger called earlier and said he would be meeting him at Guarulhos International Airport in São Paulo, Brazil. He wondered what other tricks Harbinger would spring out of his magic briefcase. He could only imagine all the luggage the guy was probably bringing.

After all these years, who would have thought they'd meet again under these circumstances. They actually had another thing in common besides Karen.

As he walked to Gate 30, posters of various Vegas shows were all over the walls. Not the great old Vegas shows like The Rat Pack, Bing Crosby, or Carol Channing, but the real bottom of the barrel stuff. Fucking Carrot Top, he thought as he raised his eyebrows. They even had the beeping one-armed bandits ready for the last minute losers, who needed just one more chance to win big.

After he found his gate number, he glanced down at his boarding pass. He was in group four, which didn't matter to him—he always waited until everyone else had boarded the plane anyway. There was nothing worse than being crowded like you were in a can of sardines. Besides, the seats were already assigned and getting on the plane quicker didn't mean you were getting to Brazil any faster. Regardless of that fact, everyone was always in a hurry to board. It's like the driver on the road that weaves in and out of traffic, only to have to stop like everyone else at the red light ahead. He didn't play that game.

After everyone had boarded and he was finally standing alone at Gate 30, he walked up and handed the male flight attendant his boarding pass. Stallings noticed the man's eyelashes were curled upward. He was also wearing a large cheeky smile. Another twinkle toes, Stallings thought. The airlines seemed to attract them like flies. You could always spot them as they sashayed down the aisle.

"Thank you, have a nice flight," the flight attendant said as he gave Stallings a one over and took the boarding pass.

"I hope so," Stallings said as he turned and walked down the ramp and boarded the plane. In the aisle, there was a hold up as a man loaded his bag into the compartment above. The guy had obviously barely made the maximum size for carry-ons and didn't want to pay seventy-five bucks either. Finally, one of the flight attendants helped him, and the line started to move again. He held up his ticket and looked for 26C, spotting it to his right up ahead. He was relieved it wasn't a seat in the middle and was an aisle seat.

He shoved his bag into the area below the seat in front of him and sat down. His knees were rubbing the seat in front of him. He was 6'1" and obviously the plane didn't take height into consideration anymore than they took weight into account. He glanced sideways at the old lady sitting in the seat next to him as he leaned back. She had wide, drawn on eyebrows that gave her a cartoonish appearance and a glazed over expression. That's what Vegas does to people, he thought. He felt a bang on the back of his seat and heard a kid cry out from behind him. Yep, it was going to be a long ride to Brazil, Stallings thought as he buckled his seatbelt. And it was going to take a hell of a lot of scotch.

CHAPTER 28

NEW YORK CITY.
SEPTEMBER 2.

"The mouth is not satisfied by speaking,
and the ears are not satisfied by hearing."
—Guru Angad Dev, in Guru Granth Sahib

I n the *gurdwara*, the sound of Sikhs singing hymns filled the air around him. His lips moved, his voice barely audible, as he sang along with them. He listened to the holy scriptures as they were recited from the *Guru Granth Sahib* and reveled in the feeling of peace it gave him. Then, he prayed for the well-being of the world.

Jaspreet Singh Bhatia gazed down at the steel *kara* on his wrist as he opened his eyes. The bracelet was a symbol of his commitment to God. He flushed the toilet and stood, he had been battling an upset stomach all morning and had already made multiple trips to the restroom. He stepped in front of the sink, staring at the image in the mirror. His eyes were dark and sunken like hollow holes in his head. He didn't recognize this sick human being in front of him.

He turned his head and grew quiet, listening. He thought he heard whispering. He'd better check to see if someone had come into the store. He washed his hands; then, cupped some cold water in them as he ran them over his face. His skin felt as hot as a tandoor oven—he could feel the warm vapor rising from his body. As he took a step toward the door, he found that he could barely move—it was as if his feet were made of concrete blocks.

When he walked out of the bathroom, he doubled over in pain. He grabbed his stomach and raised his head to look around the store. It was empty, but there was no choice but to lock the front door and close the store for the day—he was too sick. He stumbled forward, still grasping his side, and turned the lock on the door. Then, he flipped over the closed sign.

As he made his way toward the back of the store, he fell to the floor, landing on his side. Sharp jabs of pain began to stab him in the stomach. The pain was excruciating, and he was drenched in sweat. Jaspreet tugged at the turban, loosening it. He began circling his hand slowly around his head, unraveling the material. His black hair fell down to his shoulders, and he grasped the white turban in his fist. Another wave of pain began to overcome him, and he clenched part of the turban in his teeth. The pain deepened, making him cry out to *Waheguru*, the one true God.

He glimpsed up at the bags of chips lining the shelves. He'd never noticed before, but the bags were in every color of the rainbow, like the candles in the *gurdwara*. Purple, yellow, blue, red, green . . .

His eyes shifted to the green and yellow lit up neon sign on the wall as he mouthed the word HEINEKEN. He looked down at the white turban cloth in his hand, it had also taken on one of the colors of the rainbow—red.

He squeezed the cloth to his cheek as he listened to the voices singing hymns. His lips began moving as he silently sang along. He rolled onto his back, gazing up at the neon lights reflecting on the ceiling. The voices went silent as he breathed in one last breath. As his eyes glazed over, all the colored lights around him turned white.

CHAPTER 29

GUARULHOS INTERNATIONAL AIRPORT.
SÃO PAULO, BRAZIL.
SEPTEMBER 2.

S tallings waited for everyone to disembark the plane ahead of him. The lady next to him had fallen asleep and snored the entire flight. She finally woke up when someone opened the compartment in front of them to get their luggage. He, on the other hand, had gone through eight mini bottles of scotch. At one point, he was tempted to sneak some in to the bottle of the kid behind him after listening to over an hour straight of crying.

It was a bumpy landing, but that was to be expected with the heavy rain the region was currently experiencing. Even though it was the dry season, there was still plenty of rain. The Amazon averaged around 200 days of rain per year. The main problem he could foresee was that many of the waterways were inaccessible this time of year, since the water level was 23 feet lower than in the wet season. However, the good news was that the jungle paths were not flooded, and they would be able to explore easier by foot. There were also fewer mosquitoes—but that wasn't saying much, some areas were still teeming with them.

Stallings could already feel the heavy humidity and smell the scent of rain. He listened to the low drumming sound of the rain beating against the roof of the plane as he stepped onto the docking terminal. As he passed by the airbridge window, he watched the rain pouring down. It was a welcome sight after living in the dryness of the desert for so long.

After he exited the terminal, he saw long lines branching out that led to Brazilian Immigration and Customs. He grabbed an immigration form and a customs form and read the top of the first form:

DEPARTAMENTO DE POLICIA FEDERAL
Cartão de Entrada/Saída
ENTRY/EXIT CARD

Then, he held up the second form:

MINISTERIO DA FAZENDA
SECRETARIA DA RECEITA FEDERAL DO BRASIL
ACCOMPANIED BAGGAGE DECLARATION

Stallings glanced down at the one bag he was carrying and rolled his eyes as he got in the long line. After he finally reached immigration, the officer looked up at him and took his passport.

"*Motivo da sua visita?*" the officer asked with a heavy Portuguese accent. "Reason for your visit?"

"*Lazer*," Stallings said. "Recreation." The officer stamped the passport and immigration form and handed it back. Well, that was easy, he thought. Then, he approached the customs officer, who was a dark-skinned muscular man with a mustache. He handed him the immigration form, customs form, and passport.

The officer studied the passport photo and glanced back up at him.

"*Foto antiga, eu preciso de um novo*," Stallings joked, saying it was an old photo and he needed a new one. He figured the beard he was sporting in the photo was throwing the officer off.

The man stared at him with a serious expression. Then, he grabbed the bag and unzipped it, searching inside.

"*Você está trazendo alguma coisa para o país?*" the man asked in an equally heavy accent. "Are you bringing anything into the country?"

"*Não, o que você vê é o que você começa,*" Stallings said. "What you see is what you get."

The customs officer didn't seem to have a sense of humor in regards to his use of Portuguese and just handed him back his bag. He learned Portuguese in college, he didn't think it was all that bad.

"*Próximo na fila,*" the officer said as he turned away. "Next in line."

Stallings glanced up at the sky as he stepped outside. It had stopped raining, but thick clouds hung low overhead. When his eyes shifted downward, he saw a man waving his arms. It was Harbinger, who was wearing an Indiana Jones style hat and a tan Ex-officio button down shirt, complete with an array of pockets. This guy's killing me, Stallings thought as he looked down at the plain white shirt and blue jeans he was wearing. I'm closer to being an archaeologist than he is, and I still wouldn't dress like that.

Then, he noticed a woman standing next to Harbinger. She had dark hair that barely brushed her shoulders and was wearing a yellow floral print dress. He looked at her small turned-up nose and full lips, which curved into a smile as he approached. She was a beautiful woman by anyone's standards. Probably someone from the hotel, Stallings figured.

Harbinger quickly walked up, grabbing him by the shoulders in a firm grip.

"You made it," he said as he turned to the woman next to him. "James, this is Samantha Boutroux, another colleague I met during grad school at Keck."

Stallings held out his hand, taking her hand in his.

"James, Michael's told me many stories about you," Boutroux said, smiling as she stared into his eyes. She had an accent he couldn't quite place.

"And he told me nothing about you," Stallings said as he glanced over at Harbinger. "Please, call me J.D."

Boutroux cocked her head slightly to the side.

"All right, J.D., please call me Sam," she said, still wearing a smile.

"Great," Harbinger said as he clapped his hands together. "Now that we're all here, our driver's ready to take us to the hotel."

Stallings took a deep breath as they walked toward the car. The air was refreshing after the long plane ride of circulated air. He noticed that the ground was still wet from the recent rain and puddles dotted the sidewalk. In the distance, he could see the palm trees lining the airport sway back and forth in the wind. It was very humid and he could already feel his armpits beginning to sweat, but there was nothing like being out in the field again. He didn't realize how much he missed South America.

As they got closer to the car, he pulled Harbinger aside.

"Hey, I didn't know we'd have company. Might have been a good piece of information to have, since I did have to charter the plane and boat."

"I needed help and Samantha offered to come along at the last minute," Harbinger whispered. "Dr. Boutroux has a degree in bacteriology—"

"Sorry, my ears were ringing," Boutroux said, interrupting. "Actually, I have a Ph.D. in Microbiology like Michael, but I specialize in bacteriology, virology, and protozoology." She patted Harbinger's arm. "Although, Michael's right, I'm usually labeled as a bacteriologist. Which is probably why you *asked* for my help. Right, Michael?"

Harbinger nodded, his face turning red.

French. That's the accent I heard, Stallings thought. He squinted his eyes as a gust of wind hit all of them. He chuckled as he watched Boutroux wrestling to hold down the sides of her dress.

"Where we're going is no place for a lady," he said.

"I can handle it," Boutroux shot back. She balled one side of her dress in her fist to keep it from blowing upward again. Another strong burst of wind knocked her hat out of the other hand, and it went tumbling across the sidewalk. Michael dropped their luggage and ran to catch it.

"Well, I hope you brought better clothes," Stallings said as he sat in the front seat of the white Land Rover that was waiting for them. He turned around, watching as the driver opened the back door for her. She had a sour expression on her face. Harbinger got in the backseat on the other side and handed Boutroux her hat.

"*Bem-vindo ao Brasil*," the driver said in Portuguese. "Welcome to Brazil."

"*Obrigado*," Stallings replied. "Thank you." Most people from Brazil speak Portuguese since Portugal first colonized Brazil. Before the Portuguese arrived, there were six million Indians living in Brazil, who spoke over 1,000 languages. He eyed a fake shrunken head that was hanging from the rearview mirror. That's one way to welcome people to Brazil, he thought. He noticed the driver had pockmarked skin and a few deep cuts on his cheek.

"*Você é um guia turístico na selva?*" Stallings asked the driver as they pulled away from the airport, wondering if he was a jungle guide.

"*Não, eu apenas conduzir as pessoas para o hotel e a cidade*," the driver replied. "*Se você precisar de um guia sei que alguém.*"

"Oh, you speak the language, too," Harbinger said as he settled in the backseat. "That's good, because I couldn't understand anyone at the hotel. What did he say?"

"He said if we need a jungle tour guide he knows someone," Stallings said.

Harbinger leaned forward between the seats, speaking loudly. "No, we have someone. Dr. Stallings here, is an expert and has traveled into the deepest parts of the Amazon. He's quite famous in these parts." He patted Stallings on the shoulder. "Right, James?"

"*O que?*" the driver said, looking confused. "What?"

"What did he say?" Harbinger asked.

"He said 'Okay,'" Stallings said. A real expert, he thought. The truth was, he was a bit rusty and hadn't traveled much over the years. He could only hope that the Amazon hadn't become as unrecognizable as Vegas. When he turned, he noticed Harbinger staring at the shrunken head dangling from the rearview mirror.

"Can you ask him if that's a real monkey head?"

"*Meu amigo gosta da sua cabeça de macaco*," Stallings said. "My friend likes your monkey head."

"*Sim uma cabeça de macaco é boa sorte. Se você quiser que eu pode obtê-lo para você*," the driver said as he eyed Harbinger in the rearview mirror.

"He said yeah, it's for good luck. Would you like one?" Stallings said, trying not to crack a smile. Trinkets, he thought as he shook his head. *A real monkey head.* He'd let Harbinger squirm in his seat a bit thinking it was real. Dried fruit or leather was more like it. Most of the tourists who came to these countries were easily fooled, and they'd buy about anything with a story.

"No, I think I'm all right," Harbinger said, his eyes darting around nervously.

"*Meu amigo diz que ele vai comprar um antes de ele sair,*" Stallings said to the driver. "My friend says he'll get one before he leaves."

"How many languages do you speak, J.D.?" Boutroux asked as she leaned forward.

"A bit of Portuguese, Spanish, Swahili, and some languages from the tribes I worked with in the Amazon and Africa. You?"

"Four, but none of them are Portuguese. I'm fluent in French, German, and Italian. I was born in France, but I lived all over Europe before moving to the states. How about you, Michael?" Boutroux said as she turned.

"Only Latin—the dead language. It won't help me much here."

The sound of thunder rumbled through the air and everyone grew quiet. Then, it began to rain again, beating loudly against the top of the car. Stallings didn't know how the driver could see, but he didn't show any signs of slowing down as the road curved.

Harbinger and Boutroux sat back and buckled their seat belts.

"I thought it was the dry season," Harbinger said as he gripped the sides of the seat.

"It is," Stallings said as he looked out the window. He noticed the narrow road they were on didn't have guard rails and dropped straight down. He held on to the hand grip on the ceiling as the car bounced up and down, hitting potholes in the road.

When the rain finally slowed, he gazed out at the hastily put up shack homes lining the mountains. Perched at the top of the mountain was a statue called *Christ the Redeemer.* Its arms were wide open, as if it were about to dive into the homes below. He just hoped things hadn't changed too much since his last visit.

When they stopped in front of the hotel, Stallings got out of the car and stretched his legs. He leaned back into the car as he grabbed his bag.

"We better all get some shut-eye, we've got another plane to catch at 5 AM."

CHAPTER 30

NEW YORK CITY.
SEPTEMBER 2.

A white CDC van pulled up alongside the curb, parking next to an Eyewitness News ABC 7 van. Maggie stepped out of the back of the CDC van, wearing a yellow HAZMAT suit. She was investigating the death of a homeless man named Tom Franklin whose symptoms matched the other victims.

She observed the area around her through the fishbowl helmet. The other CDC workers walking around in their bright yellow protective suits looked like giant bumblebees. Yellow crime scene barricade tape wrapped around the cordoned off zone, and news crews surrounded the spectacle. If the CDC was trying to stay incognito, the cat was out of the bag now. The quarantine of Regency Hospital, Thomas Jefferson Elementary School, and the victims were being discussed ad nauseam on every news channel.

Keeping the news teams away from the Contaminant Reduction Zone, or CRZ as it was called at the CDC, was not only challenging, but damn near impossible. She couldn't believe what the news anchor field reporters would brave to get the latest story, including risking their own lives. And with the upswing of recent mysterious deaths—they were starting to catch on.

She walked past the crowd of onlookers that had gathered around the news reporters and crouched down, passing under the barricade tape. Maggie glanced over at some of the CDC crew members as they waved their arms through the air, motioning for the crowd to move back. Police car lights were flashing in every direction, and officers tried to corral the spectators and move them out of the area. The place looked like a zoo.

Maggie stopped when she reached the sidewalk where Franklin was found. She stared down at the white chalk outline of his body surrounded by blood. The report stated that he had choked to death on his own vomit—vomit filled with blood. She noticed a broken bottle of Old Crow whiskey next to a tattered blanket. There were shards of glass spreading outward. The bottle must have been dropped by accident. She wondered if Franklin was holding the bottle in his hand when he began to choke. If her theory about a slow onset followed by a swift death was correct, then the broken bottle made sense.

It wasn't surprising to find empty bottles of alcohol in the make-shift homes of a homeless person. Most homeless people either had alcohol addictions or drug addictions. A great majority of them were also mentally ill. There was also a trend among the younger generation to live on the streets. Whether it was laziness or a blatant disregard for authority figures, many of these teens sold drugs or engaged in prostitution. Unfortunately, most of them were eventually found dead. Whatever their story was, it always made her sad to see people who had given up on life—or who life had given up on.

Maggie turned her attention back to the area where Franklin was found. The police report stated that a dog was guarding his body and acted almost rabid if anyone got too close. At that point, Animal Control Services was called in to handle the dog, which had to be put down so it could undergo testing at the NC for the bacteria strain. Although many diseases can be passed between humans and animals, it varies from species to species, and they had to rule out the possibility that the dog was infected.

Based on the behavior of the dog, it was also possible that this death came from a different pathogen. There are a number of diseases that people can get from household pets: *Campylobacter* from dog feces, *Toxoplasmosis* from cat feces, *Pasteurellosis* from bites and scratches, *Echinococcosis* from tapeworm eggs, *Capnocytophaga* from live bacteria in the mouths of cats and dogs, and the list goes on. Not to mention rabies, if the dog was acting as violent as they said. But none of these diseases explained the heavy loss of blood she was seeing. However, it did match the other victims of the bacteria.

She surveyed the area around her. The gutters that lined the streets were full of trash. Behind her, there was a chain linked fence surrounding an empty lot. Directly next to the bedding, was a dark blue mailbox that was tagged with white and green spray paint. She squatted down slowly, it was difficult to move in the HAZMAT suit. She had to bend her head at an awkward angle as she tried to look from Franklin's perspective. What were you looking at, Tom? Maggie thought. She jumped when a man's voice blasted in her ear.

"Maggie . . . you're going . . . this news," Jason said, his voice sounding fragmented as it came through her headset.

"I'm all ears," Maggie said as she leaned farther down and looked outward. Her face shield was starting to fog up from her new position as her breath grew heavier. She stared across the street at a liquor store on the corner, then her eyes moved back down to the shattered whiskey bottle.

"The rats you . . . tested positive . . . they're looking for the reptile . . . owner . . . but . . . store there weren't any rats."

Maggie stood up. Bingo! she thought. *The rats are carriers.*

"It's about time, I was beginning to think the goddamn things ran off—including the dead one. Thank God the NC isn't in charge of testing people. Did you say there weren't any rats at the reptile store? He sold rats, that's where I bought them."

"Every . . . empty. Maybe . . . sold them," Jason said.

"I'm almost done here, I'll call you when I'm back," Maggie said.

"One . . . thing. We...another death . . . Red Cross worker."

"A Red Cross worker?" Maggie said, piecing his sentences together. She let out a deep breath. This was getting worse and worse. She couldn't believe it—first hospital employees, then a school bus driver, and now a fucking Red Cross worker? What the hell? she thought.

"Amina Alaoui, Middle Eastern . . . worked at the Red . . . office. She . . . misdiagnosed as food poisoning."

"You're really cutting out, but I think I get the gist. An office worker. That means she didn't work directly with blood so that's good."

"Hold on. How's that? Better?" Jason asked, his voice coming in clearer.

"Much better. Does the autopsy report on Alaoui, however you say her name, say anything about red-ringed nodules on the lungs?"

"Let me see. Yep, how'd you know that?"

"Martinez, Greene, and Howard all had the same thing—seems to be the bacteria's calling card."

"Interesting. We've got another dot connected. Not only that— Melinda Howard gave blood recently."

"No shit?"

"Yeah. They found a Red Cross sticker on one of her shirts. Now they're trying to track the blood down at the blood bank. They closed the branch and quarantined all of the Red Cross workers until they're tested."

"I spoke too soon. This is bad." If the blood supply is tainted, then the bacteria has just become even harder to contain, Maggie thought. "Did the CDC activate the Emergency Operations Center yet?"

"They just went on High Alert, Level 1."

"Finally, those bastards are listening," Maggie snapped.

"Don't crucify them too bad, Mag. They have to follow protocol. Not everyone's as tuned-in as you are."

"Obviously not. I'll call you when I'm done."

"Can't wait."

She glanced down at the blood splattered concrete as another CDC worker picked up the soiled blanket, placing it in a bag with a biohazard symbol. She recognized the worker, he was part of a different CDC team.

"Any news yet on if this guy's positive?" she asked.

The CDC worker gave her a thumbs up.

She lifted her eyes, staring across the street as a homeless man pushing a shopping cart stopped and turned around. The man held up a red bottle, took a drink, and continued walking away. A mangy white dog followed in the man's footsteps.

"Tom," Maggie whispered, watching as they both disappeared under the overpass. She refocused her eyes, studying the buildings lining the street next to where the homeless man had just stood. Most of them were abandoned and boarded up, making the Bhatia Liquor Mart an even more obvious choice for Franklin to buy liquor. She held up the yellow barricade tape, stepped underneath it, and crossed the street. As she got closer to the store, she saw a sign that said CLOSED on the door. It seemed odd to her that the store wasn't open yet, it was early afternoon. Unless, it was only open late at night, she thought.

She noticed the store was dark inside, except a glowing green light. She moved closer to the window, holding up her gloved hand to the glass as she looked inside. Then, she saw a rack that was toppled over and two feet.

Maggie waved her arm in the air frantically, calling over the other CDC workers.

"Get this area cordoned off and keep everyone back. We have another body," she said, breathing heavily into her headset. She turned back toward the store, waiting for any movement, but the shelf was blocking her view. If Franklin frequented this store, and there was a good chance he did, they may have another victim of the ancient bacteria.

Questions kept running through her mind as the other CDC members swarmed in around her. How were these groups all linked? She knew how Martinez and Greene were connected, but how did they cross paths with Howard, Le, or Alaoui? The Red Cross worker's death connected to Howard when she gave blood, Howard bought food from Le, but how did this group connect to Regency Hospital? And how in the world did they connect to a homeless man?

All of the victims had to come in contact with each other

somehow—at least in the same vicinity. Or could they have contracted the disease from different places? Franklin could have been digging through the trash bins searching for food. She thought of where she found the dead rats. It seemed too far for him to walk, but not impossible if he took a bus. *The rats*, Maggie thought. She just couldn't get the idea out of her head—especially now that she knew the rats carried the disease. If they *were* the reservoir for the bacteria—she had to find out. And the best place to start was with the reptile store owner. She had to find out where he purchased the rats from.

CHAPTER 31

SÃO PAULO, BRAZIL.
SEPTEMBER 3.

A rusty, white and yellow striped, fixed-wing aircraft was floating on the river when they arrived. The plane sat on two slender pontoons mounted under the fuselage, providing it with buoyancy. Stallings noticed the familiar honey bee logo drawn on the tail end of the plane next to the words THE BUMBLEBEE.

He glanced over at Boutroux as they got out of the SUV. She must have decided to leave the frilly dress at the hotel. Instead, she had on dark olive pants and a green blouse. She even had on hiking boots. Maybe he had underestimated her. Harbinger, however, still had on his Indiana Jones gear. At least he'd have plenty of pockets for all of those fancy gadgets he brought. He watched as Harbinger stuck his cellphone in his front pocket and some sort of small device in one of his other pockets. Then, he snapped a pack around his waist and leg with more pockets.

"What the hell is all that stuff?" Stallings asked as they grabbed the rest of their bags.

Harbinger pulled something out of one of his pockets that looked like another cellphone and held it up.

"This is a Garmin eTrex 30x Handheld Navigator. We can use the GPS, and I also plan to use it to record locations we've been to." He reached into another pocket and pulled out an orange headband with a bulb on the front. "And this is a Petzl Tikka R+ Headlamp."

"You're going to wear that orange peel around your head?"

"Yes, it's worn on the head, and it automatically adjusts to the amount of light needed," Harbinger said as he turned it on and waved his hand in front of it. "It can cast a beam of light up to 65 meters."

Stallings nodded his head, unimpressed.

"What's in the fanny pack?" he said, smiling.

"It's a waterproof airsoft tactical drop leg pouch, not a fanny pack," Harbinger said as he pulled out a small kidney-shaped box with a white fan inside. "And this is a Hymini charger. It works with a micro wind power generator or with solar power. I'll need it to keep everything running."

"A lot of that fancy stuff won't work where we're going, " Stallings said as he looked at the backpack at Harbinger's feet—it looked as high tech as the gadgets he was carrying.

"This is lab stuff," Harbinger said as he patted it. "Various sized specimen containers, a travel microscope, and recording instruments. How 'bout you? What did you bring?"

Stallings patted his bag.

"None of the above." He'd heard about some of the new high tech equipment, but he didn't like the new direction that the field of anthropology and archaeology had taken. It had all become technology based. Instead of discovering new civilizations by foot, the archeologists shot lasers into the jungles to find lost cities. Instead of braving collapsed temples, they sent in semi-autonomous robots. Half the time, they didn't want to dig in an area until they deployed magnetic resistivity meters to check for anomalies underground. He didn't like the way the new generation tossed the data from research aside if it didn't match the machines— even if it was pointing in the right direction. Things had changed since he graduated. The young punk paleoanthropologists could name all of the tools used in the field, but had little experience using them.

Boutroux, who had just finished tying her bootlaces, walked up, looking at both of them.

"Well, are we ready to go?" She turned, staring at the dilapidated plane. "That's what we're flying in?"

"That's it," Stallings said as he glanced over at Harbinger, who looked like he was going to crap himself.

As they walked across the rickety wooden dock, the pilot opened the door and stepped off the plane. He was a barrel-chested man with flaming red hair and large calloused hands. The wooden dock creaked as he stepped toward them in large strides.

"J.D," the pilot said in a booming low register as he stuck out one of his enormous hands. "It's been a long time."

"That's what I've been hearing lately," Stallings said as he took the pilot's hand and turned toward Boutroux and Harbinger. "Barry, this is Sam and Michael."

"Nice to meet you folks. You must be the scientists," Holloway said as he stared at Boutroux.

Stallings could see that Holloway's stares were making Boutroux uncomfortable. He turned to Harbinger, who was still eyeing the plane cautiously.

"Dr. Harbinger thinks he may have found a vaccine for that ancient bacteria I found years back. He's just missing a key ingredient."

"I see," Holloway said as he turned to the plane. "Well, I'll leave the science to the scientists. Never was much into books myself. Hell, what do I know? I do remember a time, though, when you were eager to visit these parts as well. It's good to see you back."

Stallings' mind flashed back to the first time he met Holloway 25 years ago. He was with a group of other anthropologists working on a burial site in Peru, and Holloway had flown the group to different isolated locations. They had some close encounters with the local authorities, and Holloway was able to sort things out, allowing the group to finish their research on time. He liked Holloway's no-holds-barred attitude and Holloway seemed to like his dry sense of humor. They had become lifelong friends ever since.

He had heard rumors over the years that Holloway was involved with wildlife trafficking transit chains based in Latin America. The traffickers traded animals that poachers had taken illegally, many of the animals were endangered or threatened species. Most of the trading took place internationally when animals were smuggled into neighboring countries with poorly secured borders. He wasn't sure if the rumors were true and he never asked.

Holloway walked toward the plane and opened the side doors. He took the seat next to him in the front, while Boutroux and Harbinger sat in the back. Stallings looked out at the dark green strip of river, watching the birds flock from the trees as the engine roared to life. Holloway grabbed the steering wheel and flipped on some more tabs on the cockpit dashboard. He was so large, that Stallings always thought he looked like a grown man flying a kiddie plane. The plane kicked to the side and wobbled a bit as it took off. Then it lifted at a slow tilt, barely skimming the water.

"Will you look at that, J.D.," Holloway said, yelling over the sound of the plane. "She's still got it after all these years. Just listen to that engine buzz."

Stallings smiled as he looked down below, watching the land move farther away. As the plane soared upward, the jungle below seemed to expand endlessly in every direction. He felt the pressure building up in his ears and swallowed to clear them. In the distance, he could see various colors of box-shaped houses and buildings in the city. And when they ascended higher, the ground below became a blanket of green. Now, this is the way to fly, he thought. He could see the turquoise ocean jutting out to the right, and in the center was a long brown river that wound through the terrain like a serpent. It was a long time since he'd seen the Amazon River.

"There she is," Holloway hollered. "All 4,345 miles of her."

Stallings nodded. The Amazon River is the second longest river in the world. It meanders through a maze of brownish channels across the northern part of Brazil before flowing into the Atlantic Ocean. He looked out over the wing of the plane. Since it was morning, the sun was still set low in the sky, casting a deep orange glow over the horizon. Holloway was right, it was good to be back.

CHAPTER 32

NEW YORK CITY.
SEPTEMBER 3.

"Every road has two directions."

—Russian Proverb

A bang next to Vladimir's head startled him. He wiped off some spittle from the side of his mouth and sat up. Then, he laid his head back down on the steering wheel. It felt like he'd been hit over the head with a cast iron pan. There was also an annoying ring in his ears. He saw an arm waving outside his side window and turned.

A man in a running suit with gold chains and a matching gold tooth was yelling at him through the glass. Vladimir watched in his side mirror as the man tried to open the back door. After another failed attempt, the man slammed the palm of his hand against the back window, rattling the cab. Then, he stomped off.

Vladimir faced back ahead and closed his eyes, ignoring the man.

"Piss off," he mumbled as he took a deep breath. He felt like shit, and he hadn't even had a drink. This was worse than a hangover, he thought. Much worse. He probably caught something from one of the fucking passengers. They didn't cover their mouths when they sneezed, and they breathed all over him when they tried to give him directions. Filthy New York pigs. All of 'em.

There was another bang and the sound of someone opening the other back door. Vladimir rolled his eyes. He should've made sure all of the doors were locked. When he glanced in the rearview mirror, he saw a woman with sharp features and short black hair sitting in the back seat. She stared back at him coldly over the top of her eyeglasses. Then, one of her eyebrows shot upward.

"808 Lexington Avenue," the woman huffed in an impatient tone. "And can you turn the air on? Jesus, it must be a hundred degrees in this car." She looked down and began texting on her phone.

He groaned and started the cab. Goddamn pushy broad, he thought as he pressed the button on the taximeter. Then, he reached over and switched on the air conditioner. It was hot in the car, he had to give her that. But even though he was sweating profusely, the cold air made his skin feel prickly. When he leaned back in the seat, some of the sweat ran into his right eye, making it sting. He rubbed his eye with his knuckle, but the more he rubbed, the worse it seemed to burn.

Vladimir looked at his side mirror and pulled out into the street. Cars honked their horns as he blocked the road. He ran his hand over his eye again, it was difficult to drive with only one eye. He leaned forward as he strained to see the road. It was pitch black out, and all he could see was a blur of red tail lights. He inched forward as the cars moved. As their speed picked up, he pressed his foot harder against the gas pedal. He just wanted to get this lady to where she was going so he could sleep.

The brake lights in front of him turned bright red, and he slammed his foot on the brake. A series of horns blared from behind him. He waited until the cars in front of him started moving again and pressed down on the gas pedal, feeling the cab jolt forward. Suddenly, a sharp pain clamped down on his chest and throat. He began coughing and found he couldn't stop. Then Vladimir realized he wasn't coughing, he was choking. He couldn't breathe.

"Hey mister, you okay?" the woman in the backseat asked.

He felt his body going into a spasm as he tried to suck in air. His foot pressed down harder against the accelerator as he fought to breathe. The ringing in his ears increased in volume as his head became lighter. Everything looked like it was moving in slow motion. As he gazed out, his mind registered the blood splattered all over the dashboard. Next thing he knew, the red lights were rushing toward him. He gave the wheel a hard yank left, and the red lights became blinding white from the oncoming cars. The last thing he heard was the sound of screaming as the white lights engulfed him.

CHAPTER 33

THE AMAZON, BRAZIL.
SEPTEMBER 3.

After hours of flying, Stallings noticed the plane starting to descend. The Amazon River was growing closer and the clouds that were once below them were now above. The jungle had also grown much denser and filled every space surrounding the river. As the plane dropped farther down, it glided over the river, barely hovering above the water. He stared out at the shadow of the plane, soaring like an eagle over its prey. There was a jolt as the plane skidded on top of the river and water rushed up the sides. Then, the plane began to slow, drifting in the direction of the current.

He heard the sound of grunting during the landing and figured Harbinger must have fully shit himself. When he turned, Harbinger was white-knuckling his bag and drenched with sweat.

"Lighten up, we made it," Stallings said. He glanced over at Boutroux, who looked equally scared. She straightened up in the seat when his eyes met hers. "How 'bout you? All right back there?" She nodded her head.

"Stings like a bee, doesn't she?" Holloway yelled out.

"She sure does," Harbinger yelled back.

To Stallings, this was a much better flight than the sardine can he had just flown in on. There was something untamed and wild about small planes. Riding in one gave him the same feeling as riding down the road in a classic car, like an old Ford or Buick. Larger planes tried to hide the fact that you were flying and seemed to do anything they could to distract you from the fact that you were 39,000 feet in the air. Including, showing you a bad movie. One thing's for certain, they had a captive audience. Maybe that's why he liked small planes—they didn't try to sugar coat what they were. When you were in the air, you knew it. Yep, if you had to fly, he thought, this was the way to do it. He glanced out the side window, noticing the wing of the plane was only a few feet above the river below.

As the propeller clicked to a stop, the loud whooping bark of howler monkeys replaced the sound of the engine. Stallings recognized the calls as a warning to stay out of their territory. With a reputation as the loudest land animal, the howler monkeys distinctive sound could be heard miles away. They rarely left the treetops, but they could be seen roaming around the ground during this time of year in search of water.

Eight of the total 15 species of monkeys called the Amazon home: capuchins, marmosets, squirrel monkeys, tamarin, woolly monkeys, ua-kari, titi, and night or owl monkey. But, unlike the Old World monkeys he'd encountered in Africa and Asia, many of the New World monkeys that inhabited this area had prehensile tails. The monkeys here were a food source for jaguars, ocelots, birds of prey, and even native tribes. Including the Huaorani tribe that he studied. The Huaorani people have very flat feet, which evolved to help them climb the trees to catch their prey. After targeting the monkey, they kill them using blow-pipes. Then, they skin them and roast them on an open fire.

Farther down the river, Stallings could see the boat that would be taking them on the next leg of their trip. It was a local native riverboat with green chipped paint and a wooden roof. At the stern of the boat, it said BARCO JUNGLE in bright orange letters. He'd forgotten how large the boat was and began to worry about how low the river would be where they were going. He hoped the boat would be able to take them all the way to their next destination, he was only familiar with one route into the jungle.

He glanced over at the sloping sides of the embankment. It was lined with holes where the water level had once been—new homes for some of the animals during the dry season. For the animal watchers, you were more likely to see anacondas, caiman, paiches, and river dolphins this time of year. But it was a real problem when you were trying to navigate a boat on a river that was 23 feet lower than normal.

The riverboat began heading for them, making waves ripple against the pontoons and rocking the plane side to side. When the boat got closer, Holloway stepped out of the plane and onto one of the pontoons. The entire plane tilted to the side with his weight as he grabbed a hold of the wing to steady himself.

Stallings could see two people standing on the deck of the boat. One of them was an older man with leathery dark skin, who was wearing a straw hat. The other person looked to be in his teens and was wearing an ear-to-ear smile. He recognized the older man as Fernando Sousa. He figured the boy must be his youngest son.

Sousa threw the rope attached to the stern over to Holloway, who caught it in his enormous hands. Then, Holloway tied the end of the rope in a bowline knot to a metal ring on the side of the plane and jerked it toward himself as if it were a pull toy. He continued to tug on the rope, pulling them closer to the boat. When the plane was within arm's reach, Sousa tightened the slack on the rope.

Holloway boarded the boat and pivoted around, opening the plane doors. Then, he reached in and helped Boutroux onto the boat as the two men grasped her arms. Harbinger had his backpack strapped across the front of his body, holding on to it like he was guarding the Holy Grail. He almost slipped off the pontoon, knocking his glasses sideways on his nose.

When the men helped Stallings onto the boat, the scent of fish and gasoline wafted to his nose. Sousa stepped forward with the boy and smiled up at him.

"*Bom ver você velho amigo,*" Sousa said as he turned to the boy. "*Este é o meu filho mais novo João Miguel.*"

The boy, still smiling a big toothy grin, took a step forward and shook his hand.

"Nice . . . to meet . . . you," João said with a heavy accent.

"Well, you speak very good English, João," Stallings said as he nodded and patted Sousa on the arm. "*Menino Bonito, Fernando.*" He stretched his hand out. "*Sam e Michael.*" Boutroux and Harbinger smiled and shook hands with Sousa and João. "This my friends is Fernando and his youngest son João." He turned to Holloway. "*E nosso piloto, Barry.*"

Holloway put one of his large hands to his head like he was saluting a sergeant.

"Well, this is where the river ends for me," Holloway said. "Safe travels my friends, see you all when you return." He took Stallings aside, speaking in a low voice. "Keep that little lady safe—the jungle's no place for a woman."

"I know. I told her," Stallings said as he glanced over at Boutroux, who jumped as she batted away a large blue dragonfly with a red tail. "She wouldn't listen."

Holloway handed him a brown leather sheath. Then, he untied the rope, tossed it back to Sousa, and boarded the plane.

Stallings pulled the knife out of the sheath and held it up.

"Thank you, Barry."

Holloway gave him a thumbs up and started the plane.

He waved his arm over his head as the plane skidded across the water, reared up, and roared into the sky. He held up his hand to block the sun as the plane disappeared amidst the clouds. When he turned back around, he saw that João still had a large smile on his face. Stallings shrugged. Maybe the kid hadn't seen many tourists, he thought. Or maybe he was laughing at Boutroux and Harbinger, who both looked terrified. She was still flapping her hands over her head, trying to get rid of the dragonfly, and he was staring down at the murky water.

He glanced down at the water to see what had captured Harbinger's interest, but he didn't see anything—which was probably just as worrisome knowing him. Most people were scared of the piranhas, but they didn't bother with humans much—they usually ate other fish or wounded animals. In fact, they were eaten by people far more often than the other way around. Usually the *Pygocentrus nattereri*, or "red-bellied" piranha, were the most common type you'd find on the dinner table. He'd eaten one of the little nippers himself, it tasted a bit like salmon with a bit of a pungent aftertaste—not too bad really.

He was far more worried about the candiru, or *Vandellia cirrhosa*, also known as the toothpick fish, which can swim into your urethra. But, as long as you didn't piss in the water—you were fine. If fish didn't scare people off, then the anaconda, caiman, or electric eel usually did. He found all of the danger more exciting than frightening. He shook his head as he glanced over at Boutroux and Harbinger. It goes to show you—when you let a couple of lab rats out with the field mouse . . . they freeze up.

Stallings watched as João picked up a coconut, vaguely resembling a head with stringy brown hair, and pulled out a long machete. He saw Boutroux and Harbinger eyeing the knife like it was their own heads on a guillotine. They both jumped as the knife cracked down over the coconut. João, with his ever-present smile, handed one of the halves of coconut to Boutroux.

She smiled nervously as she took the coconut, staring down at the clear liquid floating above the white mesocarp.

"Thank you."

Harbinger laughed uncomfortably as he took the other half.

"I hope this isn't a show of strength."

"Strength," João said with a smile, not comprehending what he meant.

"Thank you," Harbinger responded awkwardly, speaking loudly. He drank the liquid, making a sipping sound. "It's very refreshing."

"*Sim*," João said as he grabbed another coconut and chopped it in half, handing it to Stallings.

"*Obrigado*," Stallings said as he drank the clear milk. He held up the coconut, watching the light reflect in the liquid. Coconuts were often referred to as the "Tree of Life" in South America. Every part was used by natives for food, drinks, fuel, and utensils. He'd also seen some very creative musical instruments made from coconuts.

"How long from here?" Harbinger asked as he walked up to him.

"Depends on the tributaries, some of them may be dried up or too shallow," Stallings said as he leaned over the side of the boat, looking out at the river. "Just enjoy the ride—we'll get there." He glanced over as Boutroux joined them. They all stood side by side, without a word, listening to the sounds.

The orchestra of animals chirping and howling created an energy in the air—a continuous reminder that the jungle was alive. He noticed the roots of the trees lining the bank curved downward, hovering above the low river. A white heron was standing in the water, walking on its stilt-like legs in search of fish. Boutroux and Harbinger both jumped when there was a shuffle along the embankment, followed by a loud splash. He turned, watching as a long tail disappeared into the water.

"Just a caiman," Stallings said when he saw the startled expression on both of their faces. Up ahead, he saw a green shack with a corrugated tin roof. The house was built on top of a raft so it would rise and fall with the seasonal flooding, but because it was the dry season it sat on a patch of dried mud. Two small, dark-skinned boys were playing in the muddy river next to the house. As they passed, the children stared up at them with wide eyes.

"What about the caiman?" Boutroux said with a concerned expression on her face.

"Looks like they're more scared of you," Stallings retorted as he waved at the kids. The two boys smiled and waved back. "There are very few attacks on the Amazonian people. They have a symbiotic relationship with the jungle." If only everyone else could learn to do the same, he thought.

CHAPTER 34

THE CDC-IU.
NEW YORK CITY.
SEPTEMBER 3.

The New York City CDC-IU is located in a tall, rectangular-shaped building next to the NCEZID. The Isolation Unit is a high tech hospital facility equipped to observe disease in a highly contagious patient. There were others like it in every major city, but Maggie had only been to this one and the IU in Atlanta.

She froze as she stood in front of the dual iris scan until it beeped. The CDC has the highest level of security technology to protect against terrorism in all of their facilities. She was just happy to hear the eye scans didn't work on dead eyes—the last thing she wanted to be was a walking target.

Maggie pulled the door open when the green light blinked. She handed her identification badge and bag to the security guard. The man was a gruff looking man with red hair and a ruddy complexion. The CDC security guards were basically carbon copies of airport security guards, including their flat affect. The guard gave Maggie a once over, eyeing her and the badge like she had suddenly sprouted an extra ear. Then, he handed her badge back.

She signed her name on the sign-in sheet and walked through the full-body scanner. The scanner used electronic waves, which create a computerized image when they are bounced off an individual. Another security guard, a lady with an equally bad attitude, was on the other side, waiting to pounce if the scanner beeped. Luckily, Maggie didn't set the machine off and have to stand spread-eagled while the lady ran her "magic wand" up and down her body. She had learned to avoid all jewelry—it was an inconvenience she didn't have time to deal with on a daily basis. She picked up her bag and headed down to the locker area, her thoughts immediately returning to the reptile store owner.

After a lot of searching, they finally found Kaplan holed up in a rundown motel. From what she heard, he didn't come along willingly. The paradox was that he was outsurviving the other victims. He should have died before Martinez, she thought, it didn't make sense. Unless he had some sort of natural defense against the ancient bacteria. Some people's DNA made their immune systems less susceptible to certain diseases.

Maggie stood in front of the lockers and quickly undressed. She pulled on the scrubs and HAZMAT suit she'd taken from the rack, followed by the helmet equipped with a built-in communication line. She was literally traveling from one HAZMAT suit to the next since yesterday. She heard a loud buzzing sound when she donned the helmet. She adjusted the helmet and heard people talking.

"De Luca here. What room is Kaplan in?" Maggie asked as she slipped on the rubber boots.

"About time we got some help. Room 18," a man with a baritone voice huffed on the other line. "The guy's not making any sense—good luck getting anything out of him. I sure can't. He keeps mumbling something about the rats taking over."

She recognized the voice as belonging to Lionel Mack, one of the other CDC workers on her ground team. He was an okay guy, but he tended to take shortcuts, and she always had to double check his work. There was no place for error in this job. She figured that was why Lionel still worked under her leadership—the CDC didn't take well to mistakes or overlooked facts. Even though he had five more years than her under his belt, he still had to report to her for everything. Maggie knew he held it against her, she could see the resentment on his face. But that wasn't her problem, and she learned to ignore the evil looks.

"That's what they pay me the big bucks for," Maggie said as she made her way up the steps. When she met Kaplan, he already had rats in the attic—in more ways than one. She could only imagine his current state.

Her face shield was already starting to fog up as she climbed the steps. She tried to relax and slow down, concentrating as she breathed in gently through her nose. She turned right at the top of the steps, making her way down the long corridor. The cinder block walls she was passing were painted an ungodly yellow, and the red lights along the walls were glaring off of them sickeningly. She walked up to a door at the end of the hallway. It had a biohazard symbol and the words ISOLATION ZONE, AUTHORIZED PERSONNEL ONLY.

Maggie held out her identification card on the lanyard and waited for the terminal to blink. A green light lit up, and she pulled the next set of doors open. She paced her steps and ran over ideas in her head of how to approach Kaplan. Wonderful questions came to mind . . .

Did you know that you helped spread an ancient plague that could wipe out a quarter of humanity? How's that cold now, Mr. Kaplan?

She let out a small chuckle. Pull it together Maggie, she thought as she approached an observation window. When she looked through the window, she noticed the room was empty except for a bed. She glanced up and saw the number 17. She was in front of the wrong room. She turned and took a few more steps.

Through the glass partition she watched as two men in HAZMAT suits tried to strap Kaplan to a chair. She grimaced as he broke free. She was shocked at how grotesquely distorted Kaplan's face looked. His erratic eyes were bulging out, and his cheeks were hollowed-out pits. He lashed out at the men, jerked the intravenous tubing out of his arm, and then let out a horrific scream. It was an odd feeling to see a man who kept animals in glass enclosures, ultimately enclosed behind glass himself. *He* was now the main attraction at the zoo.

She stood back as Lionel caught sight of her and opened the door.

The high-pitched wails of Kaplan resonated louder throughout the corridor as the door opened.

"Your turn," Lionel said as he shut the door to the room. "That guy's crazy."

Maggie saw another person approaching in red protection gear. She immediately recognized the suit as one from the NCEZID.

"What are they doing here?" Maggie said, motioning to the man advancing toward them.

"Waiting for you. You gave them the rats didn't you?" Lionel said as he walked away.

"Maggie De Luca?" the man said as he walked up to her.

"Yes, what can I do for you?" She glanced down at the man's badge: GARY POLENSKI, NCEZID DIVISION DIRECTOR.

She tried to hide her fear. She knew there would be questions since she discovered the rats. The questions would probably pertain to how she acquired the rats and what precautions she used. If they knew the truth, they would place her in quarantine and pull her off the job while they "watched and waited" for a couple of weeks. She had to proceed with caution, or risk being taken off the case.

"I wanted to congratulate you on a job well done. The rats were quite a find," Polenski said, his eyes narrowing behind his glasses and protective face shield.

"Thank you," Maggie said uncomfortably, worried about what would be coming next.

"As you know, my job is to check what kind of precautions you took while obtaining the specimens . . . since the bacteria *is* highly contagious."

Cha-ching, Maggie thought.

"I took the highest precautions, sir," she lied, feeling like she almost swallowed her tongue. She saw this one coming from ten steps away. She also knew the NC would love to take over the case—and take credit for her work.

"When you say that you took the highest precautions, Ms. De Luca, that would be a full protection suit, I assume?" Polenski asked as he tilted his head slightly to the side.

"Yes, sir. I've been living in the suits lately," Maggie said, which wasn't a complete lie.

"Very good. I'll keep your department updated if new information arrives. Please do the same."

"I will. Thank you," Maggie said as she watched Polenski walk away. She let out a deep breath. She could feel sweat dripping down the back of her neck. She knew it wouldn't be the last time she'd be hearing from the NC.

She turned back around, gazing through the observation window again. She watched as a doctor in a HAZMAT suit struggled to hold Kaplan's strapped down arm steady so he could reinsert the IV. Maggie opened the door and entered the room quietly, she didn't want Kaplan to feel that she was a threat. His eyes suddenly shot over at her, allowing the doctor to reinsert the IV.

She was immediately taken aback by his red bulging eyes that flicked side to side. If he had any kind of immunity, it wasn't enough—he was a very sick man. It was hard to believe she was looking at the same person. He looked . . . ghastly. His ribs were protruding out of his bare chest, which was covered in dried blood. She glanced down at the floor where his bloodied hospital gown had been ripped apart and cast aside.

She nodded at the doctor, who gave her an exasperated look and left the room. Kaplan seemed to lose interest in her immediately and stared down at the floor, his lips moving as he mumbled incoherently under his breath. Suddenly he gasped, letting out a deep rattling cough. Blood began dripping from the corners of his mouth. Judging by the way Kaplan looked, she was surprised he was still alive and doubted he would be for long.

"Mr. Kaplan?" Maggie said in the softest voice she could muster.

When he gazed up at her, his bloodshot eyes had a look of recognition. He must have remembered her voice from their previous meeting. He began trying to jerk his arms out of their restraints.

"You. It's you," Kaplan said as his body arched off the seat. "All of 'em dead! Dead!" He tried to rise up farther, but the chair lifted up with him, and he fell back into a seated position.

"Who's dead, Mr. Kaplan? Was it someone close to you?" Maggie asked, wondering if there was another victim that they didn't know about. She picked up a chair across the table from him and scooted it back in case he managed to break free again. When she twisted around, she saw Polenski observing them on the other side of the glass. She glanced up, noticing the red lights on the cameras in each corner of the room. They were recording her every word.

Those NC assholes are trying to catch me making a mistake, Maggie thought. She had to tread cautiously. She turned her attention back to Kaplan, whose chair was rocking back and forth as he thrust his body around. She was expecting the chair to flip over on its side at any moment.

"The reptiles . . . all of 'em gone," Kaplan hissed.

Maggie noticed lesions all over his arms where he had been scratching them.

"I'm sorry to hear that Mr. Kaplan, you had a remarkable collection of reptiles. Do you know how they died?"

"It was the rats," Kaplan said through clenched teeth. "I set 'em loose like they asked, but it was too late. Rats will be all that's left." He began making a poof sound with his lips as he raised his chin in the air. "Everything else—gone!"

That's why they didn't find any more rats, she thought. He released them. That meant more infected rats were loose in the streets.

"You're right," Maggie said as she leaned over the table. "The rats *are* bad. I want to help you get rid of them. Mr. Kaplan, where did you get the rats from?"

Frothy red foam ran down Kaplan's mouth, and his eyes glazed over, unresponsive.

Maggie took a deep breath and tried again.

"Mr. Kaplan, can you just shake your head yes or no? Did you purchase the rats in New York?"

He began shaking his head rapidly side to side.

"No, no, no," he yelled.

"Did you order them by mail?" He began coughing again, this time more violently, and his entire body arched upward. Maggie averted her eyes away as more blood drizzled out of his mouth, and his eyes rolled back into their sockets. He looked like he was possessed. She got up from the chair as the doctor came rushing back in with two other men in protective gear. The two men helped hold Kaplan down while the doctor injected him with a long needle. Almost immediately Kaplan's head fell forward, and his body went limp.

"I think he's had enough for today," the doctor said as he looked over at Maggie.

Maggie nodded and headed toward the door.

"The . . . Rat . . . Packery," Kaplan mumbled as she was leaving.

"Rat Packery?" Maggie said as she quickly turned back around, but Kaplan was unconscious. "Thank you, Mr. Kaplan," Maggie said under her breath as she exited the room. Her eyes darted over to Polenski who stood quietly watching her. She was relieved when she saw the suited figure next to him was Jason. He was smiling behind his face shield and stuck a gloved thumb in the air.

She closed the door and pulled on Jason's arm, walking him away from Polenski.

"I'm so glad you're here."

"You are?" Jason said, his smile growing even wider.

She hit his arm.

"I need anything you can find on the name Rat Packery."

"That's easy, it's Frank, Dean, and Sammy."

"It's a rattery—where Kaplan said he purchased the rats."

"I know. Where's your sense of humor?"

"It died," Maggie said. "Let me know what you come up with. We have to find out where the hell these rats came from."

"Aye, aye, captain," Jason said, giving a salute as he walked away.

Maggie smiled and glanced over at Polenski. He had a serious expression. I did it, she thought as she turned back to the glass partition. Her smile fading as she watched Kaplan, who was roused up again and had broken free from his restraints.

"Get them off of me! They're all over me!" Kaplan screamed as he swatted at the air around him.

My God, what kind of monster have we awoken? Maggie thought as she watched Kaplan clawing at his arms and face, drawing blood. She closed her eyes as the men tried to restrain him. A feeling of panic washed over her, making it difficult to breathe. We have to stop this.

CHAPTER 35

MILWAUKEE, WISCONSIN.
THREE WEEKS EARLIER.

Waded up tissues were strewn all over the floor. Edward Langford had a cold that he just couldn't kick, and it was getting worse. He tugged at the bandage on his index finger—one of the rats had mistaken him for food a few days ago. He prodded the swollen pink skin around the bandage and some yellow pus oozed out.

Langford blew his nose, balled his hand into a fist, and tossed another Kleenex next to the wastebasket. He glanced down at the purchase forms on his desk. He had more orders to ship, and he could barely move out of his chair. He started coughing again, it was hard to stop once the tickle started in his throat. He grasped his neck as he tried to catch his breath between coughs. The pain was getting worse.

He picked up the bottle of DayQuil sitting on the desk.

"The hell with it," Langford said as he threw the plastic cup on the floor and drank two large gulps straight out of the bottle. Then, he popped four Tylenol in his mouth and took another swig of the red cough syrup to wash them down. He squeezed his eyes shut. When he opened them, his vision was filled with bright spots of light. He had a pounding headache.

He heard a grating noise and glanced over at the wire metal cages along the wall, watching as one of the black rats ran on a running wheel.

He'd lost a number of rats over the last couple of weeks and many of the cages were empty, but the new black rats were all thriving. Edward stared down at the death tally on his desk. *Twenty-seven.* Losses were common in the breeding business, but that was an astonishingly high number in such a short period of time.

He tried changing the rats' food, and even administered antibiotics to some of the sick rats, but nothing seemed to work. He made a mental note to call the vet again, maybe he'd have some more advice. He didn't want to lose his entire stock of rodents and start all over again, he'd worked too hard to grow his business. He was also sure that his clients wouldn't wait around and would find a different supplier—if many of them hadn't already.

He was getting an increasing number of complaints about sickly rats from his customers, but most of them were happy when he guaranteed to replace any rats that had died within a week of the sale. The problem was, he was finding it harder and harder to fulfill the demand—too many of the rats were dying, and he was losing money hand over fist.

Langford thought back to all of the years he worked at a rattery in New Jersey. At the time, he dreamed of opening his own rattery. Then one day, fate brought him back to his hometown of Milwaukee when his mother fell ill. She passed away soon after, but he was happy he was there for her last moments. Even though her eyes were vacant at the end, he knew that she felt his presence.

After his mother died, he found an ad in the local newspaper that was placed by a widowed elderly lady. The woman said that she needed help with her land upkeep in exchange for one of the outbuildings on her property. He jumped at the chance. The property was located on many acres and needed a lot of tending, but he enjoyed riding the John Deere lawn mower over the hilly landscape. He also found it more peaceful living away from the crowded city.

The outbuilding had a lot of old rusty farm equipment stored inside, but after he moved everything out, it was quite a large space. He slept in the loft up top while he renovated and fixed the electricity. Within a few months, he transformed the metal outbuilding into his living quarters and opened his own rattery business. He was so obsessed with rats that he even used part of his inheritance money to take a trip to China a couple of weeks ago. Mostly because both the *Rattus norvegicus*, or Norway rat, and the *Rattus rattus*, or black rat, originated in the plains of Asia. There are at least 60 species that fall under the genus *Rattus*, but he wanted to find the perfect mix. He figured there was no other way, but to go to the original source.

After searching, he'd found that too many of the American rats had been messed with by other breeders or labs, which led to a strain of inbred rats. The first captive rats were selected for calmness and docility, and this led to changes in their hormone chemistry and physiology. Many of the rats' original characteristics were lost, and he intended to right this wrong. That was why he was so excited when he found Gracie at the Panjaiyuan Flea Market in Beijing.

When he had first entered the Panjaiyuan Flea Market, he was shocked at how large it was. There was a multitude of vendors selling everything from fruits and vegetables to handicrafts and exotic animals. At first, he thought the only animals they were selling were reptiles, monkeys, or birds; then, he saw a small black rodent in a rusty wire cage.

The vendor, from what he could understand, had captured the rat in the field near his home. She had a sleek black coat, and her head was shaped differently than any rat he'd ever seen. She moved gracefully with her smaller build, so he began calling her Gracie. He figured she was a *Rattus rattus*, but some of her characteristics didn't match. She was probably some sort of hybrid mixture that they stumbled upon in the rice fields, but at least she wasn't a lab rat or one of those fancy rats that other breeders sold. She was exactly what he'd been searching for, and once he was back in the states, Gracie became his new obsession. There was also an added bonus—Gracie was pregnant. A day later, she gave birth to ten pups.

Female rats can mate over 500 times in the course of a day. They can also have up to 2,000 pups a year. As a rat breeder, he was always watching for signs that one of his rats was pregnant. They would usually start taking anything they could find and start stacking it in the corner of their cage to build a nest. He'd even found a paperclip and one of his receipts shredded in a rat's nest—he had no idea how they got there.

Rats had gotten a bad wrap, Edward thought as he wiped his nose and let out a deep breath. Some even called a group of rats "mischief," but he preferred for them to be called "packs," like the old Rat Pack with Frank Sinatra, Dean Martin, Sammy Davis, Jr., Peter Lawford, and Joey Bishop. He even named his company Rat Packery after the famous group. What most people didn't know, was that rats were smarter than dogs. Dogs were dumb animals.

He looked over at the mostly empty cages. He couldn't help but wonder if the sickness had come from Gracie. The rats were all doing fine until after he got back from his trip to China. Nothing else in their routine was changed. Edward jumped when he felt something on his shoulder and looked over.

"Did you get out again?" he said as he looked over at the black rat on his arm. "Were your ears ringing, Gracie?" Langford reached up and patted the top of the rat's head. He held his arm out as she began crawling down it. She was so healthy looking, he felt bad for blaming her. "Gracie the escape artist. I should have named you Houdin-a." He noticed Gracie's nose twitching as she stared at the half-eaten donut on the desk. "All right, you can have it."

He grabbed the jelly donut and held it in his hand. He didn't have an appetite anyway, and his throat felt too sore to swallow anything. Gracie stood in the palm of his hand while she nibbled the donut. After she finished most of the donut, she hopped down on the desk and walked across his keyboard.

"Hey, off the keys—unless you're a secretary, too." He let out a sigh. "I could sure use one."

He started coughing again, and it nearly knocked him out of his chair. He glanced down—there was red all over his hand. *Blood.* He grabbed another Kleenex, wiping off his hands and mouth. When he looked up, he saw Gracie hiding behind his computer screen.

"Sorry girl," he said as he coaxed her out of hiding with another piece of donut. The blood was scaring him, too. Was his throat that raw? Then he remembered the red cough syrup he took. That was a relief.

Gracie crawled back onto his arm and stared up at him. Then the thought hit him: What if she gets sick like the others? He glanced over at the number 27 again. He knew deep down that he had to start over. He couldn't keep selling sick rats. He picked up Gracie, walked over to her cage, and put her inside.

"Our rattery's not doing so well, girl," he said as he locked the cage. But I'm going to make sure you go to a good home."

He turned and stumbled back over to the desk chair. He felt dizzy as he scribbled the words PET WORLD on the calendar, and the words began zooming in and out of focus. He could also feel himself beginning to sweat, but that was usually a good sign that the fever was breaking. Right now, he just needed to sleep. Edward leaned back in the chair, propped his feet up on the desk, and closed his eyes.

"Say goodnight, Gracie."

CHAPTER 36

THE AMAZON, BRAZIL.
SEPTEMBER 3.

fter a few hours, the riverboat began to slow down, veering to the left side where the river began to branch off. The river was thinner in width after the boat turned down one of the tributaries. The trees and foliage were twisted around each other above them, forming an expansive green web that blocked out most of the light and a thick mist hung low over the water. Under the dim canopy, the low hum of bugs buzzing joined the calls of the birds and the howls of the monkeys.

Stallings noticed the humidity increasing as the jungle closed in around them. He glanced over as a light passed in front of him. It was emitting from Harbinger, who was wearing the orange peel light on his head as he scribbled in a notebook. Boutroux was sitting on a fishing crate with her arms crossed protectively over her chest as she stared up at the canopy above them. João was standing next to his father as he steered the boat.

Every so often, João would look out over the side of the boat and walk back over to Fernando. The boat was creeping along slowly, but at a steady pace. Then, there was a loud scraping noise on the bottom of the boat. The engine began kicking as it struggled to push them forward. There was one last jolt, and then it died. The boat made a creaking sound as it tilted to the side. Harbinger and Boutroux slid sideways a couple of feet on their crates. They both grabbed on to the crates under them, looking relieved when they stopped moving.

"*Filho, me ajude a empurrar,*" Fernando called out. João quickly walked over to the cabin and unhooked a long stick hanging on the wall.

"*Você tem outro pau?* Stallings said, asking Fernando if he had another stick. He was worried this would happen with the water at such a low level.

Fernando looked at him funny, seeming offended.

Stallings pointed at the stick.

"*Sim no outro lado,*" Fernando laughed.

What the hell did I say? Stallings thought as he walked into the cabin and came out with another stick. He joined João and plunged the stick into the mud on one side of the boat; then, moved to the other side.

"What's going on?" Harbinger called out.

"The river's too low," Stallings said as he pushed the stick against the embankment. "I think the propeller got caught on something." He turned to Fernando. "*Tente dar partida no motor.*" The engine turned over once, but it wouldn't start. There must be a branch or something caught in the propeller, he thought. "*Um ramo está na hélice.*"

Fernando glanced over at João and nodded. Then, João took off his shirt and jumped off the side of the boat. There was a small splash, and then it grew silent.

"Oh, my God," Boutroux said as she stood up.

Harbinger sat frozen, staring at the spot the boy leaped from.

As more time passed, Stallings began to get worried, it seemed like João was down there for too long. He glanced over at Fernando watching from the side of the boat. He turned back to the water, it was dark and still.

"Michael, come over here and shine that thing you're wearing at the water," Stallings yelled. Harbinger walked up next to him and leaned over the boat. He saw movement in the beam of light, but realized it was a fish.

"Where is he?" Boutroux asked as she walked over to them, staring at the water.

Suddenly, a head sprung up out of the water with a big toothy grin.

"*Sim*," João said as he held a broken branch in the air. He narrowed his eyes against the glare of Harbinger's headlamp.

"*Sim, sim*," Stallings said as he shook his head and reached down to help João out of the water.

Fernando walked back over to the wheel and turned the engine on. It kicked and sputtered for a minute, and then roared steadily. The boat straightened as it lifted and started moving ahead.

After the excitement with João, everyone on the boat became more reserved. Boutroux and Harbinger were studying the forest around them and discussing the different attributes of the plants they passed. João sat quietly near them, listening to them talk as he carved on a small block of wood with a knife. Every so often as they drifted along, Stallings would hear a faint splash of water or a rustling sound in the palm leaves. He also had the strange sensation that something was watching them.

The river wasn't the only place where dangerous animals lived in the Amazon—the deadliest land animal was the jaguar. It could measure up to 6.4 feet in length and weigh up to 300 pounds, making it the largest cat in the Felidae family that lived in the Americas. The jaguar has a bite more powerful than a tiger or lion, with teeth that could easily crush through a skull. He'd only seen the animal once in person, but the Motombu feared the animal, and he'd heard many stories of attacks on their people.

There were also nine subspecies of South American rattlesnakes. Their venom was a potent neurotoxin, and one bite could cause blindness, paralysis, or even death. The rattlesnake has distinctive stripes and can be difficult to spot, but it will only attack when provoked. They'd also have to watch out for insects, such as bullet ants, which live in the bases of the trees and can grow up to over an inch in length. The bullet ant also has the most painful insect sting known to man—hence its name—which feels like you were shot. Like they say, Stallings thought, the jungle was about the survival of the fittest. Most of the animals adhered to the eat or be eaten frame of mind—including the most dangerous animal of all—the people.

His mind drifted back to the present. He noticed the canopy above them was higher in this part of the river, allowing small rays of light to pierce through the leaves of the trees. It was much cooler than roasting in the blazing sun on the main river. He felt a sting and slapped his hand on the back of his neck. He held out his hand and looked down at the dead mosquito. Luckily, he was up to date on those shots, he thought as he glanced up at the swarm of mosquitoes buzzing around his head.

Every country has their diseases, and in the Amazon, there were plenty: malaria, dengue, Chagas disease, and Brazilian purpuric fever—to name a few. But, he didn't have to tell that to his cohorts—they specialized in this shit. It wouldn't be too smart of them to return with a vaccine to wipe out a bacteria in the states, only to succumb to one of the local diseases here.

The boat started slowing, and he walked across the deck. There weren't any markers of any sort showing his last route, but the locals knew the jungle like the back of their hands. He watched as João jumped off the side of the boat—this time wading through waist-high water—and began to pound a stake into the dry ground.

"Looks like we're here," Stallings said as he picked up his bag sitting next to him.

"Aren't they going to get us any closer?" Boutroux said as she looked over the side of the boat.

He glanced over at the embankment. They were a good 8 feet from dry land.

"This is the closest the boat can get without getting stuck again," he said as he jumped into the water. He could feel his feet sinking in the mud, but the water was a welcome break from the heat of the jungle. He gazed up at Boutroux, who was looking at him like he had the plague himself.

"You mean I have to get in that?" she said, gesturing to the dark brown river.

"Yeah, unless you want me to carry you," he said with a smirk on his face as he held out his hands.

A look of defiance spread across her face.

"No, I'm fine," Boutroux said as she pushed his hands away and jumped into the water next to him.

He chuckled at the look on her face as she waded through the water. He could hear sucking sounds from the mud when she reached the side of the embankment. He glanced up at Harbinger still standing on the deck. The man looked like he was going to vomit.

"How 'bout you? Do you need a piggyback ride?" he asked.

"No, I-I'm good," Harbinger said as he took off the pack around his waist. He gritted his teeth and carefully slid into the water, holding his backpack high in the air in front of him.

Stallings followed Harbinger through the water, chuckling as he made grunting sounds. When they stepped onto dry land, Harbinger began opening his pockets, making sure his cell phone and other gadgets didn't get wet. Boutroux took off her boots and began wiping them on the grass, trying to remove the mud.

They all turned as João walked up to them with his beaming grin. He handed a wooden figure to Boutroux. She smiled as she held it up in the air. It was a carved dragonfly like the one she had been shooing away earlier.

She glanced over at Stallings.

"How do you say 'beautiful' in Portuguese?"

"*Bela*," Stallings said.

"Oh, the same as Italian," Boutroux said as she nodded at João. "*Bella*."

"Sam beautiful," said João as he grinned.

Boutroux stood up and kissed him on the cheek. João turned pink and smiled. Then, he turned and untied the boat. He gave a final wave before hopping on the boat. Fernando waved from the deck.

"*Obrigado amigo!*" Stallings called out. They all waved as the boat motor kicked on and chugged up the river, disappearing around the bend.

Harbinger looked panicked as his eyes flitted around.

"Where's our next guide?"

"You're looking at him," Stallings said as he headed into the jungle.

"But, what about a vehicle?" Harbinger said, his voice going up an octave at the end.

"This isn't Disneyland—there aren't any roads where we're going," he called back. "You're the one who said I was an expert. Famous in these parts if I recall."

cages with bright colored tubes leading in different directions. She thought it would give Jamie hours of fun.

When they got to Pet World, Jamie was more interested in the rats than the hamsters. Alexandra kept trying to show her all the bells and whistles on the different cages, but Jamie wasn't impressed. She said that the rat was cuter, and she liked its long tail. Alexandra, on the other hand, was automatically turned off by the long tail. Rats were creatures she'd seen in horror films and were the furthest thing from cute that she could imagine.

The man that worked at the pet store claimed rats were much better pets than hamsters. He told her that if they got an older one, they were also less likely to bite. Alexandra wasn't sold at first, but after he brought out a black rat, she could see that the rat did seem to take to Jamie right away and let her hold it. She still insisted that the man bring out one of the hamsters, but each hamster they tried would fall on its back and squeal. It was a terrible sound. In the end, Jamie won.

The employee said this rat was the smartest one he'd ever seen—it would even come to you when you called it. He said it was trained by the breeder, who insisted the rat went to a good home. Jamie even liked the name Gracie, that was given to the rat. The employee was right, Gracie was smart and did seem to know her name. She noticed the rat's ears would perk up every time Jamie said it.

"Dinner's almost ready, and your father will be home soon, so let's clean up," Alexandra said as she picked up a few of the plush toys scattered on the floor. She tossed them up into the mesh net draped in the corner. One of them hit the side of the net and bounced off, almost hitting her in the face. She picked up the small brown teddy bear and tossed it into the center of the net. "Didn't know your mom was a pro basketball player, huh?"

She walked out of the bedroom. When she turned around, she saw Jamie handing Gracie a piece of Pop-Tart through the bars.

"Jamie, it's not good for a rat to eat sweets." She watched the rat nibble the edge of the cherry pastry as it sat on its hind legs. She had to admit, Gracie was kind of cute.

"But mom, Gracie likes them," Jamie said as she handed the rat another piece.

"All right, but not too much. You don't want Gracie to get fat, do you?" Alexandra said as she tousled Jamie's hair again. "Now, go wash up like I said."

"O-kay," Jamie said as she ran past her and into the bathroom.

She let out a deep breath as she stood in the doorway, watching the rat. The rat finished the bit of Pop-Tart and began stuffing seeds into its already full cheeks. She could hear Jamie singing in the bathroom as the water ran:

"Ring around the rosie.
Pockets full of posies.
Ashes, ashes.
We all fall down."

Alexandra smiled, turned off the light, and went back downstairs into the kitchen.

"Shit," she said as she looked at the stove. The mushroom gravy was dripping over the side of the pan and down into the burner below. She grabbed a potholder and moved the pan off the hot burner. She completely forgot that she left it on. She glanced down at the flour all over the floor and shook her head. She had to get this mess cleaned up before Lenny got home, she didn't want to get him started.

She opened the pantry door and grabbed the broom. As she was sweeping, she looked over at the television in the other room. There was a reporter standing in front of an elementary school in New York. She walked closer to the television and watched news teams interviewing some of the parents. She turned up the volume as a reporter came back on the screen.

"An unknown bacteria is sweeping through the streets of New York City. With at least six deaths and countless others infected, fear is mounting for parents whose children attend Thomas Jefferson Elementary School after a bus driver for the school was among one of the latest victims. The school has closed its doors while students are quarantined and tested for the bacteria. So far, five students have already tested positive. Other schools in the area are also closing until they are cleared. This marks the third closure in the New York City area. Little is known about the bacteria, except that it's airborne and highly contagious. Authorities claim that the situation is under control, but parents here at Thomas Jefferson Elementary School are concerned for the safety of their children."

Alexandra turned off the television when she heard feet coming down the steps. Jamie had just started first grade a few weeks ago, she couldn't imagine what those parents must be going through. New York was a world away from Wisconsin, but it still felt too close to home.

CHAPTER 38

LONDON.
SEPTEMBER 3.

"The man who gives little with a smile gives more
than the man who gives much with a frown."
—Jewish Proverb

London is the capital city of England and the United Kingdom, it carries a population of almost 9 million people, making it the most populous city in the European Union. Originally named "Londinium" by the Romans who founded it, London still retains most of its medieval boundaries. It wasn't until 1348 that a pneumonic plague pandemic washed up on the shores of London—it wouldn't be the last.

Ethan Goldberg tossed his briefcase and iPhone on the bed and undressed. He finally straightened everything out with Zoe Levine, but it had taken a toll on his health. After days of weeding through the lawsuits and countersuits, he finally got both parties to agree to a cease-fire. The press was having a field day with information that was leaked out on a daily basis, and almost all of Levine's demons were brought out into the the open. Things he didn't even know about—including the fact that she had worked for a high-end escort service that catered to studio execs. Even though he had put a stop to Levine's immediate problems with her manager, things were not looking good for the once bit part actress.

He looked in the bathroom mirror, it was as if he'd aged 30 years. His eyes were bloodshot, and he not only looked like shit—he felt like shit. His head was throbbing painfully, causing him to grind his teeth together—a bad habit he had had since childhood. His parents tried to rid him of the habit by taking him to an orthodontist who fit him with a teeth guard. The teeth guard worked, but lately he found himself reverting back to the behavior again. The behavior specialist said it was nerves, he was probably right. It had to be from the stress of dealing with his clients.

He worked his fingers into his temples with as much pressure as he could stand, and then rolled his neck across his shoulders, trying to loosen up. Goldberg opened the shower door and turned the faucet knob as hot as it would allow. He sat on the toilet, letting the steam fill the room, and then stepped into the shower.

The hot water burned, but it felt good beating across his sore back. Maybe I should call a masseuse, Goldberg thought as he washed his hair. His stomach began to cramp again, and he grasped the shower bar as he contemplated his options. That's what he was good at—weighing options. He figured at the very least, he was stuck in London until the final papers for the Levine case were signed. He couldn't possibly travel in this condition anyway, he was way too weak. He couldn't imagine sitting on an 8-hour plane ride while feeling like he was going to lose his lunch any minute. He could call the front desk and see if they could send up a doctor that makes house calls. Some antibiotics might help kick this thing, he thought. Then again, if this was a cold or flu, antibiotics wouldn't help.

Usually, he let the colds just work themselves out and didn't even bother with over-the-counter meds. All in all, he led a pretty healthy lifestyle—except the occasional stress cigarettes when he had to fly. He even hit the gym a few times a week and worked out with a trainer. This cold, flu, or whatever the hell it was seemed different than the others though. It felt more intense, and it didn't seem like it was tapering off any time soon. In fact, it was getting worse. It started off with him just feeling run down, but now the thing was hitting him like a freight train. He slid down the wall and sat on the floor of the shower.

"Damn it!" Goldberg said as he slammed his fist against the shower wall. A pain shot through his hand in response.

He had a meeting scheduled in less than a half hour, and he was going to be late. He didn't have time to get sick. He could already hear his phone ringing in the other room. It was probably Bethany seeing if he'd left for the meeting, or filling him in on another lie Levine told that was making its way around the press circuit. More shit that he had to handle. He began pulling himself up using the shower bar. When he was halfway up he belched loudly. He grabbed his stomach as an acidic taste flooded his mouth. He belched again and almost threw up. He turned around and opened his mouth, washing out the bitter taste. Then, he hung his head downward, letting the water hit the back of his head. He coughed and when he opened his eyes, he saw blood streaming down the drain by his feet. He coughed again and felt his entire body begin to convulse.

"What the hell?" Goldberg said as he stared down at the blood splattered all over the white porcelain tile.

He was still trembling as he turned off the shower and grabbed one of the towels. He wrapped the towel around his waist and stepped out of the shower. Then the room began spinning. He held out his hands as he walked forward and fell on the floor next to the bed.

As he laid there, he could hear his cell phone ringing, but he was too weak to move. He reached out and began pulling the bedspread toward him. He kept tugging until he heard a thump from the phone landing. He listened for the muffled ringing sound. He began coughing again as he ran his hands along the bedspread on the floor, searching for the phone. He was sweating and freezing cold at the same time. He felt something hard and picked it up. His vision was blurry, but he kept pressing the phone until he could hear Bethany on the other line.

"Ethan? Ethan are you there?"

"Help me . . . I need a doctor," Goldberg said as he turned sideways and threw up all over the bedspread. He held on to the side of the bed as his body went into more convulsions. He heard another loud thump as his briefcase fell off the bed, and papers fluttered up around him like white doves. His eyes drifted over to a blotch of red—the lone pack of Marlboro Red cigarettes.

CHAPTER 39

THE CDC-IU.
NEW YORK CITY.
SEPTEMBER 3.

Maggie took one last look at Kaplan as the men restrained him again and turned to leave. As she passed back by room 17, she glanced through the observation window, noticing that it was now occupied. She stopped in front of the window, studying the woman sitting upright in the bed. Her black hair was in a pageboy haircut with straight angles that boxed in her features. She was reading a magazine, and her rectangular-shaped glasses were balanced low on her long, thin nose. Maggie could see a cast on the woman's right arm and a white bandage on her forehead, but besides that, she didn't look sick at all.

Maggie glimpsed over her shoulder as Lionel came up beside her.

"What's going on here?" she asked.

"I was just getting ready to let you know. Diane Savage, she was just brought in after testing positive for the bacteria."

"What made them flag her for testing? She doesn't even look sick."

"Well, you're not letting me get a word out," Lionel said, agitation showing in his voice. "If you'd hold on I was going to tell you." He shook his head. "She was in an accident while riding in a cab. The cab driver died soon after the accident, but not from the wreck itself. When they saw the amount of blood loss, *he* was flagged. They tested him, and he tested positive. They just brought Savage over from Mt. Zion Hospital, and they're sending over reports on the cab driver." Lionel glanced over at her. "She doesn't know yet."

Maggie nodded her head.

"And that's where I come in . . . as the bearer of bad news."

"That's why they pay you the big bucks," Lionel said, giving her one of his looks.

Maggie ignored the snide remark.

"What else can you tell me about her?"

"Caucasian," Lionel said, pausing.

"I can see that," Maggie rolled her eyes. Since Lionel was African American, he always used the race card to explain his demotion. She hated to tell him, but it wasn't any easier being a woman in this business—she'd been stepped on more than a few times.

"You're the one who says I cut corners. I'm just being thorough," Lionel said, his voice sounding crass.

"You know I have nothing to do with the CDC's decisions, Lionel. Hell, they don't even listen to me half of the time." She could feel her temper flaring, and the protection suit was becoming almost unbearably hot.

"Fifty-six years old, single, lives on the Upper East Side, works as the editor of *EVE* magazine," Lionel said in a clipped monotone voice. "They started her on a round of antibiotics."

Maggie turned and gazed at Savage through the glass partition. *EVE* magazine, she thought. That's interesting. *EVE* magazine was a pretentious magazine that usually had a supposititious waif-like model on the cover. She saw the magazine at newsstands and at the check out aisle at the supermarket. She always thought the magazine was part of a conspiracy to bring down the obesity numbers in America—except it backfired and caused women to throw in the towel. She'd put back more than a few candy bars at the check out aisle after seeing the women on the magazine—only to gorge on a gallon of ice cream later that day.

"So, they caught her early, and they're using her like a guinea pig,"

Maggie said. They know antibiotics are ineffective, she thought. "All right. Listen in. I'll holler if I need anything."

"At your beck and call."

When Maggie knocked and entered the isolation room, she was taken aback by the hardness of Ms. Savage. It was hard to believe that this was the woman putting all of those unnaturally beautiful women on the cover of a magazine. She looked more like a Disney villainess than a princess.

"Yes," Savage said in a raspy voice that went up at the end. She lowered the *EVE* magazine she was holding in her uninjured hand.

Maggie noticed she had pink Post-its all over the pages with notes scribbled on them. Even in a CDC Isolation Unit with a deadly bacteria running through her body, the lady was busily working, seemingly oblivious to what was going on around her. Didn't she see the red flags? Maggie thought, feeling like she had just interrupted a corporate meeting. If the symptoms of the disease hadn't begun to hit the woman yet, that meant she was infected by the cab driver, not the other way around. She'd have to look at his coroner report when she was done.

"Hello, Ms. Savage, I'm sorry to bother you—"

"But you are," Savage said, cutting her off in an authoritative manner. Maggie could almost visualize the wooden ruler slamming down on her hand.

"I'm sorry—"

Savage waved her hand through the air.

"I know, I know. We established your sorry. Now, what the hell do you want?" she snapped. "Why don't you start with why you're dressed in that god awful contraption and why I'm in this cinder block dump of a hospital."

Maggie cleared her throat and spoke quickly so she wasn't interrupted again.

"My name is Maggie De Luca, and I'm an epidemiologist with the CDC—"

"The what? What does that mean?" Savage barked. "Speak English, would you? That's the problem with this goddamn country. It's also probably why I got in the accident in the first place—all they hire are foreigners in this city to drive the cabs. The dumb ass didn't even act like he knew where the brakes were."

"I'm someone that wants to help you. Can you remember what happened right before the collision?" Maggie asked.

"Of course I remember. I don't have a concussion," Savage said as she pointed her finger at Maggie. "I told you the guy didn't use the brake. He just ran right into oncoming traffic. The guy didn't know how to drive—end of story. That's what happened."

"I-I didn't mean—" Maggie stuttered. Something about Savage made Maggie feel like she was back in grade school being reprimanded by the principal.

"I know what you mean. What else did I see, blah, blah, blah," Savage said as she let out an exaggerated sigh. "Look, all I know is the guy was driving, then he started coughing—hacking up and all. I asked if he was all right, but he just kept coughing." Savage sat up straight on the bed as if a new thought hit her. "Hey, maybe he was choking or something."

Maggie nodded her head.

"How are *you* feeling? Any cold or flu-like symptoms? Fatigue, nausea, sore throat, coughing?"

Savage shook her head.

"Clean as a whistle—minus a broken arm and a few broken ribs."

"That's what I'm here to talk with you about, Ms. Savage. I'll try to explain the best I can," Maggie said as she picked up one of the chairs and sat it next to the bed. She had a crushing feeling in her chest, and her throat felt like she had swallowed a bowling ball. No matter how many times she'd given bad news to people, it never got any easier. How do you tell someone they have a bacteria that came from an ancient plague? An image of Kaplan screaming went through her head. Before long, she knew that Savage would be facing that same bloody fate. "I work for the Centers for Disease—"

"Do I have a disease? Is that why you're dressed like that?" Savage said, her eyebrows shooting upward and her eyes widening.

Maggie lowered her eyes.

"I'm sorry. There's no easy way to say this. You tested positive for a highly contagious bacteria."

"A bacteria? Am I going to die?" Savage said flatly, clearly in shock.

Maggie shook her head.

"I don't know."

"There must be some mistake. How?"

"We don't know much about the disease, except it's pneumonic— that means it spreads through the air, person to person. That's why I was trying to find out more about the cab driver, he also tested positive for the bacteria."

"You mean I caught this from the cab driver? But how? I was in the backseat and never even got a really good look at the guy."

"I understand," Maggie said, suddenly realizing how much danger she had put herself into when she walked into the reptile store. Kaplan wasn't showing signs of infection as quickly, maybe he wasn't contagious yet, she thought. "Sometimes it only takes a brief contact when a disease is airborne. And because you were in an enclosed cab . . ." Maggie saw a look of terror spread across Savage's face. "Ms. Savage, we're trying to find out how to stop the disease from spreading. Anything else you can tell us would be helpful."

Savage stared straight ahead.

"But . . . I'm . . . I'm not sure. It's all become such a big blur," Savage said as she waved her hand through the air, her voice cracking. "I just remember looking up and we . . . we were in the wrong lane. I heard someone screaming . . . but maybe that was me."

"It's okay," Maggie said as she grabbed the box of tissues by the bed and held it out. Suddenly, the woman looked like a small child, the brash exterior was gone. Maggie sat silently while the woman cried. At first, Savage wiped away the tears, then she took off her glasses and buried her face in her hands. Maggie felt herself tearing up as the woman began to shake.

Then, as quickly as it began Savage uncovered her face. She grabbed one of the tissues briskly, pushed the box away, and began blotting her eyes. She laughed uncomfortably.

"Geez, I'm turning on the waterworks now. I didn't realize the whole thing had affected me so much. It was just something that happened, you know?"

"I know," Maggie said, watching quietly as Savage put her glasses back on and stared off into the distance, her eyes still glazed over.

"Strange really—that I never got a look at his face," Savage said as she turned to Maggie. "Is he okay?"

Maggie shook her head.

"No, he died right after the accident."

"Guess I'm a lucky girl then, huh?" Savage said as she turned away.

Maggie got up to leave.

"Ms. Savage—"

"Diane."

"Diane . . . I truly am sorry. I know how hard this has to be." She reached her hand out to open the door.

"Oh, Ms. De Luca—"

"Maggie," she said and smiled.

"Maggie, I'm sorry for what I said about foreign drivers and all," Savage said. She looked up at the ceiling. "My mother always said I had a mouth like a sailor. I didn't mean anything by it."

"I know," Maggie said as she opened the door. She closed the door gently and stood in front of the one-way glass next to Lionel. Diane curled into a fetal position, her body shaking as she cried. Maggie turned and walked away. She felt like she was going to be sick. She heard Lionel following her as she walked down the steps.

"I took care of it," she said.

"I'm sorry, too," Lionel said. "It wasn't right of me to blame you. Listen, you did everything you could for that lady in there."

"Well, it's not enough. She's still going to die, Lionel," Maggie said, her face shield fogging up as tears streamed down her cheeks. She picked up speed, walking quicker down the steps. She had to get out of the protective suit, she felt like she was suffocating.

"Maggie, would you stop for a minute," Lionel said as he grabbed her arm. "They found the rat breeder." Maggie turned to face him. "A man named Edward Langford. The guy runs his business from Milwaukee."

"Wisconsin?" Maggie sniffed. "That's great news. What about the cab driver? Anything else come through about him?"

"They're working on it. The man's name is Vladimir . . . sorry I can't remember the last name, it's hard to pronounce. Russian. But they did find out that he had a girlfriend living with him named Milana."

"Did they find her? She could be contagious."

Lionel shook his head.

"Not yet."

"Thanks, Lionel," Maggie said. "Go ahead and get changed—we have a plane to catch."

"You want me to go with you?" Lionel said, surprised.

"I hear Wisconsin makes a hell of a cheese," Maggie called out as she walked into the decontamination shower.

Lionel laughed.

"The beer isn't bad either."

CHAPTER 40

SHADOW HILL, WISCONSIN.
SEPTEMBER 3.

Gracie sniffed the air. She could smell the scent of the fruit pastry in the bag next to the cage. All of her senses perked up as two large eyes moved in front of the cage, staring at her from the other side of the bars. She began breathing heavier, and her body stiffened as a large hand came closer. Her first instinct was to bite, but she'd never been hurt by these hands before.

She didn't like the hands at the last place she lived—they came at her too quickly and squeezed her too tightly. She especially didn't like it when they picked her up by the tail, it felt like the floor would rush up at any moment. But worst of all, she had to share her space with other rats. The only time she had ever shared her cage was with her babies. Some of the other rats were mean. And when one of the rats bit her on the back, she returned the favor and bit the rat's ear. Then, she was placed in a different cage with another group of rats. But, none of the rats were like her, and they all smelled strange.

Now, she had her own cage again, and these hands were smaller and gentler. They had a nice scent and gave her a lot of seeds and sweet fruity bread. Gracie waited for the intruding hand to leave the cage, and then walked over to the two containers it left behind. She started to nudge the first container, but the scent of the seeds was missing. She sniffed the next container, grasped the sides, and then knocked it over. Underneath, there was a seed. She picked up the hard seed and gnawed at it until the shell fell away, then she shoved the seed into her cheek pouch with her tongue. Both of her cheeks were stuffed with food. She hadn't picked a hiding place in the cage yet. She'd been moved too many times, and she wasn't secure enough in the new cage to part with the seeds she was collecting. Besides, the eyes were watching.

Gracie jumped when a series of loud sounds came from the figure watching her. Then, after a few minutes there was another set of eyes on her, and the sound became softer again. She glanced up as the hand came back in, leaving behind two more containers. She could smell the scent of seed. She walked past the empty container and flipped the other one over, taking the seed inside. After she removed the shell and stored it in her cheek, she watched the hand disappear. Her ears perked up at the familiar sound the figure made, it was the same sound the other figure had made when it gave her sweet treats.

She relaxed as the two sets of eyes disappeared, and the lights went out. The darkness didn't bother her, she could see clearly without light. Gracie sat frozen for a few minutes, listening to the sounds coming from close by. Then, she moved around the cage, shuffling some of the bedding to the corner. She pushed one of the seeds out of her cheek, then grasped it as she chewed the soft seed inside. She felt a tightness in her jaw and began grinding her teeth. She needed something harder to chew. She walked over to the front of the cage, stuck her nose through the bars, and began to grind her teeth on the hard metal. It felt good on her teeth and helped to ease her nervousness.

She eyed a small bar above her head. It was laying flat and looked like the bar from her first cage. Just like the small containers with the seeds, the bar did a trick—it would open when she bit it. Then, she could get to the rest of the fruit pastry next to the cage. She found the bar with her mouth and pressed her teeth against it. After a few tries, she felt herself fall forward with the metal door. She stood at the edge of the door and looked over at the bag of fruity pastry. She reached her hand out, trying to get to the edge of the table, but missed and found herself hanging by her back feet. She hated being upside down. One of her feet were caught. She wiggled the foot loose, and then tumbled to the floor.

After she landed on the soft ground, she licked her foot that was caught. It hurt a little, but the pain was beginning to go away. Around her, the floor had a different scent, and her senses were going wild registering the new smells. She passed by a large furry shadow slowly, worried it would lunge at her, but was able to run past without the creature stirring.

She ran straight until she came to a wall. She wasn't able to get around the wall and began to run alongside it. She turned and stood up on her hind legs to look around. She didn't know how to get back up to her cage. She ran some more and stopped when she came to metal bars on the floor. They were like her cage. She walked across the cold metal until she found an opening. Then, she squeezed her head through the hole, and the rest of her body followed. She was suddenly sliding downward along a slippery surface, unable to get a footing.

When she finally stopped sliding, she made her way through a long tube. Up ahead, she could see a light shining. When she reached the light, she nudged her head against the bars. The bottom came loose, and she fell forward again. This time when she landed, long blades of grass were all around her. She picked at one of the long stalks and chewed it. It was soft and reminded her of running in the fields. She stood up and sniffed the air. It smelled fresh, and she liked the way the breeze felt on her fur. She paused momentarily, looking up at the large box she had fallen from. Then, she began to run again. It felt good to have no barriers blocking her way. She was free.

CHAPTER 41

NEW YORK CITY.
SEPTEMBER 3.

Ever since the days of John Snow, who pointed out that contaminated water caused the 1854 Cholera outbreak in London, the hazards of improper sewage disposal have been well known. Most New Yorkers in the late 19th century shared facilities with their neighbors. Some of these tenement buildings housed over 100 people and only one outhouse. And many of these outhouses were festering with disease that stemmed from the unsanitary conditions.

Today, the New York City Sewage System collects over 1.3 billion gallons of liquid every day. The system is made up of a complex grid of 7,400 sewer pipes, which lead to larger pipes, joining the runoff from gutters lining the streets. The dark tunnels that lay hidden beneath the streets of New York have spawned countless urban legends over the years.

Jake Weyland had heard more than a few scary tales about the underground sewer when he was growing up. Most of the tales were about pet alligators that had been flushed down the toilet when they were babies. Now, fully grown, they eagerly waited in the murky sewer water for their next meal. He looked down at the folded rat traps in his hand. The tales he'd heard about mutant rats living in the sewer were closer to the truth.

Weyland could hear the sound of running water as it echoed through the tunnel and the faint buzz of static from his headset. It was unlikely that his communication line would work from this depth—he figured he was at least 30 feet below street level, probably much deeper in parts. When he turned his head, the ray of light from the headlamp mounted on his helmet glided along the wall, lighting up the area in front of him. He stared at the brick lining the arched tunnel, it was one of many tunnels that branched off in different directions.

This particular tunnel was more flooded, but it was the only way heading north. He didn't even want to think about what was floating in the putrescent water. He glanced down at the red HAZMAT suit he was wearing. At least the suit offered a barrier between him and whatever was down here.

He stepped along the platform, grasping the traps tightly in his gloved hand. The most surprising thing, was that he hadn't seen one rat yet—he thought the place would be crawling with them. Because of the absence of rats, he would have no choice but to put the traps farther in. He took a few more steps and ducked his head when he reached a lower curved area of the tunnel. It looked like from here on out, he would have to walk with his head kinked to the side.

He looked down, watching the light bounce off the brown water with each step. He grimaced when he came to the end of the platform. Even though it would probably save his neck from a lot of pain later, he still didn't want to wade through the water. He also knew there was no other choice. This is what happens when your job requires you to trek through a sewer, he thought.

He tried not to think about what was lurking in the dark water as he plunged one leg down, followed by the other. Once he was fully submerged, the water came up to his waist. He held the traps above his head as he trudged through the water. With each step he took, he could feel something soft under his feet. He didn't even want to think about what it could be—the pictures in his head weren't pretty.

At the NCEZID, it was his job to study animals and how they interacted with the environment. Usually, this entailed catching the animal so it could be tested. It was amazing where some of the critters showed up. One time, during a SARS outbreak that wiped out a couple hundred people, he found bats living in an old Chevy pickup on some property in Upstate New York. That one gave him a good scare when he opened the hood. There must have been over 40 of the little blood-suckers living in there. Of course, the Chevy's wires had been chewed up, and it had stopped working long ago, but it was still a strange place for them to make in to a home. He must have swept by the area 20 times before he made the discovery. Something just kept niggling at him to check under the hood, as odd as the idea seemed at the time. When he did, there they were—the carriers of SARS.

Today, it was rats. After the NCEZID found a new bacteria some of the rats were carrying, he was sent to catch them in the most likely place . . . the sewer. He took another step and almost slipped when the tunnel began to shake. It was just a subway train passing by, but the quick movement gave him quite a jolt. He let out a deep breath. When he moved his head downward, the light flitted on top of the water, and he saw an oblong shape float up to the surface. He lowered his head, aiming the light beam at the object in the water as he moved forward. He saw the long tail first, followed by a small head—it was a dead rat. First one today, Weyland thought as he eyed the gray rat and watched it float past him.

When he took another step, two more gray rats drifted up to the surface—both of them were dead as well. He pivoted around, the light floating shakily over the water surface as more rats began to emerge. He was surrounded by them. Then, he realized the soft things he was stepping on were dead rats.

Weyland could feel his heart hammering in his ears as he picked up speed, each leg jutting outward as he pummeled forward. Up ahead, the tunnel curved and disappeared into blackness. He could see another platform to his left, and he moved toward it swiftly. As soon as he reached the edge of the platform, he hauled himself up out of the water. When he stood up, he smacked his helmet on the brick archway, and the light went out. He stood motionless in the darkness. He could hear a screeching sound echoing through the tunnel.

"Damn it," Weyland said as he put the traps by his feet. He reached up and twisted the light side to side. The light flickered on briefly, and then went out again. "Come on," he said as he thumped the light a few times. He hit it harder with the palm of his hand, and the light clicked on. He shook his head and picked up the traps. That was a close one, he thought. He'd have a hell of a time finding his way out of here without light. He had to be more careful. He was in such a hurry to get out of the rat-infested water, that he forgot about the low-arched ceilings.

With his head twisted to the side, he watched the light bounce as he walked. Water was streaming down the walls, and long pieces of trash hung from some of the grates above his head like dirty icicles. When he reached the next tunnel, he stood up as far as he could, his head resting against the curvature of the ceiling. He glanced down at the canal below, it was brimming with dead rats. His eyes followed the water, watching as it funneled through another pipe. He walked along the pipeline, and the sound of water grew louder. He came to a ledge with a steep drop. Down below, the rats were piling up against the walls in large mounds as they spewed out of the pipe. No wonder I haven't seen any rats, Weyland thought. They're all dead. Suddenly, he saw a shadow flicker in the corner of his eye. He turned quickly in the direction of the movement. The stream of light from his helmet, pinpointing a single black rat. He watched as it disappeared into a small pipe in the wall.

Weyland gripped the cages tighter in his hand. He didn't want to go back empty-handed, and this rat was alive for a reason—it was a carrier. He quickly moved over to the pipe, sitting the cages next to it. He set up one of the traps next to the pipe and opened the package of rat bait consisting of fruit and nuts. He placed the bait inside, and then turned the lever to set the trap door. He stepped away, waiting quietly to see if the rat would follow the scent of the food.

After about 30 minutes of no movement, he walked over to the hole. He needed to check if the pipe ran through the wall to the other side. He reached his hand into the pipe, feeling around. His hand hit against something inside, and he tried to grasp it. He felt a sharp sting and jerked his hand out, yelling in pain as he fell backward. He held up his hand, shining the light beam on his bloody torn glove.

CHAPTER 42

THE AMAZON, BRAZIL.
SEPTEMBER 3.

There was a constant, irritating buzz around Stallings' ears. He swatted his hand through the air and turned to make sure Boutroux and Harbinger were keeping up. Harbinger was using some sort of specialized binoculars that made a clicking sound as they zoomed in and out. He kept stopping every few feet to bend down and look at a plant or a bug. Boutroux had a camera around her neck with a long lens, she kept snapping pictures of the birds and plants as they walked along.

A cloudy mist was rising from the forest floor, enveloping them in a wispy haze. The rainforest floor was covered with a thick layer of leaf litter and moist leaves stuck to Stallings' boots as he walked. He leaned his head back, gazing up at the canopy above. He could hear the *cri-cri-o* sound of the screaming piha echoing loudly through the trees and the mating calls of the cicada.

Most of the life in the Amazon rainforest lived in the trees, which soared upwards of 100 feet above them. There were five layers that vertically divided the rainforest: the overstory, the canopy, the understory, the shrub layer, and the forest floor. Each one of the layers had its own unique plant and animal species. Where they stood, at the forest floor, it was humid and dusky. Beams of sunlight were shooting down in different directions, but not quite hitting the forest floor.

"Watch your step," Stallings hollered as he stepped over the buckled roots of a strangler fig. The strangler fig earned its name because of its long roots that grow over a tree's surface, eventually creating a latticework of roots that "strangles" the host tree. After the host tree dies, all that's left are the roots of the fig tree, the hollows of which become home to an array of bats, monkeys, and other animals. He knew what it was like to be the host tree, he felt like he had nothing left for years after losing Karen.

Speaking of which, when he glanced back again, he noticed Harbinger had fallen way behind. He was standing under a plant on one of the trees, studying it.

"Find something?" Stallings called out as he stopped walking and waited.

Harbinger held some sort of gadget up to the large blue flower growing on the plant.

"Do you know what kind of plant this is?" he asked as he lifted one of the petals.

"A bromeliad," Boutroux said as she walked over to where he was standing.

Stallings stepped closer to the tree, eyeing the strange magnifier Harbinger had in his hand. It was rimmed with a blue light and had different sized slides. He shuffled through the slides like a deck of cards as he held the magnifier up to the plant.

"These things grow all over the jungle, some of them even higher up in the trees," Stallings said. "I *can* tell you it's not a *lapethria* plant—a ground-dwelling plant that grows in the highlands."

"I've never seen so many plants. They're everywhere," Harbinger said as he held up his binoculars and surveyed the area around them.

"Over 40,000 species and more being discovered all the time," Boutroux said. "The Amazon rainforest holds 20 percent of the world's natural forest." She touched a train of long red flowers with green tips that were hanging from one of the trees. Then, she reached up, cradling one of the red flowers in the palm of her hand.

"Now, you're the rainforest expert," Stallings said as he walked away. "Are you a botanist, too?"

"What's with this guy?" Boutroux said as she rolled her eyes and looked over at Harbinger.

"By the way, in case they didn't teach you this in *botany* school—that's a hanging lobster claw plant," Stallings called back. "Better watch out, it might pinch." He chuckled as Boutroux jerked her hand away from the plant.

"That's James. He's always been that way—short and curt," Harbinger said as he turned, looking for Stallings through the mist. "Hey, wait for us!"

Stallings stopped walking and listened to a sound in the distance.

"Shhh," he said, glancing over his shoulder at them after they caught up.

"What is it?" Harbinger said, sounding worried.

Boutroux moved in closer, staring at the dark jungle around them.

"Listen," Stallings said as he held his finger up in the air.

"I hear it now," Harbinger said. "It sounds like water."

Stallings pulled some large palm leaves aside and stepped through the hanging vines. He kept stopping and listening; then, he would start walking again. He passed through some large tree roots, and then he saw it—a waterfall. The cliff rose up above him and disappeared through the trees. It had to be at least 30 feet high. He didn't remember passing by a large waterfall before. He hoped that they weren't too far off from their destination.

He gazed up, watching the water beat against some rocks jutting out, before crashing down against the flat body of water below. The water was crystal clear and green moss was growing all over the rocks surrounding it. He'd seen a number of waterfalls during his expeditions in the Amazon, but none were as large or as breathtaking as this one.

"Yes!" Boutroux said as she rushed over to the water. "It's amazing!"

He watched as Harbinger went to the edge of the water and began filling a container with the word GRAYL on the side.

"It's a water purifier that kills bacteria and viruses," Harbinger said as he pressed the top down like a coffee press. "Let me know if you need to use it."

"I've got tablets. Nice name though, is it holy?" Stallings said, smirking as he watched Harbinger take a drink.

"What? No, it works great."

Boutroux had already taken off her shoes, which were still muddy, and had her legs dangling in the water.

"Just watch out for the Amazon razorback snapping turtle," he said, chortling as she quickly pulled her legs out of the water. "I'm just kidding, there's no snapping turtle in there. At least I don't think so."

"Would you quit doing that to me!" Boutroux yelled as she stood up and hit him on arm.

"Ow, all right. You don't have to beat me."

She held up her hand again playfully, and he held up his arm to block her. Then, she rolled up her pant legs and stuck her legs back into the water. He bent over the water next to her, staring at his own reflection. She kicked the water up at him, splashing him in the face.

"All right, you got me. Just watch out for the—"

Suddenly, she pulled her legs out and started screaming.

"Get it off me!" she yelled as she danced around like she was on fire.

"Leeches," Stallings said as he looked at the long worm-like thing attached to her leg.

Harbinger kneeled down to look at the leech.

"Is it still there?" she asked, keeping her head turned away.

Harbinger pulled out his magnifier and moved in closer.

"Interesting," he said as he adjusted the light.

"What?" Boutroux said, still looking away.

"For God's sake, just pull the damn thing off," Stallings said as he walked up and tugged the leech off her leg. Then he turned and tossed it back into the water.

Harbinger glanced over at the water, and then held up his GRAYL water bottle, studying it with increased interest.

"Don't worry, it's purified," Stallings said. "I've seen worse water."

After Boutroux calmed down, they continued their journey and Stallings went back to his thoughts. He couldn't place his finger on it, but something seemed different this trip. It wasn't just the waterfall or the company—there was a different kind of energy in the air. Something was off, but he couldn't place exactly what it was. He began to wonder if the Motombu tribe had changed. The elder tribe leader, Watandi, was a good leader of his people, but even 20 years ago he seemed ancient. He couldn't possibly still be alive. He only hoped that whoever had taken his place upheld the same values.

The Motombu people were a gentle people, who had gotten a bad wrap. There were a few rotten apples in the group, just like in any society, and it gave them all a tainted name: cannibals. It was true, he had twisted the truth in his writings, as critics claimed, about the Motombu not being cannibalistic. But, he saw no reason to persecute an entire tribe, based upon the activities of a few. Only a small sect of the tribe had taken the rituals too far by practicing human sacrifice, most of the sacrifices were done with animals. It was under Watandi's rule that the ritual had been changed to only using animals as a gift to the gods.

After hearing about another tribe that was killed by Brazilian militia because of cannibalistic activity, he decided it was a responsibility he didn't want to have. The whole dilemma had been so stressful for him, that it was the reason he switched his line of work to paleoanthropology. At least the people were already dead, and he wouldn't have blood on his hands.

He glanced over at Harbinger, watching as he tapped on his phone, held it to his ear, and tapped on it again.

"You won't get any cell reception out here," Stallings said. "I told you all those gadgets won't work."

CHAPTER 43

SHADOW HILL, WISCONSIN.
SEPTEMBER 3.

It was very quiet in the Taylor house, the only sound Alexandra could hear was the constant ticking of the old grandfather clock in the living room and the sound of Jamie's spoon as it scraped across her plate. Her mind wandered, drifting back to the sickness that was going around as she sat watching Jamie eat.

Normally, she would tell Jamie to chew with her mouth closed, but that was the furthest worry in her mind at the moment. She stared at Jamie's lips as they opened and closed, making a smacking sound as they moved. She glanced over at the empty plate sitting in front of where Lenny would soon be, then she turned and looked at the clock. It was almost 6:30 in the evening—he was running late.

He would probably be angry at her for getting Jamie a rat and not consulting him first. He didn't think getting a pet was important. He also thought that she spoiled Jamie too much. Every time she asked for a pet, he liked to point out that he never had a pet and grew up just fine. Alexandra would usually respond by rolling her eyes and saying, "That's debatable."

She pushed herself away from the table and put her plate next to the sink, she wasn't hungry. She leaned on the counter and took a sip of wine, feeling it lighten her head. Then, she downed the rest of the glass.

What if Lenny made her return the rat? Jamie would be heartbroken. She had suffered a pet loss as a child, and it still bothered her to this day. Regardless, even if they kept it, one day the rat would die, too. She second-guessed herself about getting the older rat, they didn't live very long as it was. Two years, she thought. Had she already caused damage to her child?

As she made her way toward the steps, her only comforting thought was that Gracie was just purchased today. The attachment couldn't be that strong, could it? I'll make it up to Jamie if he makes me return Gracie, she thought. When Jamie's older, maybe they could talk him in to getting a bigger pet, possibly even a dog. If she was older, she would be able to take care of it. Dogs lived longer, too. Then again, maybe she was worried over nothing. Maybe he would give in when he saw how smart Gracie was and how much Jamie loved her.

Alexandra turned on the light to Jamie's room. She was so lost in thought, she didn't even notice the cage was empty. Then, she saw the open door. She ran over to the cage, still hopeful the rat was inside. Her eyes darted back and forth. *The rat was missing.* Jamie must have forgotten to close the cage.

She began picking up the toys around her as she crawled along the floor on her hands and knees.

"Here Gracie," Alexandra whispered, trying not to alarm Jamie downstairs. "Gracie . . . come on girl." She made clicking sounds with her tongue as her eyes scanned the room around her. She glanced over at the bag with a piece of Pop-Tart next to the cage and quickly grabbed it, ripping open the bag. She looked down as crumbs fell on the floor and held up a larger piece in her hand. She frantically turned toward the bed and walked over to it. She tossed the pillows aside one at a time as she shook them out and pulled back the covers.

"Damn . . . damn . . . damn," she kept repeating under her breath. She had really done it this time.

She ran over to the dollhouse on the floor and bent down, staring at the miniature furniture. She thought she saw something, but it was a doll sitting in a chair. She broke off a small piece of Pop-Tart and placed it on the tiny table. Where could Gracie have gone? Alexandra thought. She eyed the dresser. The only place she hadn't looked was behind it. The dresser was heavy, so she pressed her back against the side and pushed, moving it away from the wall. She walked around it and glanced down. Then, she saw the metal floor vent with a missing louver. Gracie was gone.

CHAPTER 44

THE AMAZON, BRAZIL.
SEPTEMBER 3.

Deep in the jungle the vegetation was denser, making the long trek much more difficult. Most of the routes that Stallings could make a passage through were heavily covered in undergrowth and vines. He estimated that by foot, at the rate they were moving, it would take at least another day to get to the highlands area, where he believed the *lapethria* plant grew. Another problem was that the forest had grown increasingly darker, and soon it would be nightfall. He was already having trouble seeing where he was going and found himself stumbling more often. The night also brought out more predators.

"Ouch," Boutroux yelled.

He stopped and turned, noticing that she was holding her arm. When she moved her hand away, blood was seeping through a tear on her shirt.

"What happened, Sam?" Harbinger asked with a concerned expression on his face.

She looked up at both of them hovering over her and brushed Harbinger's hand away.

"It's nothing. I just rubbed up against something."

"Let me take a look," Harbinger said as he held out his magnifier. He adjusted the lens. "Uh-huh. I'll have to put something on it." He opened his backpack, unzipped a small first aid kit, and pulled out some bacitracin.

"I'm fine, really," Boutroux said. "It's just a scratch."

Stallings walked over to the tree she had cut herself on, running his finger over one of the sharp thorns. It was a kapok, or ceiba tree, with conical spines extending upward.

Harbinger dabbed a cotton swab over the cut and bandaged her arm.

"We have to be extra cautious here, we don't want you to get an infection."

Stallings stared up at the kapok tree, it towered over the other vegetation. Luckily, it wasn't poisonous. Some of the other plants found in the region weren't so hospitable. He'd seen the Motombu grind up a toxic plant they called "*woorari*," then dip their arrows into it before blowing them out through pipes. The toxin the plant contained could bring down a large prey quickly by shutting down its respiratory system. Although deadly, he'd also seen the Motombu use it medicinally on their tribe members when they were injured by the antler of a marsh deer while hunting. The medicine man used the *woorari* as an anesthetic for pain, before wrapping the wounds in banana leaves.

"How much farther?" Harbinger asked as he zipped his backpack and lifted it up over his shoulders.

"It's taking longer than I thought," Stallings said as he glanced over at Boutroux, who had her hand over the bandaged arm. It was obvious the wound hurt worse than she was letting on. "I'm used to traveling alone." He looked out at the dark forest around them. "It'll be pitch-black soon. I think we should find an area to set up camp and start out again at daybreak."

He began pulling down some of the vines and tossing them aside.

"I guess right here's as good of a place as any." He turned to look at Harbinger and Boutroux, who were staring at him like he was off his rocker. "There's flat ground under here." He stomped his foot and could hear the sound of dried branches and vines cracking. "Somewhere. All right . . . uh, Michael . . . if you can pull out the tent equipment." He tossed a rucksack at Harbinger's feet. "I'll start clearing out some of these vines and shrubs. Wouldn't want one of you to get injured again." He peered over at Boutroux.

She narrowed her eyes and let go of her arm.

"And what can I do?" she asked.

"Just stand there and look pretty, isn't that what all you women do?" Stallings said as he grasped on to a long vine and yanked it off the tree.

"You women?" Boutroux said, her voice going up another octave. "No wonder you usually travel alone." She mumbled something in French under her breath and walked over to Harbinger. She watched as he pulled out a tent pole, examining it as if it were a cell in one of his Petri dishes. She grabbed the pole out of his hand, pushed it into the end of another pole, and handed it back to him. Then, she gave Stallings a defiant look. "I've camped before . . . in fourth grade. At Méjannes le Clap in Southern France."

"I hear they have lovely vineyards," Stallings said as he grabbed on to the other end of the post Harbinger was holding and stuck the pole through the sleeve at the top of the tent. "Pull up," he said as Harbinger tipped the post cock-eyed.

"I'll do it," Boutroux said, taking the post from Harbinger as she glared across the tent at Stallings.

"All right, tough lady," Stallings said. "Lift it up. More . . . more. Okay, stop." He grabbed a rock and beat each of the stakes into the ground. Then, he pulled the loops at the bottom of the tent canvas over the stakes and spread the tent flat across the bottom. He stood back, surveying the tent. He noticed it was tilted at an angle. He pulled back a post at one of the corners, adjusting it.

"We only have one tent?" Boutroux asked as she held the empty rucksack in the air.

"You two lovebirds take the tent, make yourself cozy," Stallings said. "I'll sleep out here with mother nature."

Boutroux looked over at Harbinger, who shrugged his shoulders.

She watched as Stallings grabbed some branches, pulled a knife out of its sheath, and began to cut up a branch.

"Does everyone carry a knife around here?" she asked.

"I don't," Harbinger said as he put on the orange headlamp. Then, he pulled his cellphone out, holding it up high in the air as he began circling around them.

Stallings shook his head.

"I told you that mini-robot won't work out here." He tossed a few branches aside and flicked on a lighter. He held the flame under one of the branches, but it wouldn't catch. He grabbed the notebook off Harbinger's backpack and ripped a couple of the pages out, lighting them on fire. Then, he tossed the lit pages into the pile of wood, watching as the fire spread through the rest of the branches.

"Actually, it's a satellite phone that—" Harbinger said as he turned, his eyes widening when he saw the paper on fire. "Hey! I need those!" He snatched the notebook out of Stallings' hand, frantically flipping through the pages to see if something was missing.

"Just blank pages, don't get your Underoos all in a bunch," Stallings said as he tossed more branches into the fire.

He stood up and pulled a cigarette out of his front pocket. After he lit it, he snapped the lighter closed and took a long drag. Then, he exhaled deeply, sending smoke spiraling upward. He leaned against one of the trees, watching as Harbinger handed an energy bar to Boutroux as she yawned. He held another bar out, but Stallings shook his head.

"I don't like space food. Big day tomorrow, you two better rest up."

CHAPTER 45

THE AMAZON, BRAZIL.
SEPTEMBER 4.

A loud squeal woke up Stallings. When he opened his eyes, two capuchin monkeys were staring down at him from a branch above his head. They looked like two little old men with their wrinkled faces and white fur. He'd been around monkeys many times before—they usually liked to steal things and cause disruptions.

One time, while working with the Motombu, he couldn't find his sunglasses. At first, he thought one of the village kids had taken them—then he saw them hanging from the tail of a squirrel monkey in a nearby tree. He managed to get the sunglasses back, but they were badly chewed and never fit quite the same. Regardless, he continued to wear them for years, and they were quite a conversation piece.

When Stallings sat up, he noticed one of the monkeys smiling at him. He almost felt obliged to smile back, but then it bared its teeth and squealed before jumping to a higher branch. He felt something hard hit the top of his head and land next to his leg. He reached down and picked up a brown ball that resembled a potato. He turned it over in his hand, studying it. It was a *cupuaçu,* a tropical fruit that was one of the primary food sources of the Motombu. It was also a reminder of how close they were getting to the tribe's territory.

He'd eaten the fruit on many occasions during his stay with the

Motombu. It had a creamy, exotic pulp in the center of the melon. He remembered the ceremonial dance of the shaman, who would give the juice of the fruit, mixed with some blood from a pregnant woman, to women who were trying to bear children. He'd heard of people in other countries trying stranger things to have children, and the ritual seemed to work for the Motombu. The women he'd seen drink the concoction, were all pregnant soon after.

"Good morning to you, too," Stallings said as he ran his hand through his hair, making sure he didn't have any other surprises in there. The monkeys gnashed their teeth angrily as they shook the branch above him. "All right, all right. I'm up." He stood up and dusted off his shirt and jeans. Then, he took the knife out of the bag and cut the fruit in half. He held one half of the fruit up in the air and took a bite of the creamy pulp center. "Thanks for breakfast."

He glanced over at the zipped up tent. Harbinger and Boutroux were obviously still out. He reached into his bag and pulled out a folded up map of the area—or at least what he thought was the area. He figured the Motombu must be close, but they had miles to go to reach the region where the *lapethria* plant grew. The problem was, he didn't know exactly where that was—he'd only heard about the plant in stories. He figured once they reached the plateau of the highlands, they could search the surrounding area.

He knew, from talking to the Motombu, that the *lapethria* plants grew near water. He also knew the plants thrived in the higher altitude of the highlands, where it was cooler. He eyed the higher elevations on the map that were located east of them. He tapped his finger on the map. Another concern that was troubling him, was that some plants went dormant in the dry season and were impossible to find. But, he didn't want to rain on Harbinger's parade by telling him this journey may be for nothing. The fact was, so little was known about the plant in question, it may not be anything to worry about. Maybe it didn't go dormant, or at least not completely.

He heard the tent unzip and watched as Boutroux yawned and

crawled out. Then, she turned around and zipped it closed. He took a bite of the fruit and held the map back up.

"You found fruit," she said as she grabbed the other half off his bag. She took a bite, the juice running down her chin. "I hope you don't mind, eating energy bars is killing me. This is delicious. What is it?"

Stallings let out a deep breath as she bit into the fruit again.

"*Cupuaçu*," he said, eyeing her cautiously as she sipped the juice. The tree branches began to shake above them, and she glanced up at the tree.

"Monkeys!" She moved closer to the tree and made clicking sounds with her tongue. The monkeys began to make a cooing sound back at her. She broke off a piece of fruit and held it out.

"I wouldn't do that if I were you," Stallings said as he peered over the map he was holding.

"But they're so cute," she said, raising her hand higher, almost in reach of one of the monkeys. Suddenly, the monkey bared its teeth, making a loud squealing noise. She leaped back, dropping the piece of fruit on the ground.

"Cute and mean as shit. One bite from one of those fur balls and no telling what disease you'll get. But go ahead, make a buddy. Just don't say I didn't warn you."

She jumped as the monkeys leaped and disappeared in the trees. Then, she took another bite of the fruit and gave him a dirty look. They both turned as Harbinger unzipped the tent, letting out an exaggerated yawn.

"I slept like a baby." He glanced over at Stallings, then at Boutroux, registering the angry look on her face.

"I'm glad someone did," she quipped. "You snored all night long."

"I don't snore," Harbinger said.

Boutroux nodded her head.

"I don't snore," he repeated as he looked at Stallings.

Stallings let out a chuckle, folded the map, and shoved it into his back pocket.

"We should start heading out—if we're ever going to find your little plant," he said as he began pulling the stakes out of the ground. He noticed a gold band on Harbinger's ring finger as he moved closer to help. "I didn't know you were married."

"Oh, yeah. I take my ring off every day at work, I must've forgotten to . . ." Harbinger paused, his face turning red when he saw the look on Stallings' face. "I-I wanted to tell you, James. I just couldn't bring myself around to. It didn't feel like the right time, and things between us had felt like old times again and I, uh—"

"Forgot?" Stallings said nodding his head. "Karen. You married Karen, and you didn't even bother to tell me." Stallings threw the posts on the ground roughly. "How long?"

Harbinger lowered his eyes, searching the ground.

"Nineteen years."

"What's going on?" Boutroux said as she looked over at both of them.

"Ask him," Stallings said as he grabbed his bag and walked away.

She glanced over at Harbinger, who shrugged his shoulders.

He couldn't believe it. *Karen.* She married that bald, spindly shit. He should've known something was going on when she stopped returning his calls. He shook his head in disbelief as he picked up the pace, kicking branches and plants out of his way. He could hear Boutroux and Harbinger calling his name, but he just wanted everything to go away. His thoughts, his feelings, and them. *Nineteen years.* Right after the last time he saw her.

CHAPTER 46

THE AMAZON, BRAZIL.
SEPTEMBER 4.

There was an uncomfortable silence between all of them, the only sounds were those emitting from the surrounding jungle. Stallings still couldn't wrap his head around the fact that Karen married Harbinger. How come he didn't hear about it? Was everyone he knew in on the gag order? After all, he lived in Vegas—not under a rock.

When he looked it square in the eye, the hardest thing for him to accept was that there was no chance of getting back with Karen. All of these years he had held out hope that maybe they would work things out one day. But, now he realized she had made her choice a long time ago. And the truth was—it wasn't him. It was never him.

Even though he was outside in the open air, he felt trapped. Trapped with Harbinger out in the middle of the Amazon rainforest. Trapped in to finding a plant he now cared little about. Trapped with the feelings of anger that he just couldn't shake. Trapped in his head with thoughts about Karen. He felt lonely. And deep down he knew, he had set that trap himself.

Stallings was torn from his thoughts when a loud whooping noise cut through the air, followed by a low hum. A second later, something flitted past him. He could feel the rush of wind hit the side of his face—the object missing him by less than an inch. He quickly turned and saw

They were cautious, since the slightest touch could send a painful burning sensation throughout their body.

One of the men took another step forward, he had a cold look in his eyes. Stallings saw the look of recognition sweep across the face of the man, the same recognition that he now felt. The man was Kaltanda, one of the leaders of a rogue sect of the Motombu, and a firm believer in the old cannibalistic ways. This wasn't good. It also explained why they were being attacked.

"Watandi," Stallings repeated as his eyes locked with Kaltanda's. There was something dead in those eyes, like the light had gone out or one had never burned. He turned when he heard Boutroux cry out. Then, he slid the knife down into his hand and began slashing it through the air.

He saw two men lift her off the ground and another man yank Harbinger up by the hair. Stallings violently whipped the knife around, cutting through the air as he turned in circles. Then, he felt something hard hit him on the back of the head. The green of the jungle swirled as the face of Kaltanda floated in front of him; then, blackness.

CHAPTER 47

MILWAUKEE, WISCONSIN.
SEPTEMBER 4.

Dark rolling hills with silhouettes of cornfields saturated the landscape. Maggie pressed her hand against the window. She had forgotten how much she missed the open air since moving to New York. Lionel stood up, holding the hand grip above him, and sat on the seat next to her. Jason and the other team members moved down, making room.

There were six team members in the CDC van and a full police SWAT team following behind them. All of her team had their protective HAZMAT gear unzipped and hanging around their waist for the two-hour drive to the location. The suits were each equipped with a self-contained breathing apparatus or SCBA, and they didn't want to waste all of their oxygen supplies solely on the trip getting there.

"I just wanted to thank you again for bringing me along," Lionel said.

"Well partner, after we're done, you may wish I hadn't."

"Don't worry, I won't blame you," Lionel said, smiling.

Maggie's phone buzzed, and she held it out in front of her.

"Damn it," she said as her eyes scanned over the text.

"More bad news?"

"Well, not that I was expecting good news, but the GDD just

reported a confirmed case in London. A businessman whose plane departed from New York." Maggie bit at the inside of her cheek. The GDD, or the Global Disease Detection Center, tracks information coming in from other countries. If this bacteria continues to spread to other countries, they could have a pandemic on their hands—a real one this time.

"So our bacteria just went international," Jason said, his face growing more serious. "Now, how 'bout some good news. They found our bus driver's blood donation at one of the other branches and it tested negative for the bacteria."

The van hit a pothole, jolting them upward. Maggie held on to the hand pull above her head and grabbed Jason's phone, scanning through the text. She hated reading while she was riding in a vehicle, it always made her feel nauseous—as if she needed help in that area. She handed the phone back to Jason.

"They still cleared out the local blood banks as a precaution," Jason added, seeing the worried look on her face.

Maggie shook her head.

"It's not that. I was just thinking that the Red Cross worker could have been infected before the bus driver," Maggie said, contemplating the two cases. "I just can't figure out how they connect. The Red Cross worker didn't work around blood, so if she spread the bacteria to Howard, how did she do it?"

"It says on the autopsy report that only one day separates both times of death," Jason said as he glanced up from his phone. "Melinda Howard died *after* Amina Alaoui, so it makes sense Alaoui was infected first."

"Maybe the two women crossed paths somewhere else in the building," Lionel offered.

"Could be," Maggie said as she ran the information through her head. All of these people had to connect. They had two hospital workers in the same building and two women at the same Red Cross building. Howard connected to Le and the cab driver connected to Savage, but she was unsure where they all fit in. The homeless man was a question mark. The reptile store owner also felt like an outlier—there wasn't any proof that Martinez was ever in the store. But, he did live close by . . .

Since the bacteria was airborne, maybe it *was* just a quick contact between all of these people like Lionel suggested. The thought had crossed her mind as well. It was starting to be the only explanation that made sense. After all, how do you track down the path of something that spreads through the air? It could spread whichever way the wind blows. And there was no telling how many cases had been misdiagnosed that they didn't even know about yet. New cases were starting to pour in from everywhere, making it even harder to fit the pieces together. The only way to stop this thing was to concentrate on tracking the source of the disease. She just couldn't shake the feeling that it all began with the rats.

"Oh, by the way—they got a positive on the man you found in the liquor store," Jason said, interrupting her thoughts. "Jaspreet Singh Bhatia, Asian, originally from India, 38 years old, unmarried."

"Jesus," Maggie said, letting out a deep breath. She was right. It would have been too much of a coincidence with Franklin found merely feet away.

"That's what my mama always says—let Jesus take the wheel. Sometimes it's in God's hands."

"Four elementary school students from Howard's bus route have already died and seven more are infected," Maggie said. "What kind of God lets children die like this?"

Lionel shook his head.

"I don't know. They say the Lord works in mysterious ways."

They all looked at each other when the vehicle came to a stop. Maggie turned, staring out the window. It was too dark to make anything out.

"Looks like we're here . . . showtime," Maggie said, standing up as high as she could in the center of the van. "All right team. Listen up. I don't have to tell you what kind of monster we're dealing with. Stick with your partner and keep an eye on each other. That tape is there for a reason. That suit's all that stands between you and our little monster. Our decontamination area will be set up right outside."

She looked at Lionel.

"Go ahead, boss," she said.

Lionel's eyebrows shot up. She nodded her head, encouragingly. He smiled at her and stepped forward, facing the group.

"Check your communication lines and each other," he said.

Everyone pulled their protective suits up over their heads, zipping them up the front. Then they all turned, inspecting their partners. Maggie ran her hand over the back of Lionel's arms and legs. She felt a hand on her back and turned. It was Jason. She smiled and pointed at his partner. He gave her a thumbs up and grinned. They took turns taping their partners sleeves and legs, adding a few extra strips of tape on their sleeves for emergencies. Then, they all turned and hit their gloved hands to each other in the center.

"Let's stop this thing once and for all!" Lionel said as the two back doors of the van flew open.

When she stepped out of the van, two large headlights hit her. She watched as the police SWAT unit filed out of the side of the truck. She turned back around, waiting for the rest of her team to disembark. Then, she walked to the passenger side of the van and knocked on the door with her fist, giving an all-clear signal to the driver. The driver was a very obese lady, who smiled at her and waved as the van doors closed.

"Melinda," Maggie whispered, watching as the van pulled away.

"Hey, did you hear what I said?" Lionel asked.

"Yeah. Yeah, I'm coming," Maggie said, her eyes still glued to the van as it drove down the road and parked.

"No, I mean about the IDPB unit arriving," Lionel said, breathing heavily through his headset.

"IDPB? Damn the CDC. They're trying to take it away from us Lionel," Maggie said, clenching her fist into a ball at her side. The Infectious Diseases Pathology Branch of the CDC dealt with re-emerging pathogens. That meant the CDC knew of the disease before, just like Michael said. It also meant they wanted her off the case.

"I can't help but agree with you there."

"Let's get in there before they start taking away all of the evidence. I can't believe it. The IDPB. Right when we're close to figuring out how this thing started."

Maggie and Lionel caught up with the rest of the team. If it weren't for the moon casting a luminous gray light over the area, it would've been difficult to see where they were walking. She could see an out-building up ahead, it was set back from the dimly lit road a couple hundred feet. Next to the building was a pile of scrap metal, but little else, except a few trees. It was extremely quiet, all she could hear were crickets and the mating calls of frogs bantering back and forth. There was another square shape in the distance with a single light, she figured it was probably the home of the property owner.

The property owner was an elderly widow, who claimed she had no idea that Edward Langford owned a rattery business. She rented an outbuilding on the property to Langford in exchange for land upkeep and didn't know much else about him. She said he was a quiet young man and kept to himself. The property was a little over ten acres, some of which her husband used for growing crops, but she said when he died, the crops died with him.

She also mentioned that it made her feel safer having another man on the property. Eventually, she said she would sell the land, but she didn't want to lose her home as well as her husband. She also didn't want to have a bunch of loud new neighbors. Another property owner in the area sold off part of their property to a real estate investment company, and the company built sub-divisions on the land.

Little did the lady know, she was housing a deadly bacteria that was practically perched on her doorstep, Maggie thought. She looked over at the M4 carbine rifles the SWAT team were carrying. She was sure they were told to kill if necessary—no one knew the state of mind of Langford. He had a clean record, but they couldn't take a risk. Especially after trying to reach him unsuccessfully by phone.

Maggie was breathing heavily as she trekked through the grass alongside Lionel. The HAZMAT suits were cumbersome and not designed for walking over long distances. Her eyes zeroed in ahead, the SWAT team were already lined up around the outbuilding. Next to their black HAZMAT suits with the word SWAT written on the back, were four red HAZMAT suits with the words INFECTIOUS DISEASES UNIT.

She was cognizant of the CDC's concern that Langford could be running a bioterrorism lab posing as a rodent breeding facility. She was also pretty sure that they were worried someone had already beat them to the punch—forming an almost unstoppable weapon that our government could have used themselves. But, that was her conspiracy theorist side coming out.

Maggie waved, telling her team to stay back. She studied the outside of the building as the SWAT team moved in first. The metal and wood A-frame building had a corrugated tin roof, with only one window near the peak of the roof. It was painted a dark green color, which looked almost black in the dusky light. A set of double sliding doors were in the center with white, rusty metal tracks. There wasn't a company sign, and based on the rural location—Langford probably ran a mail order business.

Everyone had been briefed by the CDC, including the SWAT team, about the expected safety measures. They didn't want to unleash the deadly airborne bacteria into the air. Or even worse—cause an explosion. At that point, who knows what host the bacteria would find. There wasn't enough known about the capabilities of the bacteria they were dealing with, so it was important to tread cautiously. Some forms of bacteria had spores that stayed dormant until they found a new host and carried everything they needed with them for an invasion. That was a chance they couldn't take.

Her heart began beating faster as the SWAT team leader waved his men to the side of the building. She kept her arm in the air, holding back her team while she waited for clearance. She glanced over at the Infectious Diseases Unit, who also stayed back. She had to keep an eye on them, she didn't want evidence taken away that she hadn't seen. She had learned not to trust the IDPB—if the CDC had a "cleaner," then they were it. She'd seen too many cases swept under the rug when the IDPB were involved.

The SWAT leader quickly moved in front of the double doors, his gun jutting out in front of him.

"Police! Open up!" he yelled as he banged on the door with his fist.

She could hear her heart thumping louder in her ears, it sounded like the crescendo of a symphony.

"Edward Langford, if you're in there we need you to open the door," the SWAT leader hollered.

It grew very quiet, except her heart keeping beat. She could feel the nervous energy of the SWAT team, they were amped and ready to apprehend. Holding in that much adrenaline was difficult, and the tension was high. Maggie felt like everything was moving in slow motion—she had to do something. Without a second thought, she lowered her arm and stepped forward.

The SWAT leader stuck his arm out in front of her, blocking her way.

"Let me try. It's what I do," Maggie said as she looked him in the eyes, refusing to back down.

The SWAT leader flinched, then he lowered his arm, letting her pass.

"Edward, my name is Maggie De Luca. I'm with the Centers for Disease Control and Prevention," she said, moving closer to the double doors. The saliva felt thick in her throat. She swallowed once, then had to swallow again as the saliva quickly filled her mouth again. "Edward, we don't want to harm you or your animals."

She looked over at Lionel and Jason as they moved in next to her. Lionel nodded at her, urging her to continue.

"We have reason to believe that your rats may be carrying a deadly strain of bacteria. Many people have already died, and if you don't open this door . . . even more will." Maggie waited for a sign of some sort. A noise, anything. But there was only silence.

She turned to the SWAT leader.

"Something's wrong. What if he moved to a different location?"

Suddenly, she was pushed aside, and a man from the Infectious Diseases Unit stepped in front of her.

"I'm giving you orders to break through this door," he barked at the SWAT leader. "Do it, now!"

"I disagree, we should try another way first. What if a carrier of the bacteria gets loose," Maggie said, staring at the two men.

The SWAT leader looked at both of them.

"We're going in!" he yelled.

Maggie stood back as the SWAT leader waved his arm through the air, calling over his squad. Two of the men were carrying a battering ram and thrust it forward at the door. One of the doors caved and fell inward. The SWAT leader waved his men inside. They had light beams on their guns and began sweeping them side to side as they entered.

She waved her team forward as she looked through the doorway. It was just as Maggie feared—dust and debris had taken to the air, and particles descended all around them. She saw small flecks when the light hit them and watched as they drifted to the floor.

It was dark inside and eerily quiet. She saw a flicker of light emanating from another room. She nudged Lionel to follow her as the rest of the team moved to the back of the building. Maggie ran her hand along the wall as she edged forward in the darkness. She ran into something and realized it was a shelf. She squeezed past and saw cages housing rats in various states of decay. Even through her breathing apparatus, she could almost smell the familiar stench of death. She heard a noise as she passed by the cages and saw a rat eating the remains of another rat. She felt her stomach turn over as she backed away.

Once she made it past the cages, she saw a glimmer of light illuminating from a computer screen. Then, she saw a man with dark hair slumped over in a chair. Maggie ducked down when she heard footsteps. It was someone with the Infectious Diseases Unit, heading into a different room. She watched as they began triple bagging evidence. She waved Lionel over, pointing to the man in the chair.

She could tell Edward Langford had been dead for some time. His body was stiff from rigor mortis setting in, and his skin was gray. The front of his T-shirt was smeared with blood stains, and bloody Kleenexes surrounded him on the floor. His bulging eyes were wide open, staring outward at the computer screen. She could see the reflection of the images in his eyes as the screen saver changed every few seconds.

Her eyes shifted to the computer, wondering what he was looking at when he died. A selfie of him smiling as he posed in front of the Great Wall of China filled the screen. The next photo was a selfie of him riding in a red pedicab on a crowded street in China. Asia, Maggie thought. They had to find out if he brought the rats back from Asia. She moved closer to the screen when a photo of a black rat eating a donut appeared.

As she gazed down at Langford, it became clear: he didn't know he'd opened a portal to an ancient plague. He wasn't a terrorist trying to make a biological weapon. He was just a man who loved rats. Maggie glanced down at a calendar laying on the desk and quickly picked it up. She heard footsteps and pivoted around as two men from the Infectious Diseases Unit came up behind them. She hid the calendar behind her back and gave Lionel a look.

"We found him," she called out to the two men.

The man who gave the order to break the doors in, glanced down at Langford's body and back up to Maggie.

"I'll take over from here," he said.

Undaunted, she stared the man in the eyes.

"I'm sure you will," she responded snidely, watching as they began bagging everything in biohazard bags.

Another person from the Infectious Diseases Unit entered the room, fumigating the area.

"It's not spread by fleas," she called out as she exited the room with Lionel. She heard a wheezing noise and looked down, inspecting her suit. There was a tear in her suit leg and she could hear the pressure releasing. Her legs already looked like two deflated balloons. She saw Lionel turn and she waved him on ahead. She grabbed a piece of tape off her sleeve and taped the tear. The hole was too big and she used another piece to seal the rest of it. "Shit," she whispered under her breath. She glanced up at the dust and debris floating around her. She had to get the hell out of here.

She caught up with Lionel. She turned and saw Jason following them outside.

"I was looking for you guys, you disappeared," he said, peeking over her shoulder. "What's that? A Rat Pack calendar?"

Maggie waved her hand through the air, telling him to be quiet as she pulled him around the side of the building.

"Oh," he said. "Sorry."

She turned the calendar at different angles, trying to catch the light from the moon. She glanced down at the black and white photo on the cover of the Rat Pack. Then, she flipped through the pages quickly, trying to find the last entry. At first, she saw a lot of scribbled notes, then the pages went blank. The last day with writing was August 11th. Maggie read the words; then, her eyes shot back up to Jason and Lionel.

"We have to find Pet World."

CHAPTER 48

THE AMAZON, BRAZIL.
SEPTEMBER 4.

Everything was blurry when Stallings opened his eyes. After a few minutes, some shapes gradually came into focus. He had a throbbing ache in the back of his head. When he tried to move, he realized his arms were strapped tightly to a tree behind him.

As his vision became clearer, he watched as five naked Motombu women danced around a fire to the beat of drums. They were gyrating in strange hypnotic movements, their red painted bodies bending backward unnaturally as they danced. He noticed the women were in some sort of trance, and only the whites of their eyes were showing. A shaman wearing a carved mask began weaving between them as he rattled a ceremonial stick.

Stallings strained to see past the ritual he was being forced to attend. It was pitch black out, but he saw movement from beneath the shadows. He slid farther down the tree. From his new position, he could see through to the other side of the fire. He saw movement again. It was Boutroux, she was tied to one of the other trees. His mind began racing as he searched the other trees for Harbinger. Then he saw him, his glistening white skin was beaded with sweat. He wasn't just an observer, he was strung up on a post next to the fire like he was the next meal. How the hell was he going to get them out of this? The dancing ritual wasn't a welcome party—*they* were the party.

Cannibalism is a subject that most people find repulsive, including him. He had read historical writings about it and the people who encountered cannibals around the world. They were found from New Guinea to the Congo, and from New Zealand to the Fiji Islands, and nearly every continent in between. Then, there were the writings about the cannibals here—in the Amazon Basin.

There are still tribes in the Amazon who used to practice cannibalism. The Wari' used to practice endocannibalism, or mortuary cannibalism, in which they would eat their deceased loved ones. Other tribes, like the Motombu that Stallings had worked with, also used to practice cannibalism. But these tribes and ones like them were now peaceful people—unlike the rogue sect of Motombu they were now dealing with.

The half-possessed dancers began moving toward him, slowly parting as the shaman moved forward. Stallings' eyes darted to the side and caught Kaltanda sitting cross-legged, observing the ritual from the sidelines. Then, as if sensing he was being watched, Kaltanda's eyes shot over to meet his. He could feel the coldness of his glare, even from this distance. As the shaman grew closer, he realized the mask was in the shape of a jaguar with real fanged teeth lining the bottom. Various beads and shells adorned the neck of the shaman, each one representing the marks of his accomplishments—like the stripes earned by a military general. What worried Stallings most, was what those accomplishments were.

He knew that shamans were usually front stage and center during ritualistic ceremonies. These included rituals for marriage, birth, healing, death—and cannibalistic ones. The tribe people that practiced cannibalism didn't view it as a grotesque activity like our society. They viewed it as a way to honor the dead, absorb an enemies power, gain nutrition, or appease the gods.

For this rogue sect of the Motombu, it was the later. They viewed their gods as angry gods. Gods that caused disease and famine. Gods who took their loved ones away. To them, it was a cry of mercy to stop the bloodshed of their tribe. In their view, if blood had to be shed—then let it be someone else's blood. To not kill others, was to kill themselves.

Watandi had steered his people away from the cannibalistic ritual. He showed them that the sacrifices didn't need to be human, the gods were pleased with animal sacrifices. His followers trusted him and parted with the old ways, limiting the rituals to animals. But, everyone wasn't pleased with this new way of thinking, and they were banished from the tribe. Those outcasts began following a new leader who still believed in the old ways: Kaltanda.

The shaman drew closer. In his hands, he held a coconut shell that had been split in half. Stallings knew it was the so-called "liquid of the gods," and in this case—the blood of Harbinger. The blood-letting was part of the ritual, a way to open the portal to the gods and pre-pare them for the final act—the death of a sacrificial victim. Again, Harbinger. The shaman shoved the cup at Stallings' lips. He turned his face away, he didn't care to be that intimate with Harbinger. He just hoped he was still alive.

Sometimes the shaman struck an artery in the neck when their un-skilled hands slipped, causing more damage than intended. The ritual would still continue, but the victims were preferred to be kept alive as long as possible. The cup was shoved at him again. He turned away, but he could still taste the sweet metallic taste of blood on his lips.

"Watandi," Stallings said as he jerked his head away. "*Tati-ca os-wan-ta.*" He was demanding to see the true leader, Watandi.

The words seemed to register to the shaman, who backed away as if Stallings were a leper. He was speaking the language of the Motombu, and the shaman wasn't taking it well. They never sacrificed their own people, and only the Motombu spoke their language—or so he thought.

The shaman put his hand in the air, and the beating of the drums and dancing stopped. Suddenly, Kaltanda was towering over Stallings and struck the side of his face. A sharp pain rang through his jaw, but he still turned back to face Kaltanda again. Their eyes locked in a battle of wills.

"Watandi *tot-a*," Kaltanda spat.

Stallings' eyes moved downward. *Watandi was dead.* He had hoped that wasn't the case. He had hoped Watandi's new way of thinking was guiding the future of the Motombu. A future he had tried to protect by lying about their cannibalistic activities. If what Kaltanda said was true, then there was no hope for any of them. They were all as good as dead.

CHAPTER 49

THE AMAZON, BRAZIL.
SEPTEMBER 4.

Stallings watched helplessly as the dancing began again, the rhythm of the drums beating faster. He could see Boutroux through the flames, her head swaying back and forth aimlessly from shock. She had blood dripping down her chin, and the front of her shirt was stained red. Through the blur of dancers whipping by, the image of Harbinger burned in Stallings' mind. His head hung over his chest, and his neck was red with blood. He hoped Harbinger had just passed out and wasn't as he feared—already dead. *Tot-a.*

He couldn't help but feel completely responsible for the predicament they were in. If he hadn't agreed to bring Harbinger here to search for the *lapethria* plant—none of this would be happening. Were there signs of the Motombu watching them and he chose to overlook them? He knew they were close to the Motombu territory after he found the *cupuaçu* fruit that grows in their region. He knew about Kaltanda and the rogue sect of the Motombu. He also knew the truth about their cannibalistic rituals. Did he come here because of his own arrogance and selfish need to prove he was right about the ancient bacteria? Or was he just bored with his unsatisfactory life?

He looked over at Boutroux, her dark hair partly covering her bloodied face. He shook his head. *No.* He did it because it was the right thing to do. He brought them all here because the ancient bacteria he discovered struck again. Not because he willed it to, but because it had been there all along, hiding. Harbinger could make a vaccine from the very plant that he himself had theorized to be a cure. His theory was correct. Yes, it was true that he wanted to accomplish something major in his life. But the ancient bacteria was about more than his needs and his feelings—it was about the safety of the entire world—and Harbinger held the key.

Stallings leaned as far to the right as he could from his tied up position. He needed to see Harbinger make a movement—anything. Some sign of life. Because without him, there may not be a cure. If the ancient bacteria was taking hold like Harbinger said, then millions of lives could be hanging in the balance. He saw the devastation caused by plagues in the past, and they showed no mercy.

He scooted down farther and could see Harbinger's head hanging lifelessly. All the hope he had vanished, making his chest ache. He stared at Harbinger's still figure as a flurry of activity raged around him, blood streaming down his neck. Soon, he and Boutroux would face the same fate. They were next.

A blurry haze of bodies circled around the fire in a frenzied state, their bare skin glowing scarlet red—like Harbinger's blood. Then, he saw Harbinger's head roll across his shoulders and back down. He was alive! He never thought he would be so happy to see anything good happen to Harbinger, but here he was—happier than he'd ever been. *He was alive!* There was still hope. There was still a chance. But how was he going to get them out of this?

With new found vigor, he moved his hands back and forth, trying to loosen them. Then, he remembered the knife. It was in his hand before he blacked out. *No, they would have taken it.* He felt with his fingers along the bottom of each sleeve, wishing the knife was still tucked in its hiding spot. What was he thinking? Did he really think he could take on an entire tribe of Motombu with a measly knife? Why hadn't he hidden the knife to use later?

He closed his eyes and hit his head lightly against the tree. He had to think. He knew the rogue sect of the Motombu could be violent. Damn it, he should've brought more protection. Deep down, he knew it would have been admitting to himself and everyone else, just how dangerous the Motombu could be—a fact that he had vehemently denied.

Suddenly, a blood curdling scream rang through the air. It was Boutroux. He feared the worst as he twisted his body to the side, trying to see her. He half-expected to see her lifeless, a victim of the ritual at hand, but instead the Motombu were falling down around her. He watched as one of the men he saw beating the drums crawled along the ground. Then, one of the Motombu women tried to dash into the jungle and collapsed. The sound of the drums was replaced by a whizzing sound coming from every direction. It was the sound of blow darts.

Someone was killing the tribe members who had captured them. He saw Kaltanda wrestling a man in the distance as more victims fell around them. Were they in the middle of another fight over territory between warring tribes? He'd never seen so much violence. He saw Kaltanda break free and flee with two of the men. Then, everything grew still. The onslaught ended just as quick as it began—a lightning-quick strike. The only remaining sounds were the screams of Boutroux and the crackle of the fire.

Smoke filled the air, and he could smell the burning flesh of a Motombu man who had landed in the fire. Bodies were everywhere. He stared at the glazed over eyes of one of the dancers who had died at his feet. He saw a blow dart with the familiar crimson topaz hummingbird feather pierced through her neck. The trademark of the Motombu. Had they killed their own people?

Stallings gazed up as a single figure broke through the thick smoke. It was a man wearing a T-shirt and shorts, who seemed oddly out of place. Then, he recognized the familiar eyes. They were eyes that glowed with happiness as they looked down at him. Not the cold soulless stare of Kaltanda. No, these eyes were peaceful eyes full of spirit. It was Sunda, Watandi's oldest grandson.

CHAPTER 50

THE AMAZON, BRAZIL.
SEPTEMBER 4.

Under the black sky shimmering with the light of stars that had died long ago, laid the newly dead bodies of the rogue sect of Motombu. This strange juxtaposition did not escape Stallings as he sat there in the midst of them. He found it odd how people hung on to the ideas they created, even if they knew they died long ago. The cannibalistic ways of the Motombu died long ago, yet they tried to keep it alive. The light of hope he saw with Karen—it too died long ago, yet he tried to keep it alive.

He felt the presence of the two men next to him as they helped him stand. His legs felt wobbly under his weight as he tried to register what was happening. He saw more of Sunda's men step out into the clearing. He watched as Harbinger was carried out past him on a makeshift stretcher of twined branches, his eyes rolling around while his mouth slowly opened and closed. He noticed a bandage of medicinal leaves wrapped around Harbinger's neck, covering the gushing wound.

Without access to modern medicine, Stallings had seen first-hand how indigenous tribes like the Motombu relied on shamans and herbal healers for their survival. It wasn't unusual, over 80 percent of people living in developing countries still relied on traditional medicine. The Motombu had quite a stockpile to choose from. In the rainforest alone, there were over 7,000 plant-derived medical compounds used by modern medicine today. From anti-cancer properties to the common aspirin, many of these forest organisms served as blueprints for medicine. And more than 90 percent of prescribed drugs were directly extracted from higher plants. Which is exactly why Harbinger needed the *lapethria* plant, he thought.

A couple of other Motombu men helped Boutroux to her feet. The front of her shirt was bloody and torn open, exposing her breasts underneath. She grasped the front of her shirt, pulling it closed as she was led away. Her eyes met his as she passed. She seemed hesitant to leave with the men. He nodded his head, letting her know she would be all right.

He turned to face Sunda, who smiled as he held up his arm. Stallings glanced down at the tarnished silver band he was wearing and chuckled. It was his old Timex watch he'd given to Sunda when he was a boy. When he was staying in the Motombu village, Sunda had taken a keen interest in the watch, following him around and staring at the strange mechanism as the hands ticked along. He was sure the watch had stopped working long ago, but Sunda was still holding on to it.

The Motombu have a unique concept of time. They believe we are living in a world that is divided into distinctly different times: those of the ancestors who walk in spirit among us, the gods who are alive in everything around us, and man in the state of sleeping consciousness, who never fully awakes from a dream. They believe it is only during the ceremonial rituals that man truly "wakes up" and becomes one with time, the ancestors, and the gods. This is achieved through blood-letting and through a mixture of plants which puts them into a hypnotic state.

"Time," Sunda said as he grinned at Stallings and pointed at the watch.

Stallings smiled, remembering how he tried to teach Sunda what time meant. The boy kept asking how time can be in the past and the future, if the time was now. "That's a question that everyone wants to know," he had responded.

He reached out, placing his hand on the now grown man's shoulders.

"It has been a long time, my friend." He gazed out at the slew of bodies and the smoke billowing upward. "That's what I keep hearing."

CHAPTER 51

THE AMAZON, BRAZIL.
SEPTEMBER 5.

Numerous huts with dome-shaped roofs were visible when they came to an opening in the forest. The cluster of communal huts were aligned in a circular pattern with each hut set up against the next, forming one large unit with a large opening in the center. Each hut was made from intertwined tree branches, vines, and palm leaves. He was relieved to see the familiar layout and was hopeful that some of Watandi's ways were still being carried on by Sunda.

He remembered how the Motombu would gather in the center of the village at dusk to act out vibrant stories about their ancestors. The "actors" had elaborate body paint, headdresses made with colorful feathers, and carved masks. Many of the stories were little more than legends and folklore, some of which centered around the highly feared jaguar, but others were valuable traditions that were passed down orally to the next generation.

The use of heightened sensory to tell the stories was not only a way to pass down ways of thinking, but also a way for the elders to relive their highly exaggerated past adventures. Sometimes it was hard to tell where the line was drawn between myth and reality, but the nights spent under the stars as the tales were being spun was something to behold. The ever-present sounds of the jungle added to the stories like background music as a new world unfolded around them.

The Amazon is home to over 1 million Indians, making up over 400 tribes. Each of these tribes has their own unique culture, distinct language, and territorial region. Some of the tribes have been in contact with outside forces for over 500 years, others have had no contact at all. Stallings was hoping that the Motombu were still impervious to the outside world, but his hope soon faded as he watched the villagers walk by.

All of the men, like Sunda, had on T-shirts with company brands and logos—a surefire stamp of the work of missionaries. His fear was confirmed by a few wooden crosses hanging outside some of the huts. The entire village suddenly hit him as odd—a hodgepodge of old and new ways. He was relieved that Sunda had not guided his people down the same path as Kaltanda, but it was still heartbreaking to see that they had given in to an entirely new God, one imposed on them by outside influences.

Missionaries usually brought about the slow death of indigenous people's customs. They had not only brought new diseases that killed native populations of the past, such as smallpox and the measles, but ideas that were equally as deadly. The missionaries taught the native people that their way of life was wrong, forcing them to shed their old beliefs, and imposing a new way of thinking on them. The problem was, the indigenous people were ill-equipped to adapt to Western philosophy, and if they became reliant on the handouts from afar, they lost the traditions that had sustained them for thousands of years. When many of the shamans died, all of their vast knowledge of plants and medicines died along with them. In short, they were breeding a society that was no longer self-reliant.

When he traveled to remote villages, he was always cautious. The villagers were curious, but he made sure not to press any of his personal views upon them. From that standpoint, he could truly observe and appreciate the people as they were. He knew there was really no such thing as a "silent observer," and there was some transference from his presence alone, but to see a tribe of hunter-gatherers, who had subsisted in the jungle for thousands of years and had not destroyed everything in their wake, was a very beautiful thing.

He was positive the ancient bacteria had re-emerged in New York City because of the overcrowded population of the city. The disease called *man*. It was man's greed and insatiable appetite to conquer everything around him that would lead to their demise. Life was not meant to be a one species symphony—life was meant to be an orchestra of a multitude of living things. Indeed man was his own worst enemy.

Stallings nodded his head as one of the Motombu women led him into one of the huts. He noticed she was wearing a colorful dress, obviously given to her by one of the missionaries. The Motombu women usually wore very little, except a small covering over their lower extremities.

"*Mon-ta*," he said, thanking the woman, who in turn opened her mouth in a smile, showing her black teeth. The Motombu chewed the roots of a tubular plant called *sepca*, which they mixed with small amounts of the *lapethria* plant. The mixture caused their teeth to turn black. *Lapethria*, meaning "safe passage" in the Motombu language, is believed to be a gift from the gods to keep them safe on their journey through life. Taken alone, the *lapethria* was too strong and would cause severe stomach cramps, so the Motombu mixed it with *sepca*. When he tried the mixture himself, it had a strong taste similar to turnips.

It was after he discovered the ancient bacteria had decimated other Amazon tribes in the past, that he realized the Motombu were unscathed. He ascertained that this wasn't from lack of contact, since the Motombu traded frequently with the other tribes. It was the one thing too precious that they didn't trade that caught his eye—the *lapethria* plant.

After the Motombu woman left, he turned and saw Harbinger laying on a bed made of dried palm leaves. He was drenched with sweat, and his eyes flitted around aimlessly. He kept batting away the hands of an elderly Motombu man, who was trying to apply a plant mixture to the wound on his neck. The gash was deep and still bleeding. When Harbinger saw Stallings standing over him, he held his hand out toward him, his eyes wide with fear. He tried to speak, but his words were garbled, and the movement caused blood to flow out heavier from the wound.

"Shhh, don't talk. It's okay," Stallings said as he kneeled down next to him. "You're safe now, please let the man help you."

Harbinger's eyes widened as he stared at him.

"S-s-am—"

"She's fine," he said, even though he hadn't checked on her yet. She didn't seem to be physically injured from what he'd seen, just traumatized. Harbinger got the worst out of the three of them. He watched as Harbinger closed his eyes, breathing deeper with each breath. He continued to watch as the medicine man applied leaves, covering the bloody neck wound.

When he walked outside, he didn't have to search hard to find Boutroux—the sound of her complaining echoed throughout the village. He lowered his head as he entered the hut, smiling as she slapped away the green mixture a Motombu woman was trying to feed her. The woman was gentle, treating her like one of the village children. The woman held the mixture up again, flashing her black teeth.

"Stop touching me!" Boutroux yelled at another woman, who was trying to take off her bloody shirt. She glanced up and saw him smirking at her. Her face flooded with a look of relief as she broke past the women and ran to him.

Stallings wrapped his arms around her, feeling the warmth of her body against his. Then he pushed her away at arm's length, staring at her face, it was streaked with tears.

"It's going to be all right, they're just trying to help you," he said as he wiped away her tears with his sleeve. He put his hand under her chin, looking into her eyes. "All right?"

She nodded her head.

"Good. Everything's going to be just fine now." He stared out the window at the dense jungle, trying to find comfort in his own words.

CHAPTER 52

SHADOW HILL, WISCONSIN.
SEPTEMBER 5.

In the sleepy little town of Shadow Hill, red HAZMAT suits weaved back and forth over one of the freshly mowed lawns. A radius of two blocks was sealed off by the police. The residents outside of the barricaded zone stood out on their lawns and porches, looking upward as helicopters circled above.

Another circus, Maggie thought as she jumped out of the CDC van in her yellow HAZMAT suit. She walked over to one of the officers.

"Get those news helicopters out of the area," she yelled as she pointed at the sky. "Don't you know they're trying to capture a contaminated animal? They'll never catch anything with that loud noise."

She could barely even hear herself talk with the sound of the choppers overhead. What the hell were they thinking? It's a tiny rat, not a goddamn escaped convict, she thought. She waited while the officer went to his car and reached in through the window, pulling out a walkie-talkie attached to a cord.

"I need the news media out of the area," the policeman said in a clipped voice, glancing over at Maggie. "Call the stations and let them know they're causing interference."

"Thank you," she said, waving at the policeman as she made her way to 5535 Saddle Road.

After speaking with the manager of Pet World, Maggie learned that a rat had recently been sold that was bought from the Rat Packery. With some smooth talk and a show of credentials, she was able to get the purchase receipt and an address for the buyer. Luckily, they used a credit card for their purchase. The customer's name was Alexandra Taylor, who said she purchased the rat as a pet for her daughter.

Taylor was concerned for the health of her daughter after hearing about the string of recent deaths on the news. She had good reason to be, she had been housing a possible carrier of the disease. The problem was that the rat had escaped from its cage two days ago. They'd been searching for it ever since. The rat, she claimed, had gotten loose after her daughter forgot to close the cage. After discovering a broken floor vent, her husband had taken off the vent and even pulled some of the ducts apart, but they still couldn't find the animal.

It didn't take much convincing to let the CDC crews find the missing pet after she explained the situation—Taylor was terrified. Maggie had the family flown in for testing at the CDC's quarantine facility.

As she walked up the sidewalk to the Taylor's home, Maggie was immediately taken aback by how charming the home was. It was a white, turn of the century home with a wraparound porch, complete with two rocking chairs. She held up her hand, blocking the glare on her face shield, and noticed a green swing set with yellow sunflowers in the side yard. It was a home that would make Martha Stewart proud.

She walked up the steps of the porch and found the small rock next to the door where Taylor had hidden the house key. She lifted the rock—the key was already gone. In its place was a piece of white construction paper. She picked up the paper, it was a crayon drawing with a stick figure of a girl with blonde curly hair and a u-shaped smile. Some squiggled lines crossed each other, forming the word JAMIE above it. Next to the figure of the girl, was a small black circle with a stick tail and the heading GRACIE. On both names in the drawing, the "E" was backward.

She reached down and picked up the bag of seeds next to the door that Taylor had left. She studied the bag, it had a photo of a white rat and a brown mouse on the front and said RAT & MOUSE DIET. When she looked back down, there was also a baggie with a frosted Pop-Tart. Taylor had mentioned that Gracie liked to eat sweets. Her thoughts went back to the photo on the computer screen of a black rat eating a donut. That must have been Gracie, Maggie thought. She would send a message to have them print out the photo for comparison. They had to make sure they found the right rat.

It was unusual that Langford had sold only one rat to Pet World, the manager said they usually ordered larger quantities of animals at a time. Her team had called every Pet World, and only one order came up. She was told the invoices found at Langford's were mostly smaller stores that were out of state. The manager said he would speak with headquarters to see why it was such a small order, since he wasn't in charge of animal acquisitions. He said the store had experienced an increase in rat deaths after Gracie was purchased. There were also two employee deaths that were being investigated.

Why did he sell them only one rat? Maggie thought. Maybe Gracie was special to Langford. But why would he give her up then? *Because he knew a sickness was going around his rattery*. Then it hit her: maybe he was trying to save Gracie because she didn't appear sick. What if she didn't appear sick because she was immune? What if she was special because she was the only rat he brought back from Asia? What if Gracie was the original carrier? They had to find her—she could hold the key.

The GDD tracked down Langford's trip to China at the end of July, but they were having trouble finding out if he had brought any live animals back with him. She found it hard to believe that he could sneak rodents, or even a single rodent, through customs. He could've had them shipped to his address in the states, but so far that had been a dead end. How did you bring Gracie back, Edward? Maggie thought. How did you do it?

She glanced out across the yard, watching as a couple of the Infectious Diseases Unit team circled the property. The rest of the ground crew were from the NCEZID—her team had been sent back to

New York this morning. She moved out of the way as one of the red HAZMAT suits came barreling out of the front door. Just as she had predicted—as soon as she called in the Pet World find—they descended on the scene like vultures, and her team was siphoned out.

She walked over to the green swing set in the yard and handed the bag of seeds to one of the NCEZID crew members setting out traps. She glanced down at the small trap sitting next to the swing, it had a spring door that closed when the animal entered, trapping it inside. She held up the drawing. The little girl loved Gracie. At least the CDC wanted the rat alive if possible. Since they were still studying the mechanisms of the disease, a live host would be invaluable.

The rats they obtained from the Rat Packery weren't doing well, almost all of them had died from either starvation or from injuries from the other rats housed with them. All of the rats were infected with the bacteria, but the bacteria wasn't what was killing most of them.

She heard the traps set up by the NCEZID in the sewers and areas around New York yielded the same results—except the rats were either dead or dying from the bacteria. Thus far, the only rats that were not dying from the bacteria itself, were a breed of rat that Langford was selling. A breed of black rat that had remained hidden among the others, carrying a dark secret—an ancient plague. Scientists were still looking into the classification, placing the rats somewhere between a *Rattus rattus* and a hybrid form of *Rattus norvegicus*.

A multitude of CDC teams were tracking down where the Rat Packery animals were shipped. The list of buyers ran from one coast to the other. Even with the Emergency Operations Center in full swing, the CDC was having trouble carrying an operation on such a large scale. Finally, WHO and other international organizations stepped in to help. With the death toll rising, more and more countries were starting to sound their alarm.

As she feared, the number of infected people was much higher and more spread out than originally thought. Many public schools and government buildings began closing their doors as the death toll climbed in their cities. People were running scared. Many of them flooding out of the cities, only to discover the bacteria had no borders. Small towns, like this one, were among those infected as well.

She eyed the small trap next to the swing. So, Gracie has a sweet tooth, Maggie thought as she looked around. She opened the bag and dropped the Pop-Tart through the bars. Let's hope so.

Maggie felt her phone vibrate. It was the alarm—her flight home left in two hours. She was extremely fatigued, maybe it was better she would be handling less of the case. Regardless, her hands were becoming more and more tied by the red tape of the CDC. She turned one last time, staring at the once serene home, now surrounded by red HAZMAT suits. It looked like a scene straight out of a horror film—and it was.

CHAPTER 53

NEW YORK CITY.
SEPTEMBER 6.

The line of the epidemic curve of propagating epidemic graph, which had started as progressive small peaks, shot upward in a wide arc. Maggie moved in closer to the screen, straining her eyes to see the rise in new cases. Suddenly, the line began to look like a snake wriggling up and down. She closed her eyes, willing the line to stop moving. Sharp jabbing pain radiated from the back of her head and across her scalp. She felt like her eyes were being squeezed in a vice grip, and the light from the computer was making her headache worse.

Over the past few years she had frequently experienced migraines, and they often blurred her vision and made her sensitive to light. Sometimes, the pain rendered her into a useless heap for days and she would lay in a dark room, waiting for it to pass. This usually included many bouts of running to the toilet and dry heaving.

After she went to the doctor about the pain—worried she might have a brain tumor—she was given migraine pills. Unfortunately, sometimes the migraine pills didn't work, and this was one of those times. The doctor had her try different types of migraine pills until she found one she liked. Some of the pills with caffeine took too long to kick in— six hours when you're in pain is a long time to wait—others made her feel like she was comatose.

The prescription she was on now, Sumatriptan, seemed to work better than the others—usually anyway. She picked up the bottle, reading the label again. It said to take one tablet every four hours. She had already taken too many, and her stomach was in knots. The problem was—this headache felt different.

In some ways it felt like a migraine, but the way the pain coursed through her whole body, was something entirely new. Her muscles ached, and she had a cloudy feeling—which usually signaled she was sick. Maggie felt her nose beginning to run and reached over, grabbing a Kleenex. Another sure sign she was sick—a runny nose.

She had been feeling run down since she left Wisconsin yesterday. She had no doubt that dealing with the CDC and their propaganda had compounded her fatigue. When she returned, she was hoping to follow up on the new leads that they had established, but she was informed that the CDC thought it was more important for her to analyze the data that her team had collected. All the work she had done on the case and she was demoted to a glorified secretary—thanks to the IDPB and the NCEZID. Screw the NC, screw that Infectious Diseases Unit prick, and screw the goddamn CDC, Maggie thought. She pressed her thumbs into her temples, rubbing in circular motions. They can shove their paperwork up their ass.

She laid her head down on the pile of papers scattered all over the desk. She gazed out at the blurry computer monitor. She had five windows open, each with different charts, and none of them looked promising. They all had one thing in common—they were moving in one direction: up.

She glanced down, realizing she had hardly moved, except from her bed to the desk, since she got back. She felt too sick to shower, and she was still wearing the same old holey T-shirt and sweats. She turned off the computer, relieved to be rid of the blinding glare. She was barely able to move—more or less think. She'd have to pick up where she left off tomorrow. She looked over at the clock. It was only 4 PM, but it may as well have been midnight as tired as she felt.

She walked over to the bed and laid down, her eyelids growing heavier as she began drifting off to sleep. *Sleep.* That's all she needed.

Then, her phone began buzzing. Damn it, she thought, grabbing her pillow and putting it over her head as she twisted her legs up in the sheets. The phone kept buzzing, vibrating annoyingly on top of her side table. It finally stopped; then, a minute later started buzzing again.

She let out a moan, picked up the phone, and looked at the caller. She moved her arm up, partly covering her eyes. It was Jason . . . again. She'd been avoiding his calls, except responding with a periodic text. She tried to swallow and cringed—her throat felt like it was lined with sandpaper. She reached around blindly and pulled open the top drawer of her nightstand. She felt around and grabbed a vitamin C drop, popping it in her mouth. Then, she cleared her throat and clicked the phone.

"Yeah," Maggie said in a low voice, trying her best to hide the pain she was feeling.

"Wow, you're alive!" Jason said. "I can't believe I finally got you on the phone."

Maggie could picture Jason's face with that silly grin he always wore. She did miss him, funny enough.

"Paper duty calls," she said, feeling a cough coming on. She clicked mute on her phone, held it out, and coughed.

"Your voice sounds off, you sure you're okay?" Jason said, sounding concerned.

"Yeah." She swallowed, clearing her throat again. "Just a bit run down."

"All right, because I can come by and help. I promise I won't bring Chinese."

She started to laugh and then squeezed her hand around her throat from the pain.

"I'm fine."

"Sometimes I wish you weren't, then maybe I'd feel needed."

There was a long silence between them, making her uncomfortable. She didn't know what to say to that. Part of her wanted to be around him, another part of her wanted to be by herself. It was a constant tug-of-war of emotions that she couldn't explain. Her head began throbbing again, and she closed her eyes. Besides, the last thing she wanted was for anyone to see her like this—she looked like a beaten down corpse. She also didn't want anyone to think the CDC had gotten the best of her.

"Maggie, I just wanted to let you know you were right. You were right all along. This thing is much bigger than anyone expected and if it wasn't for you—"

"Thanks, Jay," Maggie said, her eyes tearing up. Great. Now, she was not only sick—she was turning into a mush pot. It felt nice for someone to recognize all of her hard work.

"I thought it was important for you to hear it. I'll never doubt your word again, and I'm sure no one else will either."

Silence again. Why does he have to do this to me? Maggie thought. Why does he have to be so goddamn perfect all the time? She clicked the mute button and coughed. Then she cleared her throat and clicked the button again.

"Did they find Gracie yet?" she asked, changing the subject. It was something she always did to him, but sometimes it was her only means of escape when she felt cornered.

"You mean the famous rodent on the loose?" he laughed. "No, not yet. Last I heard, the traps were still empty and they were expanding the search area. They did catch a couple of field mice and squirrels though."

"Jason, if they do catch her, can you ask them not to harm her? I know it's a strange thing to ask, but a little girl died who loved that animal." She looked across the room at Jamie's drawing on the wall. Even though Gracie infected Jamie, she still asked about her until the end. She said it wasn't Gracie's fault, she didn't know.

"I'll do my best. I think with the shortage of living infected rats they're finding, she'll be fine. They're having a hell of a time tracking down the other rats Langford sold. Not to mention, the animals and people that those rats infected. I didn't know rats could be such a hot commodity."

"That's not good," Maggie said, her eyes shifting to the area next to Jamie's drawing. It was covered with photos of victims and maps.

The entire map of New York City was boxed in red, and the map of the world had red clusters throughout the U.S. and other countries. "Well, keep me posted, I better get back to work." Her head was blaring, and she felt like bashing it into the wall behind her. Thinking about what was going on out there was making it even worse. She felt helpless to do anything, and that was the worst feeling of all.

"I will. Take care, Mag. And my offer still stands, if you need anything—"

"I'll let you know," she said and clicked the phone. She turned on her side, looking up at the world map again. South America was dotted red in many areas—except for inside the red circle in the center of Brazil. She wondered if news about the disease had reached Michael. Did he even know how bad things have gotten?

CHAPTER 54

THE AMAZON, BRAZIL.
SEPTEMBER 6.

Harbinger seemed to be healing very well under the care of the Motombu people. His eyes were no longer wandering vacantly, and the warmness was returning to them. Sunda was able to find most of their belongings, including Harbinger's eyeglasses, although the glasses were missing one of the lenses.

Stallings sat next to Harbinger, listening to him breathe. The fear he had of losing him felt confusing at times. How strange to be damn well ready to kill someone at one point, then be willing them to live the next—*needing* them to live.

Boutroux had started warming up to the Motombu women as well, despite her original protest. She would sit in a group with them for hours, learning how to weave palm leaves in intricate designs. The Motombu children were fascinated by her and would follow her around, touching her light skin and listening to her talk. Almost everywhere she went, one of the children were holding on to her leg or pulling on her arm for attention.

He walked outside, watching as Boutroux held a large blue morpho butterfly in her palm. The butterfly's wings were metallic blue and spanned more than 8-inches wide. She held the butterfly up higher, smiling. She looked so peaceful in the foreign surroundings. She was a striking woman, and watching her interact with the world he knew so well, made her seem even more attractive to him. He studied her face, she seemed almost childlike as she watched the butterfly flutter away and disappear into the jungle. She glanced over at him, catching him staring at her and smiled, her eyes holding his. He felt an overwhelming sensation come over him and turned away.

Tomorrow, he would be talking to Sunda about obtaining the *lapethria* plant. He was told the Motombu traveled to a remote area in the highlands to gather the plant. The Amazon has a diverse ecosystem with rainforest, deciduous forest, seasonal forests, and savannas where different plants and animals flourish. The highlands were elevated areas of land shaped like a table top or round like a hill from erosion. They are cut by deep rifts and clefts where they drain, and many of the areas are inaccessible.

He knew the journey would be a difficult one, and Harbinger wouldn't be ready to travel anytime soon. He was also worried Harbinger may need further medical attention. Although he was showing signs of healing, there was still a chance of infection. The sooner he could get the *lapethria* plant and get them all out of here, the better.

His other concern was that since it was the dry season, Sunda would tell him the plant was dormant. Usually, a plant's dormancy pattern is tied to its environmental conditions. In temperate areas, plants go to sleep to survive winter and conserve energy. When this happens the growth and development of the plant stop temporarily. Because the rainforest environments are diverse and very little is known about many of the plants, he could only hope the plant was actively growing. Since Watandi had given him the *lapethria* sample, he knew very little about where the plant grew and had only heard the tales of their pilgrimage to collect the rare plant.

Watandi would pick three of his strongest men to make the dangerous journey. Each of the men would be given a mixture of herbs for sight and a ritual to ward off evil. Then, the men were painted white and given special spears for protection. When the men returned from their mission with the *lapethria* plants in hand, a celebration ritual was given to thank the gods for their gifts.

Stallings walked on the outskirt of the village and noticed an area of land with plants spaced evenly apart. The Motombu used to be hunter-gatherers, but now they had become hunter-gardeners. The women would still gather medicinal plants, mushrooms, nuts, and honey, but the majority of the plants they ate now came from these designated sections of land next to the village. While the men would hunt for monkeys and wild boar or use plant-based poisons to stun the fish, the children were taught at an early age to hunt for tarantulas and other insects.

He watched as a few of the Motombu women walked between the rows of plantains, yams, manioc, beans, and sweet potatoes. There were even rows of banana trees lining the edge of the garden area. He searched the plants, wishing they grew *lapethria*, but he knew the plant only grew in cooler temperatures.

As he watched the women, some of the trees swaying above him caught his attention. Then, he saw a three-toed sloth clinging to the branches high above, its head hanging downward, facing him. The sloth is the world's slowest animal, hence its scientific name, *Bradypus*, which translates in Greek to "slow feet." An animal so slow that algae grows on its fur. It was a stark reminder that time was not on his side.

He knew the area around him was teeming with animals, and if one was patient—and had time—you could see movement everywhere. All of the jungle was alive, crawling with creatures large and small, perfectly blending into the environment that they were adapted to. He watched as some leaf cutter ants made their way down the rows of vegetables. In one of the trees farther away, he saw the slow methodical movement of an emerald tree boa as it inched along a tree branch.

Stallings pulled his thoughts back to the present. He thought of the one word Harbinger would mumble over and over in his delirium: *lapethria*.

CHAPTER 55

NEW YORK CITY.
SEPTEMBER 7.

Maggie opened her eyes slowly. As the light hit them, jolts of pain almost knocked her out of the bed. Her head ached even worse, if that was possible. The pain was piercing and throbbed heavily behind her eyes. She held up her pillow to block the light. What time is it? she thought as she turned toward the clock, squinting her eyes to read the red digital numbers. 1 PM? She had slept through half the day. She felt her hair sticking to her arm and peered down at her old, torn T-shirt—she was drenched with sweat. All night she had waves of hot and cold chills, but right now, she felt like she was burning up.

She sat up unsteadily, every movement taking great effort. She reached for the phone and fell sideways, back onto the pillow. She was barely able to hold up her arm as she ran her finger down the messages. There were ten. Seven of them were from Jason, she read the last four:

They found Gracie, she's fine.
Thought you'd want to know. J

I'm worried about you. Let me
know you're okay. J

**You're not picking up. There's
too much to text. J**

**I'm coming by if I don't hear
back from you soon. I'm worried.
Please call. J**

She didn't want him to come by, especially when she was in a state like this. She looked at the time of the last text he sent, it said 12:23. She texted him back:

**Good to hear about Gracie.
We'll talk soon, I'm really swamped
here. Everything is fine. M**

Maggie dropped the phone on the bed and reached across the table for the Sumatriptan. She grasped the bottle, but it slipped out of her hand, spilling white oblong pills all over the floor. Damn it, she thought. As she sat up, she gazed over at the map of New York City on the wall. The word RATS was streaked over it in large red letters. Red handprints and rings surrounded the photos of the victims. Had she done that? She stared at all of the different faces, their penetrating eyes glaring back at her. She raised her hands up to her face, they were shaking and covered in red marker.

She tried to stand up and immediately hunched over in pain—her stomach felt like it had sharp knives cutting through it. She heard the television click on in the other room and stumbled toward the sound.

"Hello?" Maggie called out as she made her way into the other room. She kept one hand on the wall to steady herself, while the other hand clutched her stomach. When she walked around the corner, she saw a little girl with blonde hair, wearing pajamas. She was sitting on the couch, eating a Pop-Tart.

"Jamie?" Maggie whispered as she watched her.

The girl looked over at her and smiled; then, she turned back to the television. A blue flickering light shadowed her face. Maggie's eyes followed hers to the television.

She was shocked at the chaos she was seeing. The news channel showed people laying dead in the middle of the street, their bodies left out in the open for the world to see. More sick people staggered past them, barely alive themselves—their faces bloody and clothing torn. Mobs of people were yelling as they blocked the sick people in the center of the street, some of them using long sticks or brooms to prod them. Among the sick were children, elderly people, women, and men.

Bloody sheets hung from the windows of buildings. The military had blockades set up, and police in protective gear were trying to hold back the hostile crowds. Protesters were holding up signs. She read one that said THE APOCALYPSE HAS BEGUN, REVELATION 6:7-8. Another sign had the words THE RED DEATH.

"The Red Death," Maggie said as her eyes shifted back over to the couch, but the girl was gone. "Jamie?" She turned, looking for her. "Come back." She almost fell over as the room began to spin. She held on to the wall, everything was whipping around her in a blur. She lurched forward as she began to cough. It was a deep, wrenching cough, inflicting more pain on her already raw throat. She fell to her knees in front of the television, barely able to read the words:

Warning Signs: Flu-like symptoms, headache, cough, body aches, difficulty breathing, bloody phlegm or stools. If you have any of these symptoms, you may have have the beginning signs of . . .

Maggie covered her mouth as she coughed again. She looked down at her hand, it was dripping with blood. She should have known right away. She was infected. It wasn't red marker on the wall, it was blood. *Her blood.* The room seemed to pick up speed around her. She crawled over to the wall and slid down to the floor. She had given everything she could to try to stop the bacteria from spreading, and now she would be giving up her life as well.

How could she have missed the signs? Was she in denial? She knew her protection suit had a hole in it. She knew she was at risk for infection. Her head throbbed as she thought about the symptoms. It was happening to her, just like she had thought it had happened to all of them. The slow onset, hidden behind mild symptoms while the disease took hold. Her eyes drifted down to the blood stains on the front of her shirt. Then it came in for the kill.

Tears stung Maggie's eyes as her life flashed before her. She thought of rolling in the grass when she was a child. She thought of her mother rocking her to sleep. She thought of sitting in class at the university and how alive it made her feel. She thought of Jason's warm smile and how she'd never get to kiss his lips again.

Her entire body shook as she cried. She curled into a ball and rocked back and forth. She wasn't a quitter, where did she go wrong? Was there something she could have done differently? She didn't stop the disease, it stopped her. She thought about all of the people she had let down. Maybe Michael would be able to make a vaccine and succeed where she had failed. Then, she remembered the box he gave her.

"The vaccine," Maggie said, her heart beating faster.

She rolled onto her stomach and began to scoot, pulling herself along the floor. The coughing grew more intense as she willed herself forward. She got up on her hands and knees and could feel herself shaking. Behind her, she could see a trail of blood streaked across the tile floor. Maggie stopped when she felt her head hit against something hard. She lifted her head up, it was the fridge.

She sat back on her knees and reached out, trying to grasp the handle of the fridge. Her vision was blurred, making it look like there were two handles. She swung her arm up and missed. Then, she ran her hand across the cold metal, feeling for the handle. She found it and pulled with all of her strength. The fridge door flew open, knocking her backward.

She landed on her back, squinting her eyes at the spinning images. She could see something brown sitting on the bottom shelf. She had to get the box, it was her only chance. With every ounce of strength she had left, she pushed herself up off the ground, letting out a guttural roar as she fell toward the fridge. She caught her breath and reached up, knocking the box off the shelf.

The box landed next to her on the floor. She clawed at the box, trying to open it. It was sealed shut. Her fingers fumbled clumsily over the tape, unable to loosen it. She clenched the tape in between her teeth and jerked her head upward. She heard the ripping sound of the tape as the lid of the box lifted. Inside, she saw the ready-to-inject vial and pulled it out. Her hands were shaking uncontrollably as she held the needle in her hand. She pulled down the side of her sweats, raised the needle up high in the air and brought it down into her leg. She let out a scream of pain; then, everything went black.

Darkness descended all around Maggie, she had no sense of time nor place. Her body felt weightless, drifting along as if it were being pulled toward some unknown force. A white light appeared in the distance, and her body began gravitating toward it.

As the white light grew closer, she saw people, their bodies bathed in the white light. The people were calling out to her, she could hear her name echoing as they beckoned her toward them. She wanted to join them, and her body began moving quicker in their direction, picking up speed. Then, as she approached within their reach, the white light turned red. The people were now covered in blood with bulging eyes. Their mouths were gaping open as their hands clawed through the air, trying to grab her.

Maggie gasped as her eyes shot open. She frantically turned in every direction, looking for the hands that were trying to seize her only moments before. There was nothing there. Through the darkness, she could see a stage cloaked in red curtains directly in front of her. When she glanced down, she realized she was wearing a black sequin dress. The sound of an orchestra playing began to emanate from the stage, but she couldn't see any musicians. She stared out at the empty seats, she was all alone in the dark theatre. Suddenly, the red curtains parted, and a spotlight appeared on the stage, highlighting a single point. Maggie watched as a young man wearing a black top hat and a tuxedo with coattails walked into the spotlight.

She felt a wave of panic and tried to stand up, but she couldn't. Her eyes moved downward, registering the straps binding her wrists to the theatre seat. She yanked upward and tried to twist her arms free, but the straps were too tight. She gazed back up, her eyes widening as the man on the stage waved his index finger, scolding her.

When the man took off his hat, she thought she recognized him from somewhere. She watched, mesmerized, as he waved his white-gloved hand over the hat and held it outward, showing her it was empty. As he smiled, she visualized him standing in front of the Great Wall of China.

"Edward," Maggie whispered.

She surveyed the theatre around her as the music stopped and a drumroll began. Then, the man raised his arm in the air and reached into the hat. When his hand reappeared, he was holding a large black rat by the tail. He began laughing, his voice filling the theatre as his face distorted, appearing rat-like. She watched in horror as the theatre began flooding with black rats. The creatures were crawling all over her, biting at her face, arms, and legs. She began screaming as she thrashed her head back and forth, her voice echoing through the theatre.

Maggie jolted upward, still trying to knock the rats off of her. Then, she realized she was no longer in the theatre—she was on the kitchen floor. She glanced down at her bloodied T-shirt and saw the empty vial by the box. She picked up the vial, remembering how she had thrust the needle into her leg. She ran her hand across her forehead, it was cool to the touch—the fever had broken. She placed her hand on her throat and swallowed. The scratchiness was almost gone.

It wasn't possible, Maggie thought. She held the empty vial up, studying it in the light. Unless—Michael's vaccine worked. She had taken a risk by injecting herself with an untested vaccine, but the risk paid off and it saved her life. *It worked.* And since it saved her life—it could save others. She had to let them know. They had to make more of his vaccine before it was too late. Then, she remembered Michael was in Brazil, he was still searching for the plant he needed to make the vaccine.

She grabbed the edge of the counter and pulled herself up. She was still weak and her muscles ached, but she had to get word to the CDC about the vaccine. How could she make them listen? When she stood up, she could hear the sound of the television in the other room. She held her hand against the wall and scooted her feet along the floor. She balanced herself against the couch as she came around the corner, then her eyes shifted to the words on the TV:

The Red Death toll continues to rise, over 1 million cases now confirmed.

One million souls, Maggie thought as she stared at the faces of Juan Martinez and Samuel Greene on the screen. She looked at the time: 2 AM. She had been out for over 12 hours. A female reporter stood in front of Regency Hospital as she spoke. In the background, crowds of people were angrily protesting.

". . . Greene and Martinez were both workers at the Regency Hospital and are believed to be the first confirmed cases with the deadly bacteria, and people are demanding to know why. The bacteria, which is now being called the Red Death, because of its similarities to the bacteria responsible for the Black Death plague, is now considered the worst pandemic of modern times. Over 1 million confirmed cases have now been verified globally, including cases in England, France, Germany, China, Japan, Canada, Russia, Mexico, South America, and Africa. This number is expected to grow with over 150,000 deaths and no cure in sight." The newscaster paused, turning around to the crowds. "As you can see, the crowds are protesting outside Regency Hospital after information was leaked about the connection to the hospital."

Maggie moved closer to the screen as a photo of the hospital administrator, Mr. Carter, appeared on the screen.

"We now have information that the Regency Hospital administrator,

Robert Carter, has been asked to step down. We expect to hear about his resignation at some point today."

Another newscaster appeared on the screen, a man wearing a trench coat and holding an umbrella. She immediately recognized the blue and white sign of the CDC.

"I'm standing outside the Centers for Disease Control and Prevention's main building. Authorities at the CDC stated in a press conference earlier today that they are working on an antibiotic for the Red Death bacteria. The bacteria has shown to be antibiotic resistant to streptomycin, tetracycline, and gentamicin, which are used to treat the well known Black Death bacteria, *Yersinia pestis*. The CDC is facing skepticism for their slow response, and from scientists who claim that antibiotics are ineffective against a pneumonic strain of bacteria such as the Red Death bacteria. Meanwhile . . . "

Maggie reached out and turned the television off, staring at the blank screen.

"They're lying," she said under her breath. They knew there wasn't an antibiotic that would work against a pneumonic plague. Even if there was, it would be too late for the people who were already infected.

Maggie rubbed her fingers over the empty vial in her hand, realizing what she had to do. She squeezed her side as she limped across the floor and into her bedroom. Her stomach was still knotted up and waves of pain coursed through her body with every step. She eyed the bloody handprints, rings, and maps. Then, she reached up and tore the world map off the wall. She'd make them see the truth.

CHAPTER 56

THE AMAZON, BRAZIL.
SEPTEMBER 7.

The moon was hanging low in the sky, casting shadows from the forest over the village. Stallings glanced over at Sunda sitting in front of one of the huts, watching as he bent a piece of vine over his leg. He was making a strap for a hunting bow, skillfully working the vine between his fingers. The straps were important for the hunting group, freeing their hands for other tasks during long hunting trips. He noticed a few of the other Motombu men were making blowgun pipes from hollowed out tree branches. Each blowgun takes a few days to make, and is crafted using a technique that is passed down through generations.

As Stallings watched Sunda, he realized how much the boy, who was now a man, reminded him of his grandfather, Watandi. Their eyes radiated an indescribable passion and energy. When he asked about Watandi, Sunda said his spirit walks among them in the time of the ancestors.

He touched the bow strap Sunda was making.

"*Bon-ta*," he said. The word meant "superb" or "with great skill" to the Motombu.

"*Pe-ra*," Sunda replied as he continued working the bow, which meant "with the help of the gods."

The Motombu were very humble people and rarely took credit for their accomplishments. Everything that happened to them was seen as stemming from the work of the gods. If a hunting trip was successful, then it was *pe-ra*. If a baby was born, it was *pe-ra*. The gods were seen as giving, but the gods could also be angered, and when bad things happened, it was also *pe-ra*. The double meaning of the word intrigued Stallings. Even though the Motombu believed the gods helped them, they also believed the gods caused them grief and pain. And when the grief and pain became too much, the blood-letting began—a cry of mercy to the gods.

Stallings found it difficult to broach the subject, he knew how sacred the *lapethria* plant was to the Motombu people—they didn't even trade it with neighboring tribes. How could he explain that the plant could provide a vaccine for the entire world?

Sunda glanced over at him, seeming to sense something was on his mind.

"Time."

"Time," Stallings said, sitting on the ground next to him.

There was a brief silence between them as he watched Sunda working on the bow strap.

"*Kopo*," he said, pointing at himself. The word meant "sickness" to the Motombu.

"*Kopo?*" Sunda repeated. His hands stopped moving along the bow strap.

"*Sa-pa*," Stallings replied and made a circular motion with his hand, meaning "many of my people."

"*Pe-ra*," Sunda said as he stared out at the jungle.

"*Pe-ra, lapethria loma sa-pa tot-a*," Stallings said. "With the help of the gods, *lapethria* saves many of my people from the dead."

"*Sha*," Sunda put the bow strap down and stood up. Then he pointed at himself.

"*Sha?*" Stallings said as he leaped up, wrapping his arms around him. "*Sha!*"

"What's all the excitement about?" Boutroux asked as she watched the exchange of hugs.

"Sunda will take us to where the *lapethria* plant grows," Stallings said as he made a movement from the ground up, asking him if the plant was still growing.

"*Sha*," Sunda said as he pointed to the trees around them.

"Where?" Stallings said as he pulled the map out of his pocket and began pointing.

Sunda looked down at the colors and lines on the map, not comprehending.

Stallings cleared a space on the ground by his feet and grabbed a stick, planting it in the ground, and pointed to the village.

Sunda smiled, baring his black teeth. Then, he walked ten paces southwest of where Stallings was standing.

"*Lapethria*."

"They can take us?" Boutroux said as she watched them pantomiming back and forth. "Michael will be so happy."

He glanced up and saw a look of sadness in her eyes.

"Michael will be fine," he said as he grabbed her hand. "He's still too weak to move, but we can find the plant and bring back as many as we can. He'll be safe here in the village until we return."

She nodded her head, blinking away some tears.

"Are you sure they can take us to find the *lapethria* plant?" she asked, gesturing to the two Motombu men.

Sunda was pointing at the map and saying "*lapethria*," while another man kept flipping the map over as if the plant was hiding under it.

"That's what we're going to find out," Stallings said.

He knew the *lapethria* plant existed, Watandi had given him a sample. He'd also seen the Motombu grind it into a paste. He just hoped the tales of the pilgrimage weren't just mythological and it was a plant they could obtain. Sometimes it was hard for him to separate the fantasy from the reality with the Motombu, since the myths were just as real to them. In any case, they had to gather the plant from somewhere, it didn't just appear out of thin air—even if it was a gift from the gods.

"If anyone knows where to find the *lapethria*, it's the Motombu."

CHAPTER 57

THE CDC.
ATLANTA, GEORGIA.
SEPTEMBER 8.

The dual iris scan beeped, and Maggie stepped through the front door of the CDC headquarters in Atlanta. She handed her employee I.D. card to the security guard, who gave her a funny look.

"Long trip," Maggie said as she grabbed her card back and walked through the body scanner. She had driven 14 hours straight, and she wasn't about to slow down now.

When she stepped out of the elevator on the third floor, she kept her head down as she walked past the secretary sitting behind the desk.

"Can I help—" the secretary called out, her words dying in mid-air as Maggie turned around.

Maggie knew she looked like hell—she had on the same old bloody T-shirt and sweats she'd been wearing all week, and her hair was matted with dried blood, but she wasn't here to make an impression. Well, not a good one anyway, she thought. She ignored the secretary and opened the door to the office of Harold Bowman.

Bowman was on the phone when she entered the room. He cocked his head slightly to the side, staring up at her. She could see the look of shock on his face—the normally clean-cut, squeaky clean, and straight as an arrow Maggie De Luca—looked like a raging lunatic.

"I'll call you back," Bowman said as he hung up the phone. His eyes scanned down, and then back up. "Maggie . . . what are you doing here? What happened to you?"

"I'm done playing games with the CDC, that's what happened. Time's up," she said, the hoarseness of her voice adding to the effect.

"I don't understand. Do you need help?"

"Yes, Harold. I'm happy you asked, because that's why I'm here."

"Let me call someone—" Bowman said as he pushed a button on the phone.

"I don't need that kind of help," she said angrily as she moved closer to the desk. "Cancel the call to security, Harold. I know what you're doing."

"I-I can't do that," he said as he stood up.

"You knew Dr. Harbinger had a vaccine. Why didn't you back him?"

"Dr. Harbinger? Is that what this is all about? He told me about a *research* vaccine, but it wasn't tested. In fact, he didn't even have what he needed to make more, if I recall correctly."

"But he could—if he had your help." She threw the papers Michael had given her on his desk. "You've backed other vaccines with less proof. What is it, money?" She knocked over a photo on the desk that showed him standing on a yacht.

Bowman jumped, clearly worried about Maggie getting anywhere near him. He knew she was infected, she could see it written all over his face. She had him and she knew it.

"Was it the pharmaceutical companies that paid you off?" Maggie said. "You knew about this bacteria long ago. Maybe it was the CDC, who were trying to keep it hidden for use as a biological weapon." She could tell she hit a sore note by the look on his face. "Boy, that really backfired, didn't it?"

She walked around the desk, and he backed away from her. She could see the fear in his eyes.

"How many more have to die before you'll face the truth?"

"You're . . . you're infected," Bowman said as he moved farther away.

"That's right, Harold," Maggie said as she took another step forward, backing him into the corner.

She got right in his face, and he turned his head to the side.

"Now, so are you."

She held up the empty vial.

"Except—I took Dr. Harbinger's vaccine."

She shook the vial.

"Uh-oh. I'm sorry, Harold . . . there's none left."

His eyes widened as he stared at the empty vial.

"So, what's it going to be? You can either find Dr. Harbinger and fund his vaccine, or I will tell the entire world that you were responsible for the deaths of millions of people." She yanked the curtains wide open.

He looked out the window at the hordes of people waving signs. News vans and camera crews were lined up, waiting outside. She waved and the cameras moved upward. Then, two men in security uniforms stormed into the room, immediately moving to apprehend her. She stared at Bowman, her eyes unwavering as they grabbed her arms.

Bowman lowered his head and held up his hand.

"Let her go."

She smiled at Bowman and jerked her arms away, watching as the two men left.

"Good Choice. I knew you'd come around, Harold," Maggie said as she squeezed her side with her hand, trying to hide the pain she felt in her stomach.

Bowman moved back behind his desk.

"Where is he?"

Maggie held up the world map and tossed it on his desk.

"The Amazon."

CHAPTER 58

THE AMAZON, BRAZIL.
SEPTEMBER 9.

The shaman chanted as he rattled a bloodstained stick through the air. Stallings peeked over at Boutroux, her eyes were wide as she watched. Sunda and two other men, who would also be making the journey, were on their knees beside them.

As the shaman passed in front of each of them, he dipped his hand in a white mixture and smeared it across their faces. After they were decorated with white paint, he inserted a dried herb on each of their tongues.

Stallings chewed the herb, noticing it had a mild peppery flavor. He chuckled when he glanced over at Boutroux, she looked like a deranged clown. She had a funny expression on her face as she chewed the herb and almost gagged when she swallowed.

After the ceremony, they were all handed spears decorated with colorful paint. Then, the rest of the tribe parted, making a pathway for the five of them as they made their way out of the village.

As they departed, Stallings admired the beauty of the village from a distance. The sun was just starting to peak through the canopy, illuminating the entire village in a soft yellow glow. He had thought of this place so often over the years, seeing it now felt like a dream. He knew with time, the Motombu would go through further changes as they had increasingly more contact with the outside world. Soon, there would only be a faint reminder of the people who had once lived here and had remained unchanged for thousands of years.

His thoughts turned to Harbinger. He wanted to come along, but he was too weak to move and would grasp his throat in pain when he talked. When they returned, Stallings promised him to have plenty of the *lapethria* plant with them—a promise he hoped he could keep. He was grateful that Sunda was kind enough to come along for the journey, he also brought two of his strongest men.

Boutroux followed behind Sunda and one of his men, and Stallings along with the other Motombu man held up the rear of the group. He found himself shifting his gaze more since leaving the safety of the village. He was beginning to worry about another encounter with Kaltanda, who may hold a personal grudge against them.

He felt pangs of guilt for the slaughter of Kaltanda's tribe—even if they were on the dinner menu. As an anthropologist, he tried desperately not to cause disruptions when he studied the natural world, and their presence had helped fuel a fire between the two groups. Sunda tried to reassure him, claiming the war between the split tribes of the Motombu had been going on for a very long time—the old ways versus the new. He said that they had lost a great number of their people to Kaltanda over the years. One morning, the rogue tribe left the heads of Sunda's people on posts surrounding the village. The heads of the men had their testicles shoved in their mouths—a declaration of war on Sunda's tribe.

Even though Stallings knew cannibalism existed among the Motombu, he chose to turn a blind eye to protect them. These were the types of moral issues that scientists in the field dealt with every day. Not with cannibalism necessarily, which was rare, but with all of life. Life could be beautiful and deadly at the same time. Was it right to interrupt the attack of a predator to save the prey? Would you do so, knowing the predator and its offspring could die without the meal? Predators were designed to keep nature from overpopulating. A system of checks and balances—the very life cycle nature depended on. A cycle slowly being destroyed by man's interferences. The world was in a dire state, thanks to man's tendency to intervene.

His drive to find the *lapethria* plant was marred by his own torn feelings—those as an anthropologist and those as a man. Man had overpopulated the world, sending much of the other living animals and their environments into a state of depletion. Was a plague a way of nature finding balance again? Was it a way of showing just how out of line humans had become? Was he breaking his own values by interrupting the natural process of life? The thoughts tormented him, even as he stepped closer to finding a cure for the ancient plague.

Boutroux turned around, her eyes catching his.

"Are you coming old man?"

"Old man?" Stallings said, grateful to be pulled out of his dark thoughts. "I'm not that much older than you."

She laughed, then stumbled forward, tripping on a tree root.

"At least I know how to walk," he chuckled.

Suddenly, he realized everything was zooming in and out. The pathway they were following was buckling up at him as if it were moving. He stopped and grabbed on to a tree to hold himself steady. When he peered up, he saw that Boutroux had also stopped walking and had one of her arms out to the side. Sunda and the other two men were laughing, their black teeth appearing overly large.

"*Ho-tep-a*," Sunda said.

"*Ho-tep-a*," Stallings repeated, chortling. All of their faces expanded out and back like a carnival mirror in a funhouse.

Boutroux started giggling as she leaned against the tree next to him.

"What did he say?"

"It's the hallucinogen the shaman gave us for sight," he said. "Actually, you look even better like this. Smarter too—with that big wide head."

They both started laughing and couldn't stop until they were holding their sides, and tears were streaming down their faces. Sunda and the other men walked around in a trance-like state as they pointed up at the trees around them.

After a while the drug began to wear off, and they continued their journey. The calls of birds and monkeys permeated the air, and every so often a streak of color would flash through the trees as one of the birds took flight. Stallings noticed the terrain was beginning to change—the plants and trees were different than any he had seen, and the air felt thicker and heavier. He glanced down as mist rolled in around them.

The group suddenly stopped walking, and he looked up to see what was happening. Sunda had found something and was studying the ground. Stallings walked past Boutroux and squatted down next to him. There were round indentions in the ground—animal tracks. He watched as Sunda picked up something near the tracks that looked like animal feces and smelled it.

"*Qua-te-lo*," Sunda said as he stared out at the jungle around them.

"What is it?" Boutroux asked as she walked up, registering the look of worry on their faces.

"Cat feces," Stallings said as he glanced up at her. "No, not the sweet purry kind—a jaguar." He knew the jaguar was the most feared predator of the Motombu, many of their stories centered on the animal. They believed the jaguar could shapeshift, changing into other animal forms.

"Oh, great," she said, moving in closer to the group. "What do we do now?"

They all turned when some branches snapped near them. Then, a loud screech that made the hair rise on the back of his neck rang through the air. It wasn't the sound of a jaguar—it was the sound of death itself—something Stallings wasn't a stranger to and never cared to hear again. The problem was the proximity of the sound, since a jaguar could be protective of a new kill and have been known to attack to keep others from intruding on its meal.

The jungle was dense with foliage and thick mist, it was impossible to see farther than a few feet. They were blind to anything watching them—or hunting them. Sunda and the other two men raised their spears, prepping for an oncoming attack. Stallings nodded to Boutroux, and they both held their spears up.

After some time passed without another sound, Sunda began to move again. With the heightened awareness and fear levels raised, everyone took each step cautiously with their spears held up high in the air. The animals in the jungle were well camouflaged, and imagination easily took hold: every vine became a snake, every set of eyes watching them were Kaltanda's, and every low rumbling sound was the feared jaguar.

When Sunda suddenly stopped again, everyone froze. Stallings slowly turned toward the direction he was facing, his eyes following Sunda's line of view. At first, all he saw was the hoof of an animal; then, he saw the red blotch in the middle where its intestines had been ripped out. The animal's eyes were staring vacantly outward. Boutroux gasped and covered her face.

They were closer to the kill than he had anticipated. It was a white-lipped peccary, an animal resembling a pig, except with sharp tusks. If it were with a large group, the peccaries would have been a threat to them, but they stood little chance against a jaguar.

The jaguar would still be close by, ready to finish its meal. They had to keep moving—and fast. Sunda and the men swept their spears back and forth and motioned for Stallings and Boutroux to move ahead of them.

"Quickly," Stallings said to Boutroux as he urged her forward.

"Was that done by the jaguar?" she asked, her eyes wide.

"Oh, yeah," Stallings said as he grabbed her arm, helping her past some of the large roots of a banyan tree. "But at least it won't be as hungry."

The aerial roots of the tree were draped downward in long sheets. They weaved through them until they saw an opening on the other side. He checked behind them, but he couldn't see Sunda and the other men following. He shoved Boutroux back behind some of the hanging roots. She grabbed them like the bars of a jail cell as she looked out at him. She started to speak and he put his finger up to his lips.

"Just stay quiet and wait here. I'll see if they need help."

He made his way through the banyan roots, backtracking the same way they had just taken. He kept his spear raised up in front of him as his eyes swept side to side. As he walked, he listened for sounds, but it had grown eerily quiet. He couldn't see anything in front of him because of the thick mist. When he finally reached the main pathway, he saw Sunda and the other two men coming toward him. He let out a sigh of relief.

"*Atk-ee . . . atk-ee,*" the men chanted in unison.

The chant was to pay respect to the jaguar, an animal regarded as god-like to the Motombu. It was also a protection ritual. Stallings had seen a few displays in the past, honoring the strength of the jaguar, but he wasn't sure if any of them were still practiced among the Motombu today. He was happy to see they were still hanging on to many of their beliefs.

The truth was, he was so alarmed by the change in their appearance, he didn't realize how much the Motombu had remained the same. Maybe it was sheer blindness on his part. While it was true their style of clothing was different, and some of their foods had changed—overall the Motombu were very much the same people he remembered them to be.

CHAPTER 59

THE AMAZON, BRAZIL.
SEPTEMBER 9.

Stallings stared at the empty space behind the banyan tree roots. Boutroux was gone. He felt a sense of panic wash over him. He turned in circles, taking in the area surrounding him. He was standing right where he left her, he was sure of it. He remembered her hands grasping the roots as her eyes met his. Did she try to follow him?

"Sam!" he yelled, cupping his hands around his mouth. He couldn't have been gone more than 20 minutes. His thoughts raced back to the jaguar. "Sam!" He looked over at Sunda and the other two men as they searched the area. There was no sign of her, it was as if she had vanished into thin air.

He walked through the banyan tree roots, searching the ground where she had been standing. He couldn't see any blood, but a large animal like a jaguar could easily attack without leaving a trace of their prey. As a stalk and ambush predator that weighs up to 300 pounds, they could drag a prey as heavy as 800 pounds over 40 feet in one shot. A 120 pound woman wouldn't stand a chance against such a stealthy predator. He noticed a mark on the ground next to where she'd been standing. It was a hole, about the size of the end of a spear, but it could've been the spear she was carrying. If it was a jaguar attack, the spear would still be laying here, he thought. *Unless she speared the animal.*

"Kaltanda," Sunda said as he walked up, holding a bright red feather.

"No," he said, panicking. "Sam!"

He shouldn't have left her. *Sam.* He thought it would be safer for her here in case they were attacked. If Kaltanda had her, he may not wait to kill her this time. What if she was dead already? Fear took hold of him, making his chest ache.

"Sam. Oh, Sam," Stallings whispered. He clenched his hands into fists at his sides. He wanted to hit something. He wanted to strike out at how unfair this felt.

Suddenly, all of their heads bolted upward as a blood-curdling scream shot through the jungle.

"Sam!" Stallings said, his head flipping toward the sound of the voice. "It's her!" He was relieved to know she was alive. *Alive.* Until now, he didn't realize the deep connection he felt toward her. She had awakened something in him that he thought had died long ago, like the illusory light of the dead stars.

The scream came from close by, so they couldn't have gotten very far, he thought. He stared in the direction that her voice came from—it was down a rocky cliff. Sunda pointed at a dried up gully that ran alongside it. He was right, it would be the quickest escape route through the thick jungle. If it was the rainy season, the runoff from the high cliff would carry a torrent of water and be impassable, but the water worn ravine was dry. The aerial roots of the trees hung mid-air many feet above the dried crevice, a reminder of the once bountiful water they drank from.

As they got closer, a footprint was faintly visible in the dirt path of the gulch. Stallings followed Sunda and dropped down into the dried ravine. The jungle had become exceedingly quiet and darker from their new vantage point under the barrier roots of the trees. The ground looked dried and decayed from erosion and crunched under their feet as they walked—a sharp contrast to the green vibrant jungle that surrounded them above.

His eyes searched the path of the gully, if he could only see a glimpse of Boutroux, he would feel better. Just to be reassured she was still alive—she'd been quieted too quickly—it wasn't a good sign. She had to be terrified, and he felt helpless as he stared at the dark slopes of the ravine. He winced in pain as a sharp branch sliced into his thigh when he brushed past. He glanced down and saw an inky gash of blood on his torn jeans.

Up ahead, a deep chasm dropped at a sharp incline. During the rainy season, it would transform into a waterfall, but in its current state, it looked more like a treacherous landslide. He heard Sunda emitting a a series of coughs, it was an uncanny imitation of the jaguar—and a threat to Kaltanda. Sunda's men followed the calls with hooting sounds, a war cry to their enemy. A sound echoed back from Kaltanda in answer to the call, a low growling mimic of the howler monkey, egging them on.

As Stallings followed Sunda down the steep incline, he held on to the roots jutting out of the sides of the embankment. He could feel his feet slipping with each step and was barely able to stop himself from sliding the rest of the way down on his backside. He peered over the cliff as he edged his feet forward, noticing the other men were already down below. Then the ground beneath him split under his weight. He swung his arm up, grabbing the closest root. He glanced down, his feet were dangling below him. He could see Sunda and the men at the bottom of the drop, but it was a good 15 feet down and he was afraid to let go. There was a sudden snapping sound and he felt himself falling down, the piece of dried root still in one hand and his spear in the other.

When Stallings landed he felt a sharp pain shoot through his knees. He reached down and felt the wound on his leg and grimaced in pain. The laceration was even deeper than he realized. He straightened up his back and gazed out, trying to get his bearings, but he couldn't see through the mist. He waved his hand in front of him, straining his eyes to see where Sunda and the others had gone. He couldn't see anyone as he stepped forward and figured they must have climbed out of the ravine.

He stopped walking when he heard the sound of feet above him. When he looked up, a hand reached down toward him. The hand appeared to be disconnected from its body as it reached through the thick mist. He grabbed the hand and stuck his foot into a crevice. Pain shot through his leg as he was pulled upward. He climbed out the rest of the way and fell onto his side as he stared outward. Through the haze, he could see Boutroux. She was with two of Kaltanda's men, who were holding her arms. He jerked his head upward, staring at one of Sunda's men standing wide-legged over him. Then, two sets of hands reached down and helped him the rest of the way to his feet.

"J.D.!" Boutroux called out to him.

One of Kaltanda's men grabbed her by the hair, yanking her head backward. He tried to move forward to help her, but he was held back by Sunda's men, who were holding his arms. Then, he saw the reason. Kaltanda and Sunda were both standing in a war-like stance, facing each other above the gorge. He turned back toward Boutroux as one of the men held a spear up against her throat. When she tried to move again, the man ran the tip of the spear down the side of her cheek. A trickle of blood ran down her face. She froze, her eyes wide as she stared at him.

He wanted to save her. He wanted to hold her in his arms and tell her everything was going to be all right, but he couldn't. This was a war between the two Motombu leaders, and it was a long time coming. It would be a duel to the death, and the last man standing would be the leader of all the Motombu. It was a natural progression that he would not allow himself to interfere with. Even if things didn't go the way he envisioned, this was the way of the Motombu, and he had to respect their traditions. A tradition that went back thousands of years

CHAPTER 60

THE AMAZON, BRAZIL.
SEPTEMBER 9.

Aspear thrust forward at Sunda, who leaped aside and regained his warrior stance. As Sunda aimed his spear at Kaltanda, Stallings found himself trying to anticipate the next move. It was a gruesome battle to watch. Both men had blood gushing from wounds inflicted by the sharp spears of their opponent, although neither of them showed any signs of pain or retreat. They stared at each other with fierce intent as if the rest of the world had dropped away. This was solely the world of two adversaries, who were ready to defend their way of life with their own.

Sunda had blood dripping from a deep gash on his forehead, it ran into one of his eyes and down his face in red streaks. Kaltanda had a stab wound in his right shoulder and kept his spear raised high in his other hand. To reveal any pain was a sign of weakness, and like a wounded animal, it let your opponent know what that weakness was. Both men stood with their heads held high, refusing to give any ground to the other as they paced back and forth.

Kaltanda's men kept Boutroux close, pinning her against a tree with their spears. She tried to close her eyes as the two men battled in front of her, but was forced to watch. Although no one should enter the battle of two Motombu leaders, it was equally insulting not to watch the war waged between two demigods.

To both Motombu tribes, Sunda and Kaltanda had blood running through their veins passed down from the gods themselves. Sunda, as the son of Watandi, whose ancestors came from the sky. Kaltanda, as the son of J-otan, whose ancestors came from the ground below. Two very different beliefs, but both equally powerful.

The fact that Sunda was wearing a Nike T-shirt and shorts, made watching this ancient-style battle even more surreal. He represented the new, ever-changing future of the Motombu. Kaltanda represented the old ways, sporting a bowl haircut, red painted chest, and a cloth barely covering his loins.

Even with many lives on the line, including his own, Stallings couldn't help but wonder which way was better. He shook the thought away as another spear jabbed forward. This time, it was Sunda's spear stabbing Kaltanda's left leg. Sunda tried to pull back on the spear, but Kaltanda growled, showing his black teeth as he grabbed the handle of the spear and held on to it.

Stallings felt the cold chill of fear run down his spine. Without the spear, Sunda had no chance of winning the battle. He began a tug of war to take his spear back, but Kaltanda held steadfastly on to the spear, refusing to let it leave his leg. Seeing his effort was futile, Sunda thrust forward with the handle of the spear until it completely bore through Kaltanda's leg and came out the other side. Kaltanda's eyes grew wide, like two black holes, as he gritted his teeth. Sunda began to twist the spear, first yanking the spear to the right, then to the left. The two men stood face-to-face, their noses almost touching as they both breathed heavily, a series of growls escalating from them both.

Suddenly, lightning crackled through the air, the sky opened up, and a torrent of rain poured down. Sunda looked up as the rain fell around them, and the thunder rumbled. Kaltanda seized the opportunity and raised his spear in the air. Stallings felt himself leap forward, it felt like slow motion as the spear came up behind Sunda and stabbed him in the back. He waited for Sunda to fall at the feet of Kaltanda, but instead Sunda reached his arm back, yanking out the spear. Kaltanda laughed, his head rolling loosely across his shoulders, as he tried to maintain his warrior pose.

Then, Sunda raised the bloodied spear above his head, the rain beating down on him.

"Watandi-i-i-i! Watandi-i-i-i!" he yelled as he stared up at the sky, calling out to his father for strength. As another bolt of lightning streaked through the sky, he brought the spear down swiftly, piercing Kaltanda's heart. The two men's eyes locked again as they stood face-to-face. Then, Kaltanda let out one last breath and crumpled to the ground at Sunda's feet.

Stallings watched as the blood from Kaltanda's chest seeped into the ground, joining his ancestors below. He gazed up, noticing the rain had suddenly stopped.

"Hello, old friend," he said, watching as the sun reappeared. He let out a long breath. It was over. He turned toward Boutroux as the two men released her. She ran over to him, wrapping her arms around his waist. She glanced over at the body of Kaltanda and buried her face in his chest.

"Don't tell me it's going to be all right," Boutroux said as she looked up at him, her face streaked with tears. "Just hold me."

He watched as Kaltanda's men bowed down on one knee in front of Sunda. Sunda, still showing no sign of pain, placed his hands on each of the men's shoulders. Then, he looked over at Stallings and held up his arm with the watch.

"Yes, my friend," he whispered. "Time for the two tribes of the Motombu to become one again." He wrapped his arms around Boutroux as she smiled up at him. "Now, let's go get that plant."

CHAPTER 61

NEW YORK CITY.
SEPTEMBER 9.

"But now, how few people I see, and those walking
like people that have taken leave of the world."
—Samuel Pepys
Diary of Samuel Pepys (22 Aug 1665)

Milana pulled the hood down farther, covering her face. As she passed by a broken store window, she stopped, lowered the hood, and gazed at her reflection. The remnants of the black eye and split lip Vladimir had given her still haunted her face. Now, he was gone. He left for work one day and never came back. When they called saying they needed to speak to her, she ran. She was scared.

She didn't know he had the sickness until it was too late. At first, she thought he was drinking again—then the sickness claimed her as well. She pulled back one of her sleeves, staring down at the scar on her wrist. She had tried every way to escape over the years: pills, a straight razor, and even a near jump off the Brooklyn Bridge.

In the past, Vladimir laughed at each attempt, taunting her. *Fly little birdie, fly away.* She couldn't even get that right. She was afraid and he knew it. *Vladimir.* He promised to take care of her, and now he was gone. She watched two people stumble by, their faces smeared with blood, and their eyes already dead.

Milana pulled up her hood as she glanced out around her. The streets of New York City were barren, hardly a soul in sight. The once thriving city she remembered had been turned into a desolate wasteland. People were afraid to leave their homes—except people like her, who had no home and no hope to survive. She felt the ground rumble as two large military tanks rolled through the street and over the dead bodies.

All she could do was keep walking, she knew what would happen if she stopped. She looked at the torn posters that were plastered all over the buildings. She paused in front of one of the posters, reading the words: BE A HERO, REPORT ANYONE SICK TO THE CDC.

"We're all sick," Milana said as she coughed and looked down at her hand. There was blood all over her fingers. Her chest felt hollow and ached from coughing. She gazed up at the sound of a loud bell ringing through the streets. She began walking toward the sound. She saw others beginning to gravitate in the same direction.

As the sound of the bell grew nearer, she stared up at a cross on the St. Märgen Cathedral. In the tower at the top, a bell swung gently back and forth as it rang. She watched as sick people climbed the stairs. There were many lying dead who had tried before. She followed the others up the steps of the church, carefully stepping over the bodies. She could hear the sound of moaning and turned, staring at a woman rocking a dead baby, both of their faces covered in blood.

At the top of the stairs, the doors were wide open, and the people flooded inside. Milana stopped walking, and people began pushing in all around her. She gazed up at the stained glass windows on the front of the cathedral. The images were of people in robes, their arms stretched outward. She saw a fountain inside and began walking toward it. She stumbled forward and climbed over the dead bodies lying on the floor.

As she reached the fountain, she stared up at the statue of the Virgin Mary, an adult Jesus draped in her arms. Bloody handprints were all over the white marble, and the water had turned red.

She reached into her pocket and pulled out two coins, remembering Vladimir's words before he died: *Filthy bitch.* She squeezed the coins in her hand, kneeled down, and closed her eyes.

"Forgive me, Father, for I have sinned. Forgive all of us," Milana said as she tossed the coins into the fountain.

CHAPTER 62

THE AMAZON, BRAZIL.
SEPTEMBER 10.

The two men from Kaltanda's tribe picked up Sunda on a stretcher made of palm leaves and twined branches, while Kaltanda lay dead where he landed—an unceremonious ending to his life. The men were now followers of the new ways, and Sunda was now their leader. They were returning Sunda to the village, where he could be treated further for his injuries.

Stallings walked up to Sunda to bid him farewell. Even though he was the leader of all the Motombu, to him, he still looked like a boy. He could tell Sunda was in tremendous pain, but he was still grinning up at him, showing his black teeth.

"*Lapethria loma sa-ke tot-a,*" Sunda said as he made a circular motion with his hand. "*Lapethria* saves all people from the dead."

"*Pe-ra*, my friend. *Sha, sa-ke*," Stallings said as he grabbed Sunda's hand and nodded to the men to take him away. He sure hoped he was right. He watched them disappear through the mist, while the other two men stood waiting to take them to the highlands.

As they continued their journey, he noticed the ground above the cliff they were on continued to climb upward, slanting at a tilt. The air was slightly cooler and thinner, and the wispy fog billowed around them closer to the ground, circling their knees. He used the spear as a walking stick, pressing down with each step. His knees were still sore, and the cut on his leg was burning, but considering the series of events that had unfolded—he would take the pain any day. The Motombu were one again and he had Boutroux back.

Boutroux tugged his arm as they continued their ascent and pointed at the vast jungle below. The jungle canopy was stretched out below them like a green sea with white clouds hovering above.

"It's beautiful. And look, we're higher than the clouds," she said, gazing out.

"We're in the cloud forest," Stallings said as he looked down at the tranquil jungle. It looked untouched from where they stood, only he knew that wasn't true. Not far away, the trees were cut down and wide patches of open land replaced the seemingly never-ending jungle. Soon, deforestation would engulf this serene area as well—one day the clock would stop ticking and time would run out. He couldn't help but feel a sense of sadness, thinking that he may never stand in this spot and see the same view again.

The largest culprit of deforestation is when land is converted for cattle grazing. The main reason for the increase in cattle production has less to do with beef or leather production and more to do with establishing a claim on the land itself. Other reasons for the changing Amazon landscape are due to an increase in population, mechanized farming, and the export of oil, gas, minerals, and timber. All of these developments, when combined, can spell catastrophe for the habitats of the rainforest animals and for tribes like the Motombu, who need great stretches of land to survive.

They passed through an area of low-lying vines, and then a wide grassy plain opened up in front of them. The air had a chill to it, and a brisk wind hit his cheeks. He glanced over at Boutroux as a gust of wind swept her hair away from her face. Her nose and cheeks were already pink from the cold air. The other two men stood with their spears at their sides as they stared out. It was a beautiful sight.

The plateau was layered with giant steps, and deep crevices ran up the sides. In the distance, he could see other highland areas with pointed round tops that dropped off sharply into the jungle below. The sun hung low in the sky, casting deep orange shadows over the ridges of the mesa, making the entire highland area resemble a sleeping dragon. Another shadow rose up, and he could see the massive wings of a black condor as it circled high above in the cloudless sky.

When Stallings glanced back down, the two men were already beginning their steady climb up the side of the ridge. The ground had deep cracks gouged out by surface runoff. He helped Boutroux step over them and climbed up on one of the flat areas of the plateau. Then he reached down, pulling her up to him. She lost her footing briefly, but then righted herself.

As they continued to climb upward, his face began to feel numb from the cold, and his hands felt rigid at his sides. He could see his breath when he exhaled, and the forceful wind threatened to knock him off the small pillar of ground he was standing on.

When they finally reached the top of the plateau, he heard one of the men, To-onan, calling them.

"*Se-se*," To-onan repeated, his arm raised in the air.

"He says this is where they gather the plant," Stallings said, grabbing her hand.

He noticed another plateau next to them shot higher toward the sky. He listened and could hear the sound of running water. To-onan edged down the side of the ridge, they followed him down the steep slope. When they made it down the other side, he was squatting beside a small green plant next to a stream of water. Boutroux ran up to the plant and knelt down, cradling the leaves as she examined it.

Stallings thought the leaves had the right shape, but he wasn't sure. "Is it—"

"*Lapethria*," To-onan said as he glanced up at him.

Boutroux looked up, smiling. He fell down on his knees next to her, letting out a deep breath. He felt a sense of relief wash over him. *It did exist.* Part of him had been afraid of what may or may not be true about the mythical plant, but it did exist.

"We did it!" Boutroux yelled, wrapping her arms around him so strongly it almost knocked him over.

He wrapped his arms around her, feeling elated. A charge of energy ran through him—a sense of accomplishment—something he hadn't felt in a long time. He stared down at the plant. It was so small, yet it had the power to cure. The Motombu knew it, and now the whole world would know it, too. Then the thought hit him: it was only one plant. His eyes darted in each direction, but there wasn't another plant in sight.

"How many of these plants does Michael need? Is a single plant enough?"

Boutroux turned.

"It's a start," she said, her face flooding with worry as she glanced around them. "If he can extract enough . . . or maybe he can find a way to synthesize it."

"And if not?"

Boutroux shook her head.

"I don't know. We mimic the environment, figure out how to grow more of the plant . . . and wait."

He studied the area, his eyes taking in the stream and the side of the ridge. His mind was racing. What if the plant didn't survive? What if he couldn't synthesize the vaccine? Maybe they could find more plants. *There had to be more.* He began walking in circles around them.

"There has to be more . . . this can't be it," he called over to Boutroux. "How do plants pollinate, you're the expert."

"I'm not an expert, but from what I've read it's by the wind carrying the pollen, animals, a lot of it's accidental," she said, shaking her head, as if searching for the right words. "That's if it were a flowering plant."

Stallings stared down at the flowerless plant.

"So we have no idea how the *lapethria* pollinates?"

"We believe, from what Michael and I found, that it reproduces by spores, the same method used by mosses and ferns, but without a living sample we couldn't study how it reproduced. We only had a small piece of the puzzle." She flipped one of the leaves over, examining the underside of the leaf. "Right now, we know very little about the *lapethria* plant—much like the Motombu, before your work with them."

"So this is an entirely new species of plant—"

"Capable of saving millions of lives," she added.

He knew thousands of new plants and animals had been discovered just over the last ten years, but he didn't realize how little was known about the *lapethria*. An entirely new species of plant, he thought. *The wind*. She mentioned the wind. He closed his eyes, feeling the cold breeze hit his face—it was blowing south. He rushed past them, part of his boot landing in the stream. The cliff dropped in one section, he followed it downward.

He noticed the stream emptied into a ravine below. He kept moving down the side of the embankment, periodically closing his eyes to feel the direction of the wind. He stumbled over a rock and lost his footing. Next thing he knew, he was rolling down the slope. He crashed against another rock, and felt a burn shoot through his shoulder. When he sat up, his eyes widened—green plants were everywhere. He reached down and touched one of the leaves. He was surrounded by *lapethria*.

Boutroux caught up with him and gasped. Then a chopping sound filled the air, followed by an onslaught of wind that made the *lapethria* plants sway and bend. Birds shrieked and flocked through the air, trying to escape the deafening sound. They all looked up as a helicopter came up over the crest of the plateau above them, while another one circled higher above. One of them was brown with a white stripe and the words POLICIA MILITAR, the other was white with blue letters on the side that said CDC.

"Looks like they changed their mind about that help," Stallings said as he looked over at Boutroux. He could see Harbinger waving from inside the CDC helicopter and Sunda sitting next to him. Well, what do you know, he thought as Harbinger held up his satellite phone to the window.

EPILOGUE

NEW YORK CITY.
ONE MONTH LATER.

As the lines moved forward at the vaccination tents, the realization hit Maggie—the nightmare was finally coming to an end. Thanks to Dr. Stallings discovery of the bacteria that caused the Red Death pandemic, now labeled under the name *Stallinia pestis*, and Dr. Harbinger's vaccine, Lapethriacel, the number of deaths had begun to drop. Without Dr. Harbinger's vaccine, she wouldn't be here—a high price to pay for following in the wake of the disease—always too late and always one step behind.

The biggest issue they were dealing with now, was getting people to the vaccination areas. The only way to fight this disease was to eliminate the possibility of infection. The people who couldn't get vaccinated, such as infants, the elderly, and those with compromised immune systems, depended on the rest of the masses to keep them from getting sick.

There were always religious zealots, and those claiming the vaccine could do more harm than good, but the majority of people were clamoring to get vaccinated. She gazed upward, watching as another military helicopter flew overhead. Other military soldiers, wearing Red Cross armbands, moved the lines along and administered the vaccine to the waiting people. In the war against the deadly Red Death bacteria, humanity had won once again—for now. She turned as Jason walked up behind her and handed her a styrofoam cup.

"*Café au lait,*" he said with that silly smirk he gets.

"Thanks, Jay," Maggie said as she held the cup under her nose, breathing in the steam from the coffee. She noticed many people wearing face masks, probably fearing they would endanger themselves while waiting in the long lines.

Thousands of vaccination centers were set up around the country, and WHO set up vaccination posts all over the world. In some developing nations, citizens were offered a reward for turning in infected people. An investigation was also underway, regarding the way the Red Death outbreak was handled. Lawsuits were being filed hand over fist as the dust started to clear, and the finger-pointing began. No one wanted to take the blame for the biggest disaster to rock the world.

The Red Death has gone down in history as the worst pandemic of modern times, its death toll reaching over 20 million, nearly half of the lives lost from the Black Death over many centuries. The World Health Organization was finally able to rule out bioterrorism, after an investigation into the start of the bacteria, but classified the Red Death as Category A, "A microorganism that needs to be closely monitored for future use as a biological weapon."

The Red Death is now relegated to BSL-3 at the CDC, frozen in time at -70° Celsius, next to its ally, the Black Death. Not far away on the same level, sits RR236, a curious black rodent named Gracie—a carrier of both plagues, who has a love for sweets. Maggie was reassured that the rat wouldn't be harmed, and she has made quite a few friends on BSL-3.

Maggie glanced down. A little boy with blond hair peeked out from behind his mother's legs as they stood in line. She smiled at the boy and waved, he giggled before taking cover once more.

"It's going to be okay," she whispered under her breath as she sipped her coffee. "We're all going to be okay."

Germs are all around us, and most of them are harmless. But, every so often one of them turns deadly, and when it does—she'd be ready.

Las Vegas, Nevada

Stallings listened to the floor creak as he walked across the living room. He took one step backward and pressed his weight down, listening as the floor creaked again. He thought he would fix the floor, put an end to the creaking once and for all, but hearing it now gave him comfort—it was a reminder he was home.

He turned and sat in his favorite old green chair, wincing as he felt something hard. He reached down between the cushion and armrest, pulling out the television remote. As he held it up, one of the batteries landed on his lap. He shook his head, reached over to the end table next to him, and grabbed a roll of Scotch tape. Then, he placed the battery back in the chamber of the remote, securing it with more tape. He started to lay the remote down on the table, when the television turned on, blasting sound throughout the room. He glanced down at the remote in his hand, he hadn't even turned it on.

"I'll be damned," Stallings said as he glared up at the screen and pressed the mute button. "Technology. Now, they're going to tell you what to do."

The screen rolled over twice, corrected itself, and showed an image of a newscaster. The woman was holding a microphone and standing in front of the CDC in Atlanta. The words THE RED DEATH VACCINE ran continuously across the bottom of the screen. The screen rolled over again, and when it stopped there was a photo of a bald man with a serious expression. He chuckled as the words DR. MICHAEL HARBINGER appeared under the photo. Then, his own face and name appeared on the screen. He grimaced and changed the channel.

On the next screen, thousands of body bags were stacked on top of each other. He pressed the remote again, turning the television off. As he sat the remote down, he eyed some coins on the table. One of the gold-tinged coins had an engraving of a bearded man and the word BRAZIL. Next to the gold coin was a single quarter.

"1974," he said as he ran his finger across the top of the quarter. "That was a good year."

He looked up as Boutroux filled the doorway. She was wearing one of his white button-down shirts and holding up two bottles of wine. He stared down at her bare legs.

"Red or white?" she asked, smiling as she held out each bottle.

Stallings thought about it for a moment.

"Red."